SECRET DEMON

Mirador Publishing
Mirador
Wearne Lane
Langport
Somerset
TA10 9HB

Secret Demon

C. L. Ryan

www.angelicalskies.com

FORWARD

Mother's food was always made with so much love, it was her pride and joy to keep her family, at all times, warm, clean and well fed, no matter what!!

We still are, and will always be a family of great love and have the utmost respect for one another, despite what has passed.

However distant we now are, we are a great inspiration for one another and our very gifted children.

Bless you lord for this very special journey.

Prologue

Here I am, still, quietly snoozing in the blazing Mexican sun, taking in all the warmth my body will allow me to take. A warm wind blows gently, caressing me as I fly up, up and away with the angels; playing with them, watching them, being close to them as they play. All I can hear are their songs. They are singing to each other and enjoying their music which swallows me into the divine. If this is heaven, I want some: beauty at its best. No cares, no worries; just peace, calm and beauty in everything around.

The beach is beautiful: white soft sand, waves gently pulling at the shoreline as foamy, white horses, riding up and down as they fall into themselves and disappear to start again. I take a long, lazy stretch, which stirs me and I accidentally put my foot down onto the soft, white sand. With a flash of lightning and a loud bang and crash I am brought back down to earth, to reality. This is it: me, here and now. My eyes open and I am back. Out of the corner of my eyes black shadows melt past; they are everywhere. I am seeing in 3D again, which is quite normal for me. I sigh.

"Oh well, that was lovely for a moment." I am so privileged to be here!

My 3D sight is really like having a television set in the middle of my forehead, which lets me see three things all at the same time. It can be quite entertaining and sometimes very challenging. I sit watching a gentleman on his sun bed in the row in front of me. He's about 50ish I think: tall, well built with a fine head of cropped, dark hair, just greying around the edges. He is constantly swishing his hand around the back of his head, as if trying to swat a pesky fly and this carries on for some time. I giggle to myself, because what I am actually seeing is a gentleman swishing away at an imaginary fly and a very tall lady with a buxom figure standing behind him, trying to slap him around the head as if she is telling him off. He has had enough so he jumps up sharply and heads for the cooling water, convinced he is under attack. Of course he is, but not from what he thinks!

This is how I see, hear, feel and sense. It's always there, the only time I get any relief from this curse, it sometimes seems, is when I am asleep. Even then, sometimes they get in; pulling the duvet off me, wanting to talk, wanting to touch, wanting to pass on messages or just to bloody annoy me! But it's who I am, *so deal with it girl*. I constantly tell myself," It's not the end of the world," trying to convince my inner child. I scream inside sometimes in sheer frustration, but it never goes away.

I am constantly bombarded with voices: shouting, calling, songs continually repeating over in my head. I hear music; the most heavenly music which can reduce me to tears with sinful beauty: visions, some good, some bad; loud bangs and flashes of lightning. The list just goes on and a lot of it is frustration on the angels' side. They keep telling me that I am not paying enough attention and to trust my feelings and senses. But, after all, I am only human, living in a mad, bad, sinful world which can, on occasion, keep me from being what, and who, I really am.

Then there are the visitors. Oh Lord, what a bunch! The worst are the black shadows, 'Blacks' we call them. These are the bad essences of people who have passed to the other side but who have not made it to the good side. They are trapped here to do penance until they are released to cross over to their allotted side. However, most never do. They stay and cause havoc, hanging on to people's souls, bringing misery, mischief, trouble, and fear wherever and whenever they can. It's like a big game to them. They slide in and out of our world at will and travel faster than the speed of light. Trouble should be their second name.

The Shifters and the Vamps are usually no trouble. They tend to live within their own packs. I can smell a Shifter at some distance away; they have a really strong, musty, doggy smell. I always wondered why I thought these people really smelly when I was little and now that I am older, I know why. If one of these goes rogue, oh goodness, it can get really messy but they usually sort their own problems out and only ever ask for help if they are really stuck, or in need of an Archangel.

Then there are the lost souls. These are the souls of the dead that don't really accept that they have died. They hang around family members, friends and the old homes or workplaces that they feel they are still attached to. Getting them to accept that they have died and to crossover to the light is sometimes very difficult and stressful for all concerned. But when we can get them to go, it's a beautiful moment for everyone involved.

Then, of course, you have your demons, devils and the usual big, bad boy and girl spirits that are around us all the time. They are not usually a problem but, every now and again, one will pop through and cause mayhem. We are called in to clean up and help get them put to bed, so to speak. This can be exhausting.

And then there are my friends, the Angels. Where would I be without them? They have been a part of my life since the day I was born and thank God they have! I have often wondered if I would have made it this far in my life without their help, support and intervention. I say a daily prayer to thank them for their constant companionship, love, trust and support. I am always chatting to them, asking for their help and knowledge which I always receive. But, remember! There are also bad angels: naughty little tinkers. There has to be, for balance. Life is a balance; where there is light, there is dark; good and bad: Yin and Yang. So, when you get a bad angel, watch out!

Now, children born with the essence of demon are very, very rare but it does happen and they are about. Some of them are as old as the Bible. This occurs because of that old thing, love. Usually, angels and demons never pair or mate; they live alongside one another, respecting their space. They do, however, tend to keep an eye on each other and what's going on in their world. Now, if a demon and an angel do pair and a seed is left in the angel, a child will be born and the birth is very important.

People who are born with the essence are very different. Their minds and bodies work faster than a normal human. Did you ever wonder where the word 'superhuman' derived from? Likely, it was from someone who knew a person with the essence. These people can multitask and say six or seven things all at one time. They are leaders, brilliant sportspeople, idealists and winners who always stand out in the crowd. They can be really amazing, beautiful people but it all depends if they can control the demon in them. The same applies to demons, good or bad, but watch out if you get a bad one!

Both angels and demons will be watching and waiting for the arrival of this very special child. It may not happen for years, even thousands of years, but they will still watch and wait for the signs.

To have an essence in one child is rare, really rare but to have two is almost impossible. Somehow, at some point, a very long time ago, an angel and a demon must have coupled twice. The rest, you can say, is history.

It all started the day I was born!

Book One

Birth

It was 1959 and one of the hottest Mays on record. Elizabeth 2nd sat on the throne, Harold Macmillan was the Prime Minister and, of course, who could forget the famous Cod Wars that were raging in the North Sea. This was the year that Megan was born.

In the 100 acre field, half a mile outside of the little town of Gorey in Southern Ireland the annual May Day celebrations were taking place. Hundreds of families gather there every year to celebrate the holiday with throngs of people as far as the eye could see arriving on foot, if they were local, or by carts, and donkeys if not. A special paddock was put to one side so they could be tied up while their owners were at the fair and, of course, for the very few who had money, motor cars and tractors all different colours and sizes would be parked around the lanes just off the 100 acre field.

The fair was a mishmash of fair rides, coconut shies, a Ferris wheel and, of course, a roundabout. The smell of the recently slaughtered hogs roasting on homemade spits filled the air while stalls selling homemade goods, bric-a-brac, household items, live animals and second-hand farm machinery, lined the outskirts of the massive field. The fair rides were in the middle and the cider tent was at the entrance and was already overflowing with thirsty drinkers.

The sun was hot and Patsy Murphy was sat on a straw bale with her little 14 month old son playing at her feet. She wiped her brow, sweat trickling down her back. Two weeks overdue, the child stirred inside and her swollen ankles, released from the pressure of constant work and walking, thanked her as the pain ebbed away and she sat looking over the busy show. She bent down and picked up her beautiful baby boy, cuddled and kissed him, wiping mud and straw from his face and offering him a drink of water from her bag, which he gulped down greedily.

She was watching her husband, her beautiful man mountain, Tom

Murphy, in a ploughing match. Trying to get some shade from the burning rays, she watched as he skilfully tilled the turf in perfectly straight rows. He gently encouraged the two massive shire horses that were pulling the very heavy and very sharp plough, manoeuvring them in exactly the right position to enable them to effortlessly turn the topsoil in perfect, straight lines. It was a beautiful sight to see. He was hers, all hers. Married only 15 months, a son was born to them just 14 months after their wedding and sealed their bond. Another was on the way any day now but at 2 weeks overdue she was tired and restless; her belly was swollen and now becoming very painful. She wanted to be at home with her feet up, but she had to stay. She noticed the other girls watching her man, calling out to him and trying to get his attention. Anger stirred in her but faded quickly when he waved and smiled at her on a round turn. The other girls turned to see who this handsome young man was giving his attention to and spotted Patsy and her son. Her very pregnant condition embarrassed her and she turned away sheepishly. Patsy flashed her big, green, menacing eyes.

"Yes he's all mine, you bitches," she said assuredly to herself. "Come on, Tinker, let's go and find Daddy, he's finishing now." She picked him up and put on his walking reins, which Tom had cleverly made a couple of weeks ago. This saved her carrying him while heavy with child.

Patsy and a toddling Tinker made their way past the rows of stalls and hog roasts which, by now, were making her feel quite hungry. They started to make their way up and along a specially constructed path which was scattered with tiny pebbles, just in case of a rainy day. This led to the ploughing finish line which was at the very top corner of the 100 acre field.

As they were slowly making their way up the hill she noticed a small woman sat on a tiny wooden milking stool. She was dressed in a grey linen skirt and top. Her apron was well soiled from that morning's work and her headscarf threadbare.

"Cross my palm with silver," she called out to Patsy, holding out her bony, hard and calloused hand. Patsy stopped and took a silver sixpence out of her purse.

"It's all I have, I'm sorry," she said to this fragile looking woman as she placed it in her hand.

"Thank you kind demon child," she replied looking deep into Patsy's eyes, which now glowed a deep green with shock that this woman could detect her secret. "Your child is late?"

2

"Yes," replied a shaky Patsy.

"It's a girl," the woman hissed. "She will also have the essence. It is written: *the first born daughter to you will have the essence. You need to keep him away for all of your sakes. He will never let you go. She will be beautiful, break many hearts and be more successful than you ever will.*" She pressed a 4 leaf clover into Patsy's hand. "Take this child and keep it safe. May the angels be with you for protection. You will need it!"

"How do you know this?" Patsy spat angrily back at her, her fangs now threatening to drop. "It is written in the stars, believe child." A howl filled the air. "He is here with you now, waiting, waiting for her, waiting to ingest her and he will if you let him." They both looked around nervously for the source of the howl. Patsy saw Tom walking quickly down the pebble path towards her and Tinker; he waved, and she waved back. Turning back around to the gypsy woman to ask another question she found she was not there, or anywhere to be seen.

"You okay, Pat?" asked Tom as he made his way to the both of them, picking up Tinker and gently placing his legs around his neck to sit on his huge, broad shoulders.

"Yes, I was just talking to the gypsy; she tells me that the new baby has the curse as well." With that she burst into tears. "I don't want it," she screamed at him. "Get it adopted!" Patsy screamed even louder, throwing herself at the ground and falling directly on to her stomach as if she were trying to harm the child inside.

"Pat, for God's sake!" Tom picked up his crying mess of a distraught wife, with Tinker still aloft on his shoulders. "It will be fine, stop worrying, she could be wrong."

"I know she's not!" his wife screamed back at him. "More trouble, always trouble with demons," she sobbed into his sweaty shirt.

"Come on now, Pat, you know it will all be fine, anyway, it could be another boy." Tom gently rubbed Tinker's chubby legs, trying to smile at her at the same time. "Come on, Mam will be waiting at home with tea." He lovingly put his arm around her waist and, with Tinker up top, they started to make their way to the paddock where their donkey and cart were tethered.

A change was in the air, it smelled of fresh rain coming from the south; after a long, hot day it would be a relief. The ground was dry and burnt from weeks of sunshine; the crops were thirsty and yellowing. A wind blew gently but was beginning to gather strength and they would probably get home just in time.

Half a mile from the cottage, the sky lit up with lightning flashes which seemed to spread like forked tongues in every direction.

"Walk on." Tom instructed the donkey to lengthen and quicken his pace as large, warm drops of rain were released from the sky and bounced off the dusty road. The first crash of thunder could be heard in the distance. "Nearly there," he called back to Patsy who was cuddling Tinker in the back of the cart and covering him with a little crochet blanket. As the donkey turned into the cottage gate the rain increased to a steady flow, soaking everyone and everything. Tom lifted his wife and son down from the cart and towards the doorway of the cottage which immediately opened.

"Come in, come in," cried Tom's mother, as she picked up Tinker and carried him inside. She placed him in a chair covered in fresh dry towels.

"Go on, I'll see to the ass," he called out to them, leading the donkey and cart to the stable to put them both away for the night.

With the cart untethered from the tired, old donkey, Tom took the collar off him, gave him a scratch under the chin and thanked him for all his hard work, the poor old thing. He couldn't have much longer; he was already 15 years old and now getting very tired and occasionally lame. This was a worry as Mam relied on him to get about, something he would have to chat about with his brothers when they met up. He finished tidying everything away and closed the stable door. Out he went into the storm. The thunder and lightning was putting on a show in the sky which was better than any firework display.

On opening the cottage door he found Patsy bathing Tinker in front of the fire in a large tin bath, getting him ready for bed. The table was laden with sliced, boiled ham, boiled potatoes in their skins, cabbage and carrots which had been cooked in the ham water. There was a mountain of soda bread with homemade goats' butter.

When Tinker was done they all sat around the table and filled their empty bellies, tired from the long day.

"Are you sure you have to go home tomorrow, Tom?" asked his mother. "Can you at least stay until the child is born?" she asked.

"Sorry, Mam, we have to get back. I have work next week and the rent to pay. Don't worry me and Pat will leave you enough to get you through to the end of the month. I'll ask Andy and Anne to come in regularly and keep an eye on you, okay?"

4

"Okay," she replied miserably. Margaret loved her son and Patsy staying with her.

"Don't forget that brother Jim will be back to stay with you soon," said Tom.

"That will be nice," said Patsy as she was feeding a hungry Tinker with some mashed potato and cabbage in between him feeding himself with the odd carrot.

"It'll be fine, Mam, don't worry, we'll write and let you know when the new babs is here. Perhaps you could come over and stay with us later in the year?" Margaret perked up at this comment.

"Oooh, I thought you would never ask! Right, that's it, I'll be over. Let me know when you want me." She smiled to herself, cutting more bread and spreading it thickly with the goats' butter.

Next morning, they were all up early, as Johnny Byrne would be calling to collect Patsy and Tom and take them and their luggage to the station. Margaret was busy packing a small bag. "I'm coming. I'll get the night boat from Rosslare tonight."

"Mam, are you sure?" Tom asked, grabbing her and cuddling her to his side with love.

"Be Jesus I am that!" she replied, her stomach in knots, knowing that this would be a perilous journey for all. "I have the feeling that you are going to need me!" she smiled. "See you some time tomorrow," she said watching them as they waved goodbye.

They waved goodbye and started their long journey home back to England. There was still no sign of the child appearing, it had become quiet and wasn't moving around so much.

"Oh please, God let me get home before it decides to come," Patsy quietly prayed.

After an eleven hour trek by rail and sea they eventually made it back home. Patsy's grandmother greeted them at the garden gate; she had been waiting for them.

"Oh my goodness, I thought you would have had that bairn by now, come in and put your feet up my girl," she instructed her. The house was clean and tidy and a fire was crackling in the front room. A cot had been erected in the dining room, ready for the new arrival and the smell of a bubbling beef stew wafted through the house. Tinker was changed, fed and put to bed then the three of them sat in front of the fire, eating beef stew off trays and chatting about the trip to Tom's beloved Ireland. They passed messages back from the other members of the family before heading up to bed.

Patsy was woken early by Tinker crying out in his cot. When she got up and hurried to his room, his smile said it all. She picked him up and went downstairs into the kitchen to warm a bottle that was waiting in the fridge. This was his normal routine: a bottle first and breakfast later. She made two mugs of strong tea and carried everything back up to the bedroom where Tom was just stirring. She sat Tinker in bed propped up with a pillow in between them. He gurgled with delight as he greedily emptied the bottle of warm milk. Patsy and Tom smiled at their beautiful baby boy as they sipped their tea, both wondering what the new arrival would be and looking out of the window to a grey start to the day.

A dog could be heard howling in the distance. Trying to ignore it, they played with Tinker who was now cooing and trying to talk and giggle at the same time. It was raining heavily but a mist was also closing in, which made the air feel damp.

"I'll get up and make up the fire. You and Tinker stay there for a while." Tom dressed and washed then made his way downstairs, gathered in wood and coal and relit the warm embers. The fire was quickly re-established; throwing warmth into the small room and making it feel homely again.

He put the kettle on and started to make breakfast: eggs, bacon and flat mushrooms for him and Patsy, Weetabix with hot milk for Tinker. All would have warm soda bread and tea, slightly weaker and cooler for Tinker.

With the luggage unpacked and the washing done, Patsy started on the evening meal. Tom had been down the allotment nearly all day, digging and sowing winter veg, so reaping the reward of his earlier work in the spring. His wheelbarrow was full of carrots, lettuce, runner beans and heads of cabbage as well as tomatoes; a real feast for any family. It was now late afternoon and he was just cleaning down his garden tools and putting them away when again he heard the dog howl, but nearer this time. He stopped and looked around. *Time to go* he thought to himself and, locking the allotment gate behind him, he started to make his way up the muddy lane. Once again, the rain started to fall with a vengeance. Suddenly, a strong wind whipped up from nowhere and a lightning flash cracked open the sky.

"Tom, Tom!" called a lady at the top of the lane. It was Mrs. Winters, the next door neighbour.

"Freda, what is it?" he asked, calling back to her.

"It's Pat, the baby's coming!"

"Oh God in heaven, on my way!" he called back pushing the heavily laden wheelbarrow up the lane like it was an empty doll's pram.

He arrived back at the house, via the kitchen at the back, to see his beloved Patsy sat on her stool in the kitchen. Her face was ashen with pain and fear. Freda stood holding her hand and counting the minutes between the contractions.

"I've rung the midwife; she says it will be hours yet." Cottage pie was cooking in the oven, the soda bread was cooling on top and the buttered mashed swede and runner beans were keeping hot on top of the stove.

"Has Tinker been fed?" Tom asked.

"Not yet," came the reply.

"Well there's plenty to go round; let's all eat now while we can, then I will put Tinker to bed; it's going to be a long night," he said, laying the table and dishing up the beautifully cooked meal. "Freda stay, please join us."

"I will, thank you, Tom," came the reply, as she helped Patsy into a comfortable chair at the table. "Try and eat something if you can, you are going to need all your strength," said Freda to Patsy. Rightly enough, Patsy was starving hungry and ate a whole plateful.

While Patsy and Freda washed up and cleaned the kitchen, Tom took Tinker upstairs. He changed and bathed him then settled him down in his cot to sleep, leaving the bedroom door ajar, with the landing light on. He looked back and whispered to him,

"You might have a new baby sister by the morning." Tinker looked up at him and cooed.

Patsy's contractions were now coming every five minutes: strong and regular. The midwife arrived and confirmed that she was indeed in labour but stated that it would still be hours. There were another three ladies in the same stages of labour as her in the area, so she would fly around all four of them and call in another midwife, should she need to.

Patsy had a warm bath, changed and got into bed to wait for the arrival of her new child. And wait she would.

The rain poured outside and the wind howled around the small house. The thunder and lightning was ravaging the sky and somewhere in the distance a dog howled. The pain grew worse. Tom and Freda sat on the bed comforting Patsy who, by now, was in pain and distressed. This would turn out to the longest wait of her life!

New Beginning

After three days there was still no sign of the birth happening. The storm raged outside, the wind howled and raindrops the size of almonds beat against the thin window pane like little drums. The thunder and lightning seemed to be right above the house, shaking it violently with every crash of thunder. It was as if the devil himself was trying to get in. It seemed to all present as though a cauldron of evil was brewing. A dog could be heard howling somewhere in the distance and Tom looked nervously at Blodwyn and his mother Margaret who were mopping Patsy's brow.

She had been screaming constantly now for the last three hours; the pain and contractions were unending. The two midwives, who had stayed with her constantly for the last two days, were chatting quietly in the corner of the room, looking at paperwork and writing notes. They were assessing this as a likely tragedy rather than a happy arrival. The doctor arrived shivering and feeling quite sick. As he made his way upstairs to the bedroom he thought he saw an angel out of the corner of his eye as he entered the room, but when he turned to look there was nothing there. His spine tingled.

"Right then, Patsy, how are we doing?" he asked, looking at her splayed out in the bed. Her stomach was heaving and her face was blue and distorted as she screamed at him,

"Help me please! This child is trying to kill me!" Rage and tears flowed at the same time as she cried out.

"Now, now, Patsy, get a grip, and deal with it!" said an exhausted Blodwyn, trying not to be embarrassed at her daughter's outburst. "It won't be long now, love," she whispered lovingly.

The doctor was quietly speaking with the two midwives in the corner of the room, looking at the notes they had made.

"We could have a dead child here," he warned them quietly. "How long since you have detected a heartbeat?"

8

"About five hours now, Doctor," one of them replied, looking over to Patsy who was wriggling and writhing on the bed and foaming at the mouth.

"We could even lose them both if we are not careful!" he said in a very worried tone. Tom was now sat next to the bed holding Patsy's hand trying to calm her. Still the storm raged outside and the thunder and lightning crashed. The house shook and Patsy screamed in pain even louder.

One by one the angels gathered. Blodwyn was praying hard and silently, asking for help and a new arrival sooner rather than later.

She walked over to the doctor, who was still talking to the midwives.

"It doesn't look good, I'm sorry," he said speaking in a low voice.

Blodwyn looked at him and pleaded,

"The child is coming very soon and it will live I am sure. Please don't give up on her, she's so close now." The two midwives shrugged their shoulders as if to say, *well, we have tried everything with no result.*

"There is something," the doctor said, looking into his bag. "It's a little unusual, but we haven't tried it yet. I warn you this will be the last resort. Patsy is losing strength and is absolutely exhausted."

He looked directly at Blodwyn, then over to the bed where Tom was soothing her after another contraction; both were praying really hard. The doctor took a syringe from his bag, along with a small glass vial.

"Prostaglandin, let's see if this helps," he said to Patsy, gently pushing the needle deep into her thigh. More angels were now gathering in the room. They were quiet; just standing and guarding, watching and waiting for Patsy to produce the long awaited child.

One by one, the room filled with the most wonderful angelic hosts; they knew who was coming of course: the special angel child who they were to protect and welcome into the world. Still Patsy screamed but the atmosphere in the room started to change. It was noticeable to everyone present and made the doctor once again feel sick. The two midwives felt shivery and looked around the room, as if they were searching for something but, of course, they could see nothing. All the neighbours could hear next door was the screams of a woman who really thought she was dying and the crash of thunder which shook the house. It was a tense and worrying situation for all. Then suddenly, without any warning, but with the most terrible scream from Patsy, she was born. Thunder and lightning rocked the house; angel dust fell from the ceiling covering everyone present and flashes of gold and blue light lit up the room just as though a sparkler had been lit. Blodwyn was wailing in fear while the

9

two midwives were on the floor, covering their heads with their hands. They feared the roof of the house would be taken off.

"Everyone calm down now!" The doctor rose to his feet and attended to Patsy by pulling the infant from her mother's body with the help of the two midwives who were now at his side.

It was done. She was here: beautiful, small and perfect with all her fingers and toes accounted for and a head of dark, fine hair. All her father could do was cry and coo at his beautiful new little girl. Blodwyn was crying with joy and praying at the same time with thanks for the safe arrival of this special and long awaited child. Meanwhile, poor Patsy was still screaming out loud that the child was a devil child. She hated it instantly.

The angels had gathered to protect this child at her birth but she was born into fear. It's the one thing they really did not want, because it causes a chasm in the aura. When we are born our auras are complete; just like a shield protecting us. When there is a chasm, or a little chink out of the armour, *they* can get in and that's exactly what happened here. An essence of demon crept in at the last minute of the birth, just as the child appeared into the world and there was nothing anyone could do. It was done; she was born an angel child with an essence of demon. It is a very rare occurrence and hardly ever recorded. This was just the start. The Church had spies everywhere and they knew of the imminent arrival. They knew when she would be born, but not where. They had their work cut out and would have to find this child urgently.

Megan's life was dictated from the start. Her mother hated her and wanted nothing to do with her. She was born into a very poor, very strict, Catholic family who were driven and controlled by the Catholic Church. Their daily lives, thoughts and actions were utterly dominated by what the parish priest would deliver in his weekly sermons. The nuns from the local convent would back everything he would preach, acting as his sidekicks and assistants. They would follow fervently in his footsteps and aggressively deliver his word.

The Murphy house was adorned with sacred ornaments and pictures; on every wall there was something sacred to remind you of the Church's presence. There was even a little font filled with holy water; you could buy the water every week when you attended mass and it was supplied in a little blessed bottle. The font was filled so you could bless yourself as you left or went into the house. Weekly contributions were essential to the church. They needed their coffers to swell so made all Catholic households in the diocese agree to a weekly sum to which they were strictly held. Specially numbered envelopes which would be matched against a register would be delivered every month and every week, after mass, the register was checked to make sure your contribution had been received. The Murphys' agreed sum was 10 shillings, a huge amount for any poor family, and woe betide if they missed putting their specially numbered envelope into the collecting plate on a Sunday. The very next day the parish priest would call for it and the family would go hungry. The Church and God were bigger and more important than everyone or so they thought.

Every day became a fight for survival in the Murphy household as Patsy was now not working. With only one wage coming in, things were tough. The poorer families in the area would pay for their gas and electricity by meter to the South West Electricity Board (SWEB) on a weekly basis. Filed down halfpennies were kept for emergencies in a little blue egg cup on top of the dresser in the kitchen. The meter man would call to empty the meter and, if there were any halfpennies in it, he would always give them back, smiling to himself. The SWEB would not miss two shillings worth of electric every now and again, he reasoned.

Food became a priority in the Murphy household and Patsy was an excellent cook. They were very fortunate to acquire and rent from the local council two very large allotments which needed much attention but, after countless hours of sweat and toil, produced the most beautiful fruit and vegetables. With hungry mouths to feed, even in the poorest of times, Tom could always find something from the allotment to feed the kids and keep the family going. All the fruit and vegetables were grown naturally and no sprays or chemicals were used on them. In later years it would be Megan's job to help her father with the allotment work and picking off all the caterpillars and bugs would be one of the jobs which she would grow to love. She enjoyed collecting the bugs and taking them to the school playing field, releasing them into the long grass on the edge so they could live in safety. Then she would watch her mother weave her magic spell which would always result in beautiful, tasty, home cooked food. Megan was proud of her mother's cooking and determined she would follow in her footsteps. Even when food and money were short Patsy managed to make the food stretch longer so that no one ever went hungry except herself. She would often go without, just to make sure the children and her husband did not.

Early life for Megan was not easy. She was often left alone for hours at a time in her cot and was a lonely little soul. The only attention she had was when Granny Blodwyn, Patsy's mother, would call in to feed and change her. Patsy still refused even to acknowledge her but every night her father would sing an Irish lullaby at bed time. It was the very same one he sang to Patsy the first evening they met and Megan's little angels would keep her company, flying around to amuse her. They began to watch over her in the loneliest times. This was a turning point in Megan's life; the angels would now never leave her and would play a very large part in her life. With a life-changing trip to Ireland coming she would need them and they knew it.

The day finally arrived for a visit to Tom's mother Margaret in Gorey, southern Ireland. Megan was now almost 9 months old. Blodwyn's health was deteriorating and the decision was made that the time had come to take Megan to live with Margaret. It was a very sombre day for Tom but a great relief for Patsy. Now she could unburden this little bundle, a secret kept totally safe here, to grow up with her large, and loving, Irish family. Tom and Patsy would return to England to maintain some kind of family bond.

Megan, meanwhile, was growing bigger, stronger and more beautiful by the day. She adored her cousins and played with them for hours on end. You always knew where Megan and her cousins were playing; screams of high-pitched laughter would fill the air which made her Irish family laugh. She loved them all and they loved her back, making her feel very safe and secure, for the moment anyway. Granny Margaret would look at her and wonder: *what was it about this lovely special child that Patsy hated?* It was something she could not work out, and often wondered how Patsy would be with her when she had to return to England, *that's if she lets her go back!* she thought.

Even at the age of 5 you had to work; everyone worked, it was how you survived. One of the greatest pleasures and rewards for a hard day's work was a ride home aloft a massive shire horse called Thomas who had been pulling the plough all day. He loved the children and never minded giving them all a ride. He was always untethered first and then the farmer would put five or six of them up top to have a slow, but rewarding, ride home. It was a sight to see: screaming children willing the old horse to trot on, which of course after a long hard day's work he never did. The children, laughing and feeling like they were on top of the world, was a regular, happy sight around this village.

The Murphy family had two carts: one with hard wooden wheels which was always used just for work and the other one which was painted in shiny dark green with soft rubber tyres. It was very smart and just right for shopping, going out or going to mass on a Sunday. When they went to work, it would be picking fruit for the local jam factory or picking the Godly potatoes, or even haymaking. This was as well as all of the other chores that needed attending to around the cottage. Every day Granny Margaret would pack a small bag and inside would always be: soda bread, cheese, apples and a clean jam jar, so you cold drink water from the streams. They were the freshest, clearest waterways you could ever see; totally pure and clear and very safe to drink from as it was mineral water which descended down from the mountain ranges in the area. In those days they were full of small wonders like fresh mussels, oysters, and brown trout which have all but disappeared today because of pollution.

The trout were a cherished treat for tea. Megan would sit for hours watching her uncle Jim fish in the local chalk streams which were teeming with them. He would fish the very old fashioned, but very skilful way, by trout tickling. Few managed to catch fish this way; you had to have patience, fast reflexes and a brilliant eye. This method was used by the poorer families who didn't have rods and when you actually managed to catch one it was a big celebration. The usual boiled bacon and cabbage cooked in the bacon water, served with fluffy red poppies, Chef brown sauce and soda bread was a staple diet in southern Ireland and could, of course, get boring. When money and work were short and times were really bad, people lived on only bread and tea.

First thing in the morning the two goats were milked, providing the warm creamy milk for the tea and porridge. Any leftover would be churned into butter. Then Megan made what seemed like a hundred mile hike to the well for water with a huge stainless steel bucket. In reality, the well was probably only 250 yards away but when you are small carrying a heavy bucket of slopping water, it seems further. This was one of the chores Megan hated the most because it hurt her arms and fingers, but she did it without question or complaint. Water was a precious commodity the whole family needed and, with none on tap, this was the only way it could be collected.

The cottage was situated at the very end of a long, woody lane which had a sandy, peaty bank on either side where wild flowers and strawberries were abundant in the summer months. To one side of the cottage was a forest, where the wood for the fire was always collected. Behind the cottage was a peat field. This was where they dug and dried their peat, the essential fuel to get them through the winter. To the other side were large open fields that were mainly laid to crops of beet or hay. To Megan it seemed that they were in the middle of nowhere. They had no running water, gas or electricity and no toilet. The way of life was easy, very quiet and relaxed. If you wanted food you caught it or reared and slaughtered it or grew it. They went to town for the staples when they had money. If you wanted peat for the fire, you dug it whilst logs were collected from the forest next door. You foraged for wild food; the autumn was a wonderful time because Granny Margaret was a master of making jams and pickles and would preserve fabulous mushrooms and vegetables in jars for the bleak winter months. Wild strawberries and blackberries would often be a surprise pudding when the fruits were in full flow and Granny Margaret would turn all of this food into a feast, making each meal as special and as tasty as possible.

This really was a beautiful way of life with no cares and Megan felt safe. No one here hurt her and her Irish family adored her. Still, the reality of it all was she was growing up and getting older and wiser; a real little girl now. She loved her family and her way of life but it would only be a matter of time before her father would come to take her back to England. Her Granny Margaret worried all the time, trying to think of a way she could keep her there in Gorey, safe with the rest of the family. She knew in her heart that the day her father would come to take her back to England was drawing near. His letters were coming every month now and always the first question was, *how's Megan*? In the last letter she received he told her that Megan had been enrolled in a new local school at which she would be eligible to start the following year. Margaret held the letter to her heart. Spying Megan playing outside, she crumpled the letter and threw it onto the fire with a tear falling from the corner of one eye. *Not long, just enough time to get her strong*, she thought, noting a very large angel in the corner of the room with a sword.

Megan had her own special place to play. It was at the bottom of the garden, just behind the dung heap where a lovely clear spring trickled. Animals were very attracted to her and they seemed to be everywhere she went. Small flocks of birds would often sit and chirp away on the wooden fence opposite the front door; ignoring the wide eyed cat, without a worry in the world. Huge clouds of brightly coloured butterflies would swoop into the garden and cover the lavender bushes to produce a multi-coloured spectacle. Each night a gathering of frogs and toads, which would normally be seen around the small pond in the garden hopping around underfoot, would drive her granny mad. It seemed the nightly choir could be heard all around until early morning and, on hot summer nights when the windows were open getting to sleep could be a problem. It seemed that they all wanted to be around Megan, to protect her and be with her.

Once all the chores were done, she was free to play and often went missing for hours but Granny Margaret and the family always knew where she could be found; her special place at the bottom of the garden, past the dung heap down by the trickling stream. It was here she would sit and watch the fairies at work, gathering spider's webs to make beautiful garlands that glistened with raindrops and sparkled like precious gems. They would wrap them around plants and small shrubs for all to admire. Dragonflies, which are really dragonfairies, would make her laugh. They would race around like sparkling darts, chasing little insects and generally making mischief which really irritated the hard-working land fairies. The fairies also spent some time talking to and teaching Megan about the real world outside, what to expect, how it would be living back with her own family and eventually going to school. Where she currently was, they told her, it was all countryside, animals, flowers, and peace. The reality was that soon she was going home to England and, at first, it might be frightening. So, by gently talking to her, they guided Megan as to what to expect and faithfully promised there would always be someone there to love and protect her.

Lately, she had been noticing odd black wispy shapes that seemed to creep past the corners of her eyes. She was starting to sense odd things and people. She often wondered why she could feel and hear their thoughts and senses. Sudden, odd sounds in the night would wake her when she cried out. Her granny would turn over and cuddle her, telling her not to worry and that she was safe. But her granny knew that the time was coming fast, a lot sooner than she had hoped. It would soon be time for her to be called back home to England. The constant questions were becoming harder to answer and large, beautiful, gold and black angels with massive wings started appearing around the house, even frightening granny one night when she bumped into one as she went into the larder. She must have blessed herself fifty times and said a hundred Hail Marys after that encounter.

The family would always comment on the strange phenomena at the cottage and noticed that it was always when Megan was around. Granny dismissed it by saying how lucky they were to have the blessings of the Lord with so much wildlife here and angels to protect them all.

Granny always told Megan that she was going to be a really special girl.

"Remember," she said, pointing her finger directly at her, "people will always come to rescue you!" Megan was still only 5 and put it all to one side, in the back of her mind just like locking it into a safe. There it would stay to be released when she needed it and that day would surely come.

Big Tom Murphy

Tom Murphy was a big man. Standing 6'8" tall he looked like a man mountain with thick, dark hair, a strong Irish jaw and big brown eyes. All agreed he was a handsome man; gentle as a kitten but strong as an ox.

Tom lived with his mother, Margaret Murphy, his brother Jim and his two sisters, Pauline and Joan in a tiny village called Gorey, County Wexford. They lived in a tiny cottage with a tin roof and just an acre of land to support them.

Pigs were kept in the sty and slaughtered twice a year for meat. Chickens were kept for eggs and, as an occasional treat when guests arrived, meat. They would be killed by Margaret who always thought it her job to kill and prepare the birds as painlessly and quickly as possible. Water was collected from a hand pump well at the bottom of the lane and peat, which was used as the main source of fuel for the fire, was dug behind the house on a daily basis in the summer and laid out in huge slabs to dry, by Tom and his brother Jim.

They led a simple life: reading by gaslight, sleeping together in big brass beds and peeing in a potty from under the bed as there was no toilet. This would be emptied daily into various pits that were dug around the wild land behind the farm to be used as cesspits and filled in when full. In the winter, to add warmth, extra coats would be piled on top of the bedclothes and waking to freezing breath was quite normal.

The staple diet was bacon and potatoes, or 'poppies' as they were called because of their lovely deep red colour. These would explode into a fluffy ball when cooked and worked beautifully with the boiled bacon and fried cabbage that would accompany it, topped off with Ireland's own famous 'Chef' brown sauce. Soda bread was also a staple and every week Tom or Jim would drive their mother into the town to shop with the donkey and cart. The wholemeal flour, white flour and sugar would be scooped out of great vats, weighed to order and put into sturdy brown paper bags which would then be tied with string. Butter was sliced from a huge block, weighed and wrapped in greaseproof paper; something that just didn't happen in England. The smell in the shop of drying herbs, spices and curing meats was something never to be forgotten. This weekly shop would be the basis of the food which would keep them all going although, when money was short, hunger was a common sensation.

Tom became the head of the family at 10 years old when his father Miles, suddenly died in an accident on the farm he was working for at that time. Tom's father was Head Horseman and Master Ploughman. He was known as the best around the whole county and his job was to plough the fields and attend to the shire horses that worked the land. Two farms used his skills and he was so adept at ploughing that he was often offered jobs around the county for bigger estates with vast amounts of land. He would often win ploughing competitions when he actually had time to get away from his job to attend; usually at Bank Holiday fair times. His heart, though, was in Gorey, his home town. With the two farms being relatively close to one another, he could walk to either in just over an hour which meant he always managed to get home to his beloved family every night. He would often put Tom aloft the shires as he was ploughing, just to train him how to move the horses. Once aloft, he could work out how the horses moved and how to rein them, to turn, to straighten and to be the eye of the horse. This was why Miles was such a master and the training rubbed off on his son who would never forget it. He loved his gentle father who had such a special way with the horses. A local racing yard asked for his services to help with yearlings by calming them when they were being broken. He often put his beloved son atop while he was working with them; they became a great team.

Miles's death was a massive shock to them all. Suddenly no money was coming in to buy the staples. Both Tom and Jim tried in vain to get jobs. They left school barely able to read or write and with no qualifications at all. As potato blight had virtually wiped out the crops, recovery was slow and that meant no jobs for young boys, only for men who were needed to work farm machinery.

Two terrible and hungry years later, the decision was made; Tom would leave for England. Perhaps work could be found there and he could send money back to support the family. He could not read or write but a family member made contact with a friend in Bristol who said he could find work for this big, fit young man and that he would take care of him and help him.

So it was done; he packed his bags, hitched a lift to Rosslare and caught a ferry to Fishguard in Wales. From there he stole away on a train headed for Bristol Temple Meads and arrived late at night, not really knowing who he was meeting.

Almost instantly he was working. His new-found friend, who had met him at the station that night, was amazed at the size and the strength of this 12 year old who easily passed for an 18 year old. He could easily do the job of two, or even three, men and the die was cast. He was able to send money home every week and, as soon as he was paid, he would run to the Post Office and send money to the Post Office in Gorey where he knew his mother would be waiting for it to shop and feed the family.

As he grew, and he did grow, into a huge 6'8" man of solid muscle with hands the size of boxing gloves, this gentle boy became a man of conscience with love for his family at home whom he missed greatly and wrote to every week. The Church ruled him with a fist of iron. He would often go to 6 o'clock mass in the morning on the way to work and again to 7 o'clock mass at night on the way home. But when they were not looking, or so he thought, he would take the odd bare knuckle fight, which he would almost always win. These would boost his wages and allow him to send more money home to his mother with a little bit left over for a few pints of the black stuff and maybe some new clothes.

Then one night at the local dancehall, he set eyes on the most beautiful girl in the whole wide world. Her name was Patsy. She had long blonde hair and big green eyes, beautiful long slim legs, and a smile that could melt any man's heart, it made her interesting and alluring. But best of all, she could dance, really dance, Tom was mesmerized and hooked that very night by this tall green eyed beauty, who would in time become his wife, and Megan's mother.

Going Home

The time had come for Megan to return home to England and start school. The family went very quiet when Megan's dad, Tom, suddenly arrived one day without notice. Margaret hugged Megan and Uncle Jim picked her up and cuddled her like a precious doll, whispering to her that it was time for her to grow up in England now and not to worry about anything. Fine words for a 5 year old; it really never registered, but she kept all this information in the back of her mind.

Megan loved her dad and went willingly with him to work on the cart the next morning. They were off to pick potatoes for Joe McGenny so Granny packed her usual soda bread with cheese and jam and a jar for the water. Tom was quite amazed how his little daughter had settled into the routine of farm work and she willingly worked alongside him all day; fetching water and bringing food when they stopped for breaks. It was hard work for them all but she enjoyed every moment of being outdoors in the sunshine and her reward would be a ride on the back of Thomas the shire horse along with her cousins when they had finished at the end of the day.

Uncle Johnny Byrnes announced that day that the next evening would be a special evening for the children; a real treat as Megan would be leaving soon to go home to England. He would be taking them into Gorey to the very first chip shop that had opened, the only one for miles around. They all screamed with delight and it was as much as they could do to concentrate on the rest of their chores that day with the excitement of the coming outing. Chips were the new fast food in Ireland; people from the countryside lived off the land and chips were really frowned on by the elders in the family but times were changing and you have to accept changes: some good, some bad. So, the little town of Gorey was grasping this new way of eating the Godly potatoes.

At the allotted time of 6pm, which was considered late for country children, Uncle Johnny Byrnes pulled into the farm in his bright red, brand new Volkswagen Beetle. Behind it he was pulling a rough, beaten up old pig trailer. This was their mode of transport for the night. Everyone used the trailers for practically everything and some of Megan's cousins were already in it, screaming with excitement at the ride they had just taken and calling for the rest of them to get in.

The men sat in the car with all the kids in the trailer whilst the women stayed at home to finish the chores and enjoy some peace and quiet. It was a boys' night with the excuse of keeping the kids amused and getting them out of the house, which would allow the women some time without them. After a shortish drive into the town and along to the high street, just the other side of the cattle market was a newsagent and general store called Paddy's News. Paddy Nugent, the owner, had announced the coming of chips for sale by buying a revolutionary, as it was then, deep fat fryer. It was the best money could buy, a table top version, and he was selling crinkle cut chips for tuppence a bag with salt and pickled onion vinegar.

He was inundated; there were queues of people as far as the eye could see, all trying to be served in front of one another. Everyone was excited and waiting to taste this new sensation which was sweeping the country.

Megan's dad treated all the kids to their bag of chips and the pickled onion vinegar was a hit. The kids agreed that when they were next in town to buy some chips, only the pickled onion vinegar would do. Megan and her cousins finished their chips and started playing on the small green; managing to dodge the ever oncoming donkeys, carts and horses. Meanwhile, the dads settled in for a few pints of the black stuff in the Royal Oak public house just opposite. They were enjoying their Guinness while managing to keep an eye on the kids at the same time, as the pub had a very large plate glass window. Morale was high all round with the dads telling tales of adventure and Tom telling of his work in England. The throng inside the pub made it quite difficult to converse but, somehow, they all managed.

Eventually the men decided that three pints of the black stuff was enough for the night and it was time to gather the kids and say goodnight to everyone. Tom was looking out of the big plate glass window, just to see where the kids were, when he felt a chill go right down his spine. He was looking over to where the kids were playing, especially his little Megan, and all he could see was a tall, menacing figure staring at her intently. The figure was dressed in unusual, old fashioned clothes and his eyes were glowing yellow green. He was licking his lips and snarling with his fangs slightly

21

showing, and drooling with delight. He was watching every move Megan made and listening to every sound she uttered. Tom could not quite gather who, or what, he was but did notice his tall top hat and long, snakelike, gold tail twitching in anticipation and pointing directly at Megan. At that moment, Tom suddenly felt sick and sure that Megan was in danger. The stranger called to her; she looked, stopped and looked deep into those horrible eyes that seemed to burn with thunder. Still, she didn't feel afraid of this evil looking man. Why should she be? Her angels always told her they would protect her, she was with family and, of course, her dad was there. He called again, curling his big index finger towards himself and inviting her to go to him. She returned the signal, calling,

"You want me?" He nodded. Everyone went quiet and looked. They all saw this menacing figure. Megan gulped and her stomach lurched; she flinched, feeling that something wasn't quite right.

"Don't go!" shouted little Shaun Byrne but Megan was caught, caught in the creature's stare. The big, serpentine tail whipped up and around his body, as if excited by the sight of her. With a flutter, a massive pair of black wings unfurled.

"I've been waiting to meet you!"

"Who are you?" Megan asked.

"I'm someone who has been waiting a long time to meet the future mother of my spawn."

"What's a spawn?" Megan asked. He leaned towards her. "Pooh! You smell." She pulled away in disgust at the stench.

"Megan, Megan!" screamed her cousins. He reached out to take her hand and, with a swift blow to his face, big Tom arrived to scoop up his precious girl into his arms.

"Fuck off, you bastard! Leave her alone, you won't have her, she's mine!"

"No, she will be mine! Maybe not yet, but I will have her," he screamed back at Tom and, with a grimace, just puffed into thin air, leaving a dark vapour trail.

It seemed the whole street had witnessed this episode and everyone scurried away to go and tell of this little girl talking to a weird looking man with wings who was punched in the face by her father after a screaming row! And what about the horrible looking man just disappearing into thin air? The work of the devil was around and everyone felt frightened, running to the church to light candles and say prayers.

Tom cuddled his little girl, who was very confused and upset now. For the first time she had felt fear; fear of the unknown, so he soothed her by saying she was safe and that he would look after her. Just to cheer everyone up, and lighten the mood, he bought everyone another bag of chips, which went down well with all the kids. Their parents frowned; perhaps the whispers had been true, and little Megan was different. They had all just witnessed something no one could explain.

"For God's sake, don't tell Father Andrews about this," whispered Johnny to the others. "He'll have us all exorcised!"

They crept out of the house in darkness at 5 o'clock the next morning, before anyone could see them. Granny kissed Megan and Uncle Jim was crying. This was the last time Megan would see Uncle Jim, she somehow knew that. Her bags were full of little gifts from Gorey and sandwiches for the journey home. They were taken to the train station to be whisked to Rosslare and the ferry home. It felt as though they had left in shame.

Our House

Megan arrived back in England in time to start school. For the long journey back to Bristol from Ireland they had caught the train at 5:20 that morning to the ferry port of Rosslare. From there Irish Ferries took them to Fishguard in Wales. It was a rough journey as the sea swirled like a boiling cauldron, rocking the boat from side to side and up and down troughs like it was a Dinky toy. At one stage they locked all the outside doors of the boat, asking people to sit in the centre alleys and not to go outside at all. After an arduous and stomach churning journey, they finally docked and made their way to the train that was waiting at the adjoining station to take them back to Temple Meads in Bristol and a short ride to their house in Stockvale.

Megan's stomach started to churn and she felt sick as they made their way up the hill and across the road to the big set of steps that would lead them up to their house. A funny sensation curled in the back of her neck and she almost cried out with fear, as if she knew what she was walking into. On entering the house with her father, who was holding her hand, she was introduced to her new baby brother and sister who had arrived in the years she had been staying in Ireland. Not to say it was a shock, no not really, but they all still seemed to have attention lavished on them and she was barely noticed by her mother and grandmother when she walked in. Her new baby brother was beautiful and her sister was gorgeous. She loved them all immediately and the little family of two was now a very proud little family of four. This made her very happy inside because she knew if no one else would, they would love her.

From the minute she stepped into the house, she saw grey fog swirling all around. Everywhere she looked it was there and she could hear whispers in the corners of every room, which unnerved her. They were quiet at first and sometimes, when she was busy doing the chores, she forgot them, but knew they would return. She also felt he was watching her, you know him, that man, the one on the green that day. She never really forgot about that encounter and thinking of it made her stomach churn with worry. *Would he really come back and get her? Was he really watching her?* She sometimes felt he was but when she was caught up in the frenzy of the household she could put it to the back of her mind. Still, she would often pray to the angels to be with her and protect her from him. She should have guessed that they were already.

The house was small, but breathtakingly clean; scrubbed every day by her mother and granny. Washing was scrubbed on a board over the old Belfast sink and a boiler bubbled away in the corner: popping, bubbling and misting up the little windows above.

The kitchen was small and functional with a larder and store cupboard, a small cooker and a fridge. The washing line hung above the dresser; this was for the school uniforms which were pressed and hung there every night with great pride for the next school day.

To the front of the house was a small, neat garden. There was a front room with an open fire, a hallway leading into the kitchen, a back dining room and a door leading to the garden of which Megan would become so fond. To one side was a large pigeon loft with about fifty racing birds. On the other side were a veg patch and a rabbit hutch where Fudge the rabbit merrily chewed his way through carrot tops. At the end of the garden was a lovely greenhouse filled with juicy tomatoes and beyond that the playing fields of the school that Megan would attend and views of the countryside with fields full of wild flowers and beautiful trees. At the side of that were two acres of allotments which kept the family fed. The downstairs of this house was a lovely, homely place to be.

Funnily though, the one place Megan did not want to be was upstairs. She would often stand at the bottom of the stairs and look up. At the top were a separate toilet and bathroom, her parents' room and a small box room which her brothers shared. Her room, which she shared with her sister, overlooked the back garden. But there was something else, something dark, something that looked at her; it felt bad and made her shiver even when it was warm. Something was lurking and there were noises, like growling, not really loud, just in the background. Something just felt wrong and it frightened her. She hoped the big angels with their sparkly wings could protect her; she was going to need them.

There was no central heating in the house, so when it was cold her mother used to wrap small towels around Corona fizzy pop bottles filled with hot water and put them in all the beds to warm them up. It was quite normal to wake up on a cold day and find ice inside the bedroom windows and be able to see your breath as you breathed in and out. On mornings like these they would all get up, rush downstairs and gather in the kitchen in front of the open oven door which was giving out heat for warmth. They would stand and eat Shredded Wheat with hot milk, or porridge, just to warm up and have mugs of sweet, warm tea before they set off to school.

Megan started school when she was 6 and school was a release for her. She could write but was found to be very dyslexic and backwards with figures. Still, this never stopped her from trying very hard, as hard as she could. She could also think about different things, run, play and forget the house. Sleeping was difficult for her and her sister, as the noises were getting louder. The nights were often disturbed and Megan's sister started to get very frightened at night because she knew that Megan was also frightened and it very soon became a vicious circle. They would often sleep in the same bed together to keep each other warm and give each other comfort when the noises were really loud. Occasionally, when the bed started shaking, they were far too frightened to get out of bed and go to the toilet when they needed to. So, quite often in the morning the bed was wet which absolutely infuriated their mother who would land a hefty slap on both, calling them 'spring rusters' and threatening them both with the doctor to find out what was going on. What was going on was right under her nose but she chose to ignore it. She also knew it would get worse.

So, going to school for Megan was freedom: freedom from worrying about the house and what was in it; freedom to be appreciated as a very bright little girl who was artistic and musically talented. The teachers loved her and she put every possible ounce of effort into everything she did.

But as time went on, things started to change. Megan was changing, she was becoming more alert, seeing wispy black shadows on a daily basis, hearing whispers, seeing odd people suddenly appearing and then disappearing for no reason. She never questioned it when it was daylight; it was at night that the fear started to grow even worse.

Megan's family were very strict Catholics. Her mother was a sensitive (had psychic ability to see, sense and hear). Her mother and grandmother had the gift but you never ever spoke to anyone about it. If you did they would think you were reared abnormally and ready for the loony bin. Unfortunately, the Catholic Church would have none of it. They were nasty and cruel; frightening people to death. To them this was the work of the devil and anyone who said they had the gift was a Satanist. Well, we all know this is not true now but years ago the Church ruled with a fist of iron.

One day a new girl started at the school along with about ten other friends. Very posh they all were, their families obviously had lots of money and they all wore the best and newest clothes and shoes. Megan never worried about her uniform: it was hand-me-down but always clean and smart, if a little bit old-fashioned.

The girl who seemed to lead this gang was called Sharon and she was an attention seeker. The girls in her gang all wore similar clothes, jewellery and make-up which, at this school, was quite unheard of. A fleet of cars would arrive to bring them to school and take them home. Megan's family didn't have a car so the bus, train or walking was their family mode of transport. Every day these mothers would parade their jewellery, high heeled shoes and designer clothes in front of everyone. The playground became a central meeting point for all. Sharon and her gang were the girls in school who wanted to be noticed and, very soon, they started to make sure everyone *would* notice them.

Megan was quite a plain little girl but always clean, well-mannered and liked by most of her fellow pupils. Her mother kept her clean and fed but had no liking for this girl: the one she spawned; the devil child. So, hairstyles were basic and boyish. Nothing, absolutely nothing, was girly about her. She was a good tomboy, she had to be, there was no one to take any interest in her except her little fairy friends who would visit her in the garden late in the evening when everyone else was inside. She would make little houses for them, pick flowers for them and they all gathered down by the greenhouse. It was out of view of the kitchen, where her mother worked most evenings, so this little spot was beginning to be a little haven for her.

Every now and again a lovely lady dressed in blue and white robes would appear. She said her name was Mary. She would just stand, look at Megan and smile. Megan often thought she looked like the lady that they had in their religious pictures - you know, Mary, Jesus's mother. But that would be outrageous, so she decided that she was just a friend. She told Megan that if she needed her to call she would come and that she was just there to make sure Megan was safe. She would often tell her not to worry about anything and to look after her brothers and sister to which, of course, Megan said she would. She often wondered why Mary appeared, especially when there was some kind of trouble in the family. Irish tempers were nasty and fights in the family were common. Mary would have her work cut out over the next four years.

Bad Times

Megan was now 7 and things were so tight in the household that her mum had started working at a sweet factory in Brislington called Drake's. With so many mouths to feed Patsy felt she had to bring in more money. Megan's dad now worked away and he was still sending money home to Ireland. So, not only was he keeping his poor, Irish family going, he was trying to support his own but, as always, something had to give. What gave one night was a massive fight between Tom and Patsy who agreed to temporarily separate, but to keep in touch for the sake of the children. Tom would continue to send money home. Fights between the parents were regular and would often result in all the children huddling together whilst they fought, blow for blow, as the children screamed with fear.

Patsy's shifts sometimes started at six in the morning until two in the afternoon, or it would be two in the afternoon until ten at night. Megan's chores depended on what shift her mother was on. The early shift meant that Megan had to get everyone up, fed and dressed ready for school; making all the beds and tidying through before she left for school herself. Also, if there was a meal to prepare, she would get up early and prepare the vegetables or cook off the soda bread. But God help her if something was not done to Patsy's exacting standards; she often came home to a swift clip around the face or ear for being lazy.

If Patsy was on a late shift, Megan would come home from school, sort out the clean school uniforms for the next day and put back the washing before cooking the evening meal, doing a shop if a list was left with some money, washing up and getting everyone in bed before mother came home. On top of all this she was being bullied at school and it was getting worse. Megan was heavy with burden, having to keep herself together to fend off the rage of her mother, as well as avoiding the girls in school. They would chant at her in a circle in the playground, odd slaps and thumps were coming and there were days when Megan really did not know where she was or who she was. On top of that, strange nightly activity was haunting her. A grey fog would appear and was even commented on by her sister and brothers, who asked her if she knew what it was. Each night she could hear a baby crying and footsteps up and down the stairs. Worse yet was the growling which was always outside her window. Megan and her sister never went to bed without saying their prayers, asking for protection and blessing all the family; something the Church had instilled into them.

One particular day when the bullies were, once again, having their fun, an elderly teacher called Mr. Mountford decided that this was not the sort of behaviour he wanted to see, or others to see, in the school playing field. He called over to the girls to break it up and to go to their classrooms. The bell rang for class and, at that point, she was released with only a few grazes and tangled, pulled hair. *Phew,* she thought, *thanks Mr. Mountford* and made her way to her classroom, where Mr. Mountford was waiting.

"Are you all right, lass?" he asked.

"Yes, sir," she replied. A kindly man, Mr. Mountford was a brilliant English teacher. He wondered how Megan could produce such brilliant poetry and stories when she was so dyslexic. He often saw her chatting to herself and when he asked her what she was doing she would reply,

"Oh just chatting to the angels," and then get on with her work. He never really thought anything of it, just childish imagination he would put it down to, but in the last couple of weeks he could see she was suffering. He had witnessed two or three bouts of bullying which he had reported to the headmaster, only to be told,

"It's just children playing, stop being so sensitive."

"Well," said Mr. Mountford, "if I had children at this school and one of them was being bullied like that, I would call the bloody police."

"And what would they do?" the headmaster replied, "give them detention?"

Getting nowhere with the headmaster, he decided to have a private little chat with Megan just to see if he could do anything to ease her situation. Well, as you can imagine, Megan did not get much affection or consideration, so when Mr. Mountford sat her down and asked what was going on at home and with the bullies she just burst into tears.

"Where do I start?" she cried.

Two hours later she felt much better and, after a cup of sweet tea which

Mr. Mountford had brought from the staff room, he allowed her to leave five minutes early to avoid the bullies, promising her that he would try and help with the situation at home and in school. He would also have a strong word with the headmaster. She quickly gulped down the last of the tea, munched the crumbs of rich tea biscuits he had brought, thanked him and ran downstairs. She carried on out of the gym, across the school playground in front of the mothers and fathers who were waiting to pick up their own children that day. *Down the steps, turn right...* she quickly ran up the hill and in through the little gate to her house; safe for a while.

The next evening, after the usual horrible school day, she had fed her siblings and was just washing up the dishes, asking her siblings to start getting ready for bed, when there was a knock at the door. Now, Megan's mother and father had always told all of them never to answer the door if either of them were not there so Megan ignored it. Once more she shouted out for them all to get ready for bed but the door knocked again, louder and more forcibly this time.

"Megan, Megan!" a lady's voice called out. "Megan, it's Susan, Susan Nicholls from Social Services. I'm outside, with a policeman, could you let us in, love? You are not in trouble, we are here to help." Megan was frozen with fear, rigid, not really knowing what to do or how to respond. Then the letterbox opened.

"Megan, it's Joyce here from next door, love. Joyce, you know me, love. Come on, Megan open the door, there's no trouble, I will come in as well, darling! Open the door, there's a good girl." So she did.

The sight which greeted the visitors would melt any responsible, loving parent's heart. Here were four children all washed with their teeth cleaned wearing pressed pyjamas, ready for bed. They were all hugging each other out of sheer fear.

"Right then you lot," said Susan as she ran over to them and put her arms around them all at once. The house was spotless, clean and tidy and it would appear they were all ready for bed. *I bet they do this a lot on their own*, she thought. "You can leave now," she said to PC Whitemarsh. "I will take it from here."

"Where's Mum?" demanded Megan.

Susan had a quiet chat with her away from her siblings, then said,

"Bedtime, everyone!" With them all tucked in after saying their prayers together she told them not to worry and that she would see them again later in the week. With that she turned off their lights, closed the doors and went downstairs to wait for their mother to return. As she stepped off the last stair a key went into the door and it opened. Patsy just stood there staring at Susan. She had been drinking, but was relatively sober.

"Hello, Patsy," said Susan. "Can we have a chat?"

There were no raised voices that night, only the sound of their mother sobbing downstairs. Megan kept awake, waiting to hear her mother go to bed, but she had a bad feeling: something was wrong. The baby started crying again, something really was wrong. She suddenly felt quite sick and the air thickened in the bedroom. A mist started swirling around the ceiling and it suddenly became viciously cold. The footsteps grew louder and louder, walking directly to her door, but everyone was in bed. The door handle started turning, and the door shaking, as if someone was trying to get in. Louder and louder sounded the footsteps, the door shook even more. The beds now started shaking and she could hear a growling, once again, coming from outside her window. With that, the next door's dog started barking; almost screaming as if in pain.

Megan screamed out to her mother,

"Mum, Mum!" There was no reply, the whole room was vibrating. "Mum, Mum!" Megan screamed again. By now her sister Trixie was also screaming and hardly able to believe what was happening.

"Shut up, shut up!" screamed Trixie, as little hailstones and marbles appeared to be flying around the room. The door was now moving violently, as if someone was trying to shoulder it.

"Help, help!" screamed Trixie, as loud as her little voice would go. Just then something changed; Megan's beautiful little sister was really being hurt by something. She was thrown into the air; she had no idea by whom or what it was. This made Megan mad, really mad; in fact super mad. When the anger came she felt different, taller. Her neck thickened, her eyes glared, her talons lengthened, her tail flips and the bumps on her neck stood out and her fangs were drawn.

"Angels," she screamed. "Where are you?" And with that she turned to the door, which was now almost on its hinges. "Come on you bastards," Megan screamed at the door, "if it's me you want, come and get me!"

With that, the door bashed in and a flurry of gale force wind, with angel dust and grey fog rushed into the room. It threw Megan and her little sister over the side of the bed and onto the floor. *If this is hell*, thought Megan,

I'm not going there. A massive fight of winds, fire and lightning with growls and screams was happening right above them. Then, after two more bursts of lightning and an explosion of angel dust and feathers, nothing. All was quiet.

Two angels landed in front of them with swords drawn and worried faces.

"Are you two okay?" the one Megan knew as Michael, asked.

"Yes, I think so," she said, looking at Trixie who had fainted. "Who am I?"

"Someone very special with a lot of work to do in the future," Michael replied. "Don't worry," he continued, looking down at her little sister, "I will make sure Trixie will remember nothing."

"Who was that?" Megan asked.

"Someone from your past, whom we are trying to protect you from," he replied, looking directly at her and smiling a look of angelic love. With that the angels curled their beautiful wings around both girls and lifted them gently back onto their beds. The whole house suddenly settled, there were no noises and peace had returned to the little bedroom. They left promising to be there when she needed them, and not to worry. Trixie stirred so Megan got out of bed and went to tuck her in a little tighter.

"Ooh! You look better," gasped the little girl. "Your eyes were glowing green and you nearly whacked me with your tail!" she said, then rolled over and went to sleep.

The next morning, Patsy had not gone to work. Instead, she was down in the kitchen making soda bread and cooking breakfast. The kids washed and dressed as usual, ate all their breakfast, packed their schoolbooks and made their way to the front door. Just then there was a knock. Susan Nicholls stood outside and waited for them to leave, noting how clean and looked after they seemed. She was accompanied by a man; very official looking.

"Have a good day children," she said as they all started to leave with very worried faces.

"Go on," shouted their mother, "off you go." So they did. On the way to school no one spoke. All of them were quiet in thought and praying hard that their mother would still be there when they got home.

On arriving at the school gates they dispersed and, once again, the bully girls were there waiting.

Oh not again, Megan thought but within a split second she was surrounded by twelve girls all screaming and chanting at her. They liked to do this in front of the parents who seemed quite proud of their little pack for teaching one of those Murphys a thing or two. *Smelly children*, the mothers all thought, *second-hand kids*. The girls had gathered in a ring around her and were chanting,

"Rhinoceros Mucky Megan," over and over and over again, almost making her giddy. Feeling suddenly quite sick, and humiliated, she called to one of the teachers on playground duty to help, but she just looked the other way and smiled at the posh mums who were looking on and acting like nothing was happening. The bell went and the group dispersed, doling out the odd slap around the face and kick in the leg as they were leaving.

Every day Megan started school with fear in her heart. *What will happen today? What will they do, shall I walk around the other way? No, that would make me late.* It was all going on in her little head and that was before school had even started. But today was her favourite day, so after registration her heart lifted. Today's singing lessons would get her through the day. She sang her heart out, as though singing to the Lord and his angels, whom she knew always came when there was music. The bullies were now focusing on her even when she walked from classroom to classroom. They would run up behind her and hit her in the back or pull her hair or even kick her in the shins so every lesson now was becoming a nightmare. Once again, no one was taking any notice, or trying to help. Hiding in the nurse's office, feigning sickness (she did actually feel sick most of the time) did not help. The nurse, at times, was quite nasty to her.

"Get back to you lessons you lazy girl," she would say, not even bothering to look at Megan's grazes and bruises. Spitting on her food at lunchtime was another of their little tricks but Megan was so hungry that, at times, she would just eat around the spittle. She, like the other children from poor families, relied on the free school meals and had no other food or money and the bullies knew it.

The teachers just looked the other way, much to the disgust of the dinner ladies. One of them, Eve Branson, saw this happen a few times so would keep a couple of sandwiches back and pass them to her when she handed her plate in.

"Thank you," Megan would say.

"Oh, no trouble, but don't let the buggers get you down, love, they are just not worth it!"

That afternoon, Megan was, once again, jumped on in between classes and an old deep scab on her knee broke open. She was bleeding everywhere: all down her socks and on the hem of her summer dress.

"Oh, God, my mum will go mad!" cried Megan, as the school nurse quietly dressed her leg. *What on earth is going on here?* she thought to herself. *Something's not right, I know the head said to ignore these girls but all this is making me feel unwell, something is definitely not right.*

That night, when Megan left school, she walked out the back of the school totally avoiding the bullies which meant a two mile walk home, as the path skirted the perimeter of the school playing fields. She just did not have the strength to face them again today, much to the disappointment of the girls waiting at the school gate. After a wait of twenty minutes the mothers called to their girls,

"Never mind, you can get her tomorrow." They all got into their waiting cars and drove off.

When she got home, her brothers and sister were already there. As soon as she walked in the door she was greeted with a slap across the top of the head.

"What was that for?" Megan cried.

"You fucking little bitch," screamed her mother. "Who have you been talking to? You've got us all in trouble now you fucking demon!"

Very shaken and upset, Megan cried out,

"What have I done?"

"You told someone, I would like to know who, I was drunk, you fucking little cow!"

"No I never!" she replied.

"Don't lie you little bitch, it's all your fault. You've split the family up. Always fucking trouble, demons are always fucking trouble."

Her three siblings all started to lash out at her, arms and legs and screaming everywhere in the kitchen, calling her a demon. With that the back door of the kitchen opened.

Everyone stopped and their mother glared at everyone to be quiet; they knew the look! Megan stood still, with tears rolling down her face which was smarting with red stinging marks. The other children looked fearful but no one said a word; you could have cut the air with a knife.

Susan Nicholls entered with her sidekick: the important looking man.

"Hello, Patsy, hello children, everyone had a good day?" she asked, noting the state of little Megan, but not acknowledging it.

Oh, God, let's get this bloody family sorted, she thought inwardly.

35

"May we come in?" she asked. She was already in but that was politeness on her part and also ensured she could get access to the children. Just be polite and nice, that's how she worked. Patsy nodded.

"May we go through into the front room?" She directed everyone with an outstretched arm pointing to the front room. "We can have a nice chat and a cup of tea."

Tea was made and they all settled in the front room. Susan noted the marks on Megan's face and everyone sat quietly, not saying anything just looking at their mum with unanswered questions that were flooding through their little minds.

"Now, Patsy, have you told them?" asked Susan.

"Was just about to," replied Patsy.

"Well," said Susan, "let me tell them."

"Megan and Tinker, we are placing you both in the care of a lovely couple for a little holiday for about two, maybe three weeks to help your mum. She's not feeling very well at the moment and her health is poor. It's nothing to worry about; you actually won't be very far away, just down in Brislington. Your mum and dad, when he's back, can visit you as often as they wish; in fact every day if they want to."

Megan screamed at Susan,

"When are we going?"

"Tonight my darling," smiled Patsy who was pleased now this bitch was out of the way. She could have more to drink and enjoy her nights she thought to herself. *Get rid of my own demons,* she thought. With that, Tinker and Megan started crying.

Oh, Lord, this is always the hard bit, thought Susan, but she was used to it. She saved little children from the clutches of evil, unloving parents every week and the end result was always so wonderful for the children who got to be loved and well looked after by foster parents whose dreams had come true by having children to care for.

Yes it will all unfold wonderfully, she told herself inwardly as she picked up a quite hysterical Megan and Tinker. Megan screamed and kicked but the car engine was running and they were both unceremoniously put into the back of the car and driven off with both the social workers trying their best to calm and reassure them. The last sight from the back of the car for Megan was of her mother standing in the road looking at them driving off. Her eyes glowed green and there was a smirk on her face. Her brother, Seamus, was crying and hanging around his mother's leg whilst little Trixie was in floods of tears, running after the car. The neighbours watched, open mouthed, feeling for the poor children that had been taken away. Megan could see her mother mouth something to her in the distance. *Suffer you little bitch, just like I had to.* And with that they were gone!

Away From Home

Tom was sat on his bed in his digs, writing to his mother in Ireland. Worry and guilt flooded the words in the letter. He missed his gorgeous Patsy and, most of all, his wonderful children. Having to support two families, one there and one in Ireland meant that he had to take the higher paid work which, on nearly every occasion, meant working away from home. His thoughts were constantly back at the house. *How were the children;, was there any trouble; how was his Patsy coping with everything he had left her with; was Alan Winters his next door neighbour looking after his allotments properly?* All this was whizzing around in his head on a daily basis. At times he was considered edgy and bad tempered when, in fact, he was worrying about his family at home and his elderly, frail mother in Ireland. It was a really heavy burden.

Old Mrs. Brown ran good digs. Berkley Power Station had done a deal with her to put up workmen at a cost to them of £5 per week for bed and an evening meal. It didn't include breakfast as the men were always on site at 6am. So, an evening meal was substituted, which suited her fine. She was in her late 60's; an ex chef who was a spinster and had no family that she knew of. So, when the power company contacted everyone in the area, asking if there were any spare rooms they could rent for the workmen, she jumped at the chance. She had three large, spare, double rooms and there were three to a room. Nine workmen brought in £45 per week in rent. It was a fortune to her and the work would be guaranteed to last at least another eight years, which paid all her bills, along with the mortgage, so she would be quite comfortable by the time the contract ended. She found cooking for nine every night was easy, everyone had the same; take it or leave it she told them all. Of course, they always all took it. The tired workmen would arrive home every night looking forward to their evening meal which was always served piping hot and cooked to perfection.

Tom always counted his blessings as being there in that cosy, clean and comfortable house helped keep him sane and focussed. He soon realised what a great cook his wife was. Old Mrs. Brown was a chef, a really good one, but Patsy's pies and stews were better. He especially missed the roasts with the massive Yorkshire puddings and luscious thick gravy. He was lucky to be there, though, and he thanked the Lord in his prayers every night. Most of his workmates were in cold, mediocre lodgings with horrible food and they moaned like buggery. Most would go out every night to the local pub, tie one on and fall into bed in oblivion, having wasted their precious money. Tom, on the other hand, had good digs and he needed every penny he earned. He would hide his cash in the bedroom under one of the floorboards which he had specially cut under his chest of drawers. He could sleep well, knowing his hard earned money was safe and unspent. It was not the same for some of the other workers but, unless someone left, there were no other lodgings available. Every single, free room was taken so it had been a lottery and Tom knew that he had one of the top prizes; for that he was very grateful.

Tom started doing little odd jobs around the house for Mrs. Brown and they soon became friends, often spending the evening in the garden chatting over a cup of tea. Then, with her approval, he dug a patch in the garden and started growing vegetables. This thrilled Mrs. Brown as she could use them in the evening meals. It was a good deal for both; as soon as the vegetables started to be picked, unbeknown to the other men, she lowered his rent to £4 per week. It also gave Tom something else to think about and life became a little better for them both.

Tom arrived home late one night. After a really heavy day he was exhausted and all he wanted was a nice hot bath and to fill his belly. The local parish priest for Thornbury, Father Ryan, was sat in the kitchen chatting away with Mrs. Brown.

"Ah, here's the man I've come to see. Tom, how are you?" he said, standing up and putting his hand out in friendship.

"Fine, Father, and yourself?" Tom asked politely, feeling a little unsure and nervous as to why he was here.

"Just popped in to see how you are. Being away from the family must be hard, especially for your wife. How's she coping?" he asked.

"Fine, fine," Tom replied nervously.

"I hear she's not been well, Tom; can the Church help in any way?" the priest pressed him.

"Not well, what do you mean?" Tom was worried now.

"It's a delicate matter, Tom, shall we speak in private?" He nodded to Tom.

"Oh don't mind me," said Mrs. Brown, wiping her hands on her pinny. She left out of the back door and up the garden path to the veg patch.

"What do you mean?" Tom again asked Father Ryan.

"Patsy has been drinking heavily, acting strange. There's been funny goings on in the house being reported by the neighbours and the social workers are now involved. They're helping her to manage the family as best she can. It seems the two young ones may be going on a holiday for a few weeks to ease the pressure on Patsy. Then the social workers can get in there and see what the problems are. Father Thomas has called over a couple of times; he tells me her eyes glowed green and he thought she growled at him. Is there anything, anything, Tom you want to tell me? Does she need our help?"

"I don't know what you are talking about!" Tom replied fiercely. "I write every week and, as for the growling, are you sure he hasn't been on the wine? He's bloody known for that!" Tom was trembling, and feeling sick to the core.

"Look, I know this is difficult for you, Tom, but people are talking, whispers in every direction, all pointing to Patsy. They say she's possessed and harming the children."

"She would never hurt those kids; she loves them all; they are her world. She's a great mother and a wonderful wife!" he shouted back, speaking to Father Ryan directly in his face. Fat tears were now welling up in that big Irish face.

"It doesn't look like that from where I am standing, Tom. It's not what I am hearing," he replied. "Look, Tom, let us help her. I could get a couple of priests, who actually specialise in these things, down from London. They deal with this all the time; we can help get this curse of demonic possession gone and make everything better, for you, for the children and especially Patsy." He was now pleading with him.

"Fuck off, Father, you can get out. Who the bloody hell do you and the bloody Catholic Church think you are? My wife, my family and my home are my business; nothing to do with you and your lot and if I find you busy bodies interfering in anything at all I will personally contact the bloody Pope myself, do you hear me?" He was screaming now and slammed his fist into the kitchen table so hard it shuddered. Tom's tears were flowing, reducing the big man to a humble man who was trying to protect his family.

"He knows of our suspicions already, Tom," said Father Ryan. He rose sadly to his feet, put on his hat and looked out of the kitchen window to where Mrs. Brown was pulling carrots in the veg patch. "You know where we are if you change your mind, Tom," he said as he made his way outside into the garden. He left via the path which led down to the road to where his car was parked. Behind him was a sobbing, crumpled man.

Oh, God in heaven, where are you when I need you now? Tom thought to himself. *What the bloody hell has been going on while I've been away?* He felt physically sick that the secret was now out. He had promised to keep it with all his heart, mind and body to Patsy's mother, the night that he asked for her hand in marriage. He knew it would be tough, really tough, but always, in his heart, he thought that he could manage the problem. Now it seemed that the problem was becoming worse and, perhaps, Patsy might need help. His contract still had another twelve weeks to go and he really needed the money. With no car and no direct way of getting home he had to rely on the lift that brought him there to also take him home but that would be in twelve weeks' time. He resolved that as soon as he was able he would go home to his family and seek help. *Perhaps the doctor could do something; perhaps medication could help keep it at bay?* He would have to make a plan and the only real friend he felt he had in the whole wide world was back in Gorey: his friend and confidant, Father Thomas Jones. In Tom's opinion he was a true man, a man of his word, one he had sat with for over four hours the week before his wedding, letting Tom spill out all his worries. He had opened his heart, letting out all his secrets and talking about his beautiful fiancée, Patsy, and what this marriage really meant to him. They had also discussed what it would mean if this bloody curse of a secret ever got out. How would he cope? How would she cope? And what about the families? *Oh, God, what a mess.* But he loved her with a passion and couldn't let her go. He had begged for the Father's help and help he did, reassuring Tom that everything would be fine and that everything would work out for them. Their love and the love of God would see them through and out the other end. Tom had believed him.

They had prayed together that night for over two hours. Finally, Father Thomas Jones had blessed Tom and his forthcoming marriage to Patsy. He told him four rules he must live by to keep the bloody curse of a demon at bay.

1. *Have any house you live in blessed.*

2. *Read the Bible regularly out loud in the house and always keep it in your bedroom.*

3. *Say daily prayers, not just you and Patsy, but the children as well: this will help protect them.*

4. *Always attend mass as much as you can. This will weaken the demon and keep him at bay.*

"Your strong love for one another, your family and the Church will get you through all of this," he had reassured him. Father Jones had promised Tom that he would always be there for him and would only be a letter away. Tom, on the other hand, promised Father Jones that he would keep his part of the bargain and *please God* he would never need to write that letter. They had hugged as friends before Tom left, knowing he would be leaving for England in the morning.

Old Mrs. Brown sat in the kitchen with Tom. She didn't ask any questions and got on with making tea. She gathered that trouble was brewing. She liked this humble, strong man with great virtues and quietly wished she had bloody met him herself years ago. She really did not want him to leave. Neither spoke as they sat at the kitchen table, preparing the veg for the evening meal. She could see the pain in his eyes and realised that this big man mountain was feeling the pain of being away from his wife and family. She was suddenly jealous; nobody had ever felt that way about her. *It must be a wonderful feeling to be so loved*, she thought in a daze while taking the steak pie out of the oven to let it rest. Tom was miles away; he ate his evening meal in silence then did his usual job of helping with the washing up before making his way upstairs to write a very important letter.

Mr. & Mrs. Smith

Sally and Harold Smith seemed a lovely couple. They lived a very nice life with good jobs, which kept them comfortable in a large ground floor flat on a good estate on the edge of Bristol. There were three large bedrooms, a bathroom, a large kitchen, lounge and a small office. They also had a back garden which was big enough for the average family. However, they lived alone. They had been married for nearly twenty years and one of Sally's dearest wishes was to have children. Unfortunately, after years of trying and various tests, the doctors had told them that Harold had virtually no sperm and that children were just not possible. With heavy hearts they accepted the news and decided to try for adoption. Harold absolutely did not want to go down that road but was quite happy to appease Sally by agreeing to the possibility of fostering. It appealed to Harold, as he would not be stuck with the same kids all the time and this, in his mind, would make things more interesting. With Harold working flexi time for the council, in a managerial position, he could virtually choose his own hours and Sally was a nurse, doing shift work, so there would always be someone home with the children.

Sally was a beautiful and mumsy looking lady, standing 5'4" with short blonde hair, cut into a sensible bob and a smile that could melt an iceberg. She had a heart bigger than an ox and would help anyone if she possibly could. She was always putting herself out to be the best neighbour anyone could possibly want. She worked in the local community hospital on the psychiatric and elderly wards, looking after all the old people who could not be nursed at home in their final months. The job entailed shift work, which suited her because it always gave her some time to herself, whilst helping to fill the void in her life. She so desperately wanted children around her; sometimes the pain was more than she could bear, and she would bury herself in projects that quite honestly, she didn't really need to do, just to keep her sane.

She met Harold when she was 17 and, after a three year courtship, he eventually asked her to marry him. One thing she made very plain while considering his proposal was that there must, in some way, be children involved in their life. Harold struggled with this as he was an only child who had been brought up very strictly. He was actually a bit of a loner. His father had been a barrister and his mother a lady of leisure, so state school was out and he attended boarding school from the tender age of 8. He suffered bullying and buggery on a constant basis but kept his head down, passed all his exams and soon got his first job working for the County Council. Starting as an office junior, he had progressed and made his way up to senior management which afforded him flexible hours and a very good pension.

Sally was a good and loving wife who never really questioned anything. She would, however, have bitter outbursts of screaming and crying when she found her husband's pictures of naked ladies and, sometimes, men. She would scream at him, "What if your employers ever found out about them? Oh, God, the shame of it all!"

She would cry and knew they would never get a chance of fostering if this ever came out. He always apologised and promised never to do it again. This was the regular ritual but, in her heart, she knew he was hiding something and that he would hurt her again.

The three bedroom flat was spotlessly clean, homely and very modern, all ready to welcome and help some needy children. Thick, wool carpets adorned the floors and a large, colour television stood on a very modern table in the lounge. There was central heating and a kitchen to die for with a large range cooker, fridge and freezer. The beds that were already made up waiting for the two children to arrive had thick, brushed cotton sheets and there was a radiator in each room and a small television for them to watch. This would be sheer, utter luxury for them. Finally, there was a power shower in the beautiful, big and modern bathroom. Oh yes, only the best for them!

Harold and Sally kept themselves to themselves most of the time. They had one holiday a year, usually two weeks in Cornwall in the same hotel, and owned a very nice car. They had all the things that most people would die for really, except the one that constantly pulled at Sally's heart: that she didn't have a child of her own to love and look after. She had friends who had nothing compared with her and Harold, but they had children and companionship, love and cuddles. They also had laughter, something that was totally missing in her life. All there seemed to be for her was work,

work, work, and where would she be without it? *In the bloody hospital myself,* she sometimes thought. So, when the chance arose for her and Harold to attend a fostering meeting, she jumped at it. They were very quickly, because of their standing in the community, invited to be part of the fostering program. When completed, it would give them a chance to be considered for actually fostering a child or two. They both had to attend the local authority community building a mile down the road for ten weeks; two nights a week for two hours per session. When this was completed, they would be eligible, with supervision of course, to be considered for fostering, on a temporary basis, any children that needed emergency evacuation from a situation. The children would remain with them until they could return to the family home or be adopted. Of course, there would be monetary help from the council for their services. This made Harold sit up even straighter in his chair even though, as a working couple, they were very comfortable. Harold was already spending this new gotten gain on a new car or television. His head was really in the clouds now.

It was a difficult time for them both, getting to grips with this course and, a lot of the time, Harold really did not want to go. By the time he got home from work and had his tea, he was ready for TV but, no. Some nights Sally literally dragged him, moaning and groaning, out of the door; such was her determination to finish this course and get some kids into her lonely life.

Harold really struggled with the session on nudity, bathing and dealing with children who needed trustworthy adults around them. *Oh, he's just shy*, Sally thought to herself. Momentarily, she questioned it in her mind and then dismissed it just as quickly.

Still...

Finally, she was handed her official fostering papers. They had finished the course and passed with flying colours. Sally was so proud and dreams of a new future filled her mind with all sorts of exciting things. *I will bake every day*, she thought to herself, *and take them to school and when I pick them up from school we can all go to the park and perhaps a visit to the zoo at the weekend.* Yes she had it all planned.

They had spent the last couple of weeks decorating and sprucing up the flat for the new arrivals, especially the two spare rooms which would be used for the children. Sally insisted on two new single beds with fresh, new child-friendly coloured bedding and a brand new, seven-seater three piece suite. The one they had was nice, and very comfortable, but would be no good when they all got on to have a cuddle and watch TV. Much to Harold's displeasure, it had to be new and bigger.

They had informed both of their employers that they would now be foster parents and would need some flexibility in their working hours. It didn't matter to Harold, as he was his own boss and was on flexi time. The hospital was not so accommodating. Sally had given them twenty-five years of her working life, always helping out when someone went sick and always there if there was an emergency because, in all honesty, it was all she had. She really had no life with Harold so, if the hospital called, she went. Her job ruled her life but Harold never minded; he only thought of the extra money. Harold had been thinking about the family finances. Money would be coming from the council, to help with the upkeep of the children, but he really did not want to dig into his savings to treat or look after these brats. No, he would have to have a word with Sally.

Sally and Harold sat nervously waiting. They had received a phone call the previous evening to say two children needed urgent placement away from their family home for a while. The mother was very ill, were they up for it?

"Yes!" screamed Sally, excitedly nervous on the phone. She looked up and thanked the Lord at the same time. Immediately, she rang the hospital and took the next three days off, which they were not much pleased at but still owed her. The office girls were really very pleased for her; they knew how much she wanted a family of her own. They often had deep discussions about families and children when out socialising on their skittle evenings so when Sally had excitedly finished telling Susan Hayward, the office manager, all about their course and the two new children arriving, she whispered to Sally, "Don't worry if you need more time off, but make sure you always speak to me. This bloody lot would have you working into your grave!"

"Thank you so much," replied a teary Sally; and it was done. Blissfully, she had baked jam tarts and a fruitcake for when the children arrived. She would serve that with hot sweet tea and a lovely chicken pie with new potatoes and garden peas for their evening meal. She and Harold sat and waited. And waited!

Finally, there was a knock at the door. Harold and Sally jumped up with fright.

"That must be them," she said to Harold, nervously making her way to the front door. "We are being greeted with a very sad situation, Harold," Sally said. "This is what we have trained for."

"Yes, dear," he replied. "Right then, deep breath!" With that, she opened the door.

Sally's heart melted the minute she saw the two little children sobbing on her doorstep; their little faces were swollen as they clung to the social workers who held them close. "Sally, Harold, I am Susan and this is Norman; I believe we met on your course. This is Megan and this is Tinker."

"Hello, Megan, hello, Tinker!" gushed Sally.

"Say hello to Sally and Harold," Susan urged the two children. They managed a bleak 'hello'. "Right then, let's get you in and sorted with something nice to eat. Sally's a great cook just like your mum," Susan enthused to the two distraught children. "And oh, Sally," she added with a wink, "Megan is a great little cook so let her help you!"

"Oh really!" said Sally. "Well, Megan, me and you are going to get along fine. What's your favourite food?" With that the ice was broken. The ravenous children devoured the jam tarts and half the fruit cake, to Sally's delight. Sally picked up Megan when she had finished the last of her fruit cake, and gave her a big hug. Megan turned and looked at Harold holding Tinker. Her stomach lurched; something was not quite right here. She looked at him and thought, *I don't like you, I don't know why, but I don't.* "Now, you two, we love you loads and you will have fun here with us," Sally told them. "You are quite safe and dinner will be at seven; let's show you your rooms and get you showered and changed, ready for your tea. After tea you can watch TV for an hour, then bed. You start at a new school tomorrow but we'll talk about that later; let's get you sorted." The two social workers quietly slipped out of the house while Sally and Harold settled the children in.

Well done you two, thought Susan as they left. Sally instantly took to both the children. It was as though she already knew them both. Being a psychic medium really helped; she instantly sensed Megan was special, but Tinker was beautiful too. Megan and Tinker were absolutely blown away by their rooms. More important for Megan was that this was the first time since she left Ireland that she had enjoyed a cuddle and any affection. It felt good to have positive vibes around her again. She liked Sally and the light that was around her head. Not so Harold, though; still she wasn't sure why. "Oh please, angels," she called out, "look after us both and bless the family while we are away. Especially, please make Mum better."

Tea was a triumph. There was chicken pie with new potatoes smothered in butter and garden peas. The two children ate as if they had never eaten; the atmosphere was homely and calm. A quick telephone call from Susan just made sure that the children had settled. "Yes," replied Sally, "what beautiful children. Oh how could anyone ever hurt them? I love them already."

"I knew they would be fine with you," replied Susan. "It's a good match but I will warn you, we are trying to keep them away from their mother for much longer, even permanently if we can. Are you okay if this happens?" she asked.

"Oh my goodness," replied Sally, "I feel like I have a family already."

"Now don't get your hopes up," cautioned Susan, "but good luck, and I will be in touch in a week or so." Sally's heart was aglow.

The children were exhausted but managed, despite nearly falling asleep, to sit in front of the television and watch a natural history program before being taken to bed and tucked in by both Sally and Harold. They slept a deep, dreamless sleep for the first time in years. Just before she nodded off Megan called to her angels and thanked them for this lovely house, the warm bed, her beautiful room and Tinker's. Then she asked that the angels look after her little sister and brother because she wasn't there to look after them. Finally, she asked again that they look after her mum. *Thank you, Lord for a real homely home, thank you so much,* she said inside her head so as not to attract attention. *I think it will be lovely here...* But as she said it a little doubt crept into her head, then sleep grabbed her.

*

That night after the children were put to bed, Sally and Harold sat in the front room. They were in shock really, not saying much to one another. They realised that for the first time in twenty years of married life they were not alone. Harold gave Sally a glass of her usual sweet wine, which they normally saved for weekends, while he had a very large whisky. He needed it; there was too much temptation around. *I could do with seeing Veronica this week,* he thought to himself, sipping his whisky in big gulps. Sally, meanwhile, thought she heard a dog howling and was busy looking out the window. She turned around to see a very large, very beautiful, navy blue and gold angel walk into Megan's room. *Ah,* she thought, *I was right, she is special, and that bloody dog is not a dog. Don't worry little Megan you are in the right place now; I'll keep you safe.* She downed her wine in one and went to bed, leaving Harold pouring another whisky. "Don't be long please, Harold," she called. "The children need their sleep."

"Okay, dear," he replied. *Bitch*, he thought then downed his whisky and followed.

Over the next couple of weeks, Sally got Megan and Tinker into a really good routine that fitted in with them all. The new school was great and very welcoming. Sally looked through all the clothes that their mother had sent with them and binned them all, cursing their mother for the worn out clothing these children were wearing. *No wonder Megan was being bullied*, thought Sally, *a new wardrobe it will be*. "That's going to cost at least a hundred pounds!" Harold spat at her one night after tea when the children were doing their homework out of earshot. "We can afford it. These kids have nothing," Sally countered, "and anyway, the council are paying us for their upkeep!" With that Harold sauntered off, got his car keys and went out. *Bastard*, she thought. *I know where you are going*. The next day was a Saturday. Sally got up early, washed and dressed Megan and Tinker then got the bus into town with a big shopping list. She was determined that these children, if and when they left her, would not stand out in the crowd as being poor. Wearing the clothes their mother had sent, it was obvious that Megan did. For some reason Tinker's clothes were better and he could take care of himself but Megan was a gentle little child: very sensitive. She seemed to take everything to heart and had a nervous stomach. Sally resolved she would make sure they had lovely, up to date clothes which would make them the new kids on the block in school.

Sally rang Harold to pick them up from the city centre; laden with bags there was no way she was getting the bus home. Megan and Tinker were in seventh heaven. Yes the clothes were lovely but, better yet, Sally had taken them to a Wimpy Bar where they had burger and chips with a milkshake: their first ever. They were ecstatic! *Oh my*, thought Sally, *these kids really haven't lived in the real world at all.*

Harold was late so Sally and the children were waiting nearly one hour for him to pick them up. "Where the bloody hell have you been?" cried Sally when Harold finally showed up. "Been to see Veronica," he replied. "Oh, that bad?" Sally asked sarcastically. Harold just looked up to the sky and shrugged his shoulders. "Come on, kids get in," said Sally. "Seat belts on!" And off they went.

You fucker! she thought. *Hurt these kids and you're dead!*

Susan Nicholls called next day, which was a Sunday. She had a quick meeting with Harold and Sally in the kitchen before going through to the lounge where Tinker and Megan were sat watching the television. "Everything okay my little darlings?" she asked, looking at the beautiful children, all in new clothes. They looked like real, up to date, modern, well-kept and loved children. It ran a note through her heart. *Thank God we have so many brilliant foster parents who really help these kids in need*, she thought to herself.

"Good news, all is well at home and Mum is responding well to treatment. Your brother and sister send you their love. Any messages to go back?" asked Susan. "Yes," they both replied. "Tell them we will see them soon and we love them and love to Mum." This hit Sally hard. How could these kids, who were treated so badly by their parents, still love them so much? "Would you like to write a letter to Mum?" Sally asked. Much to the delight of them both Sally sat and helped them draw pictures and write little notes that could be passed on to their brother and sister and their mum.

Susan kissed both the children goodbye, took the letters and told them she would deliver them herself. *No chance!* she thought inwardly. *If you can't be bothered to visit, or even ask me how your children are, I hope you never get them back.*

"Fucking little bastards!" Harold said to Sally. "After all we have fucking done for them, they still want to be at home." Sally felt a lurch in her stomach. "Shut up you evil man; it's children here not some fucking whore you deal with, children! They are real people, they can't help it, it's who they are, where they are from. It's only been six weeks, how can you expect them to forget everything in that short time?"

Sally felt elated. Susan had said it was possible that Megan and Tinker could be staying

even longer. "Oh, God, please make this so. I love these children and I know they love me. We could be a real family," she prayed out loud. Originally it was 3 months, then possibly 6 months. Finally, after psychiatric assessment, it was deemed that Patsy was really unstable. She was drinking too much and, with an unusual blood group which could not be matched, the less pressure on her the better was the thinking of Social Services. Megan and Tinker were doing so well with Harold and Sally, *let's leave them there!* It seemed a good solution all round.

Things were going well; Sally was now leaving Megan to cook the tea when she was on a late shift, much to Harold's annoyance. She was amazed how well this little 7 year old could cook even better than her with some things. Megan had actually started teaching Sally how to make bread, pastry and quiches! *Bloody hell,* thought Sally, *I had better buy some cookery books!* Everything was working well and Sally's shift pattern was suddenly starting to worry her. She did not want to leave the children at night, especially Megan. That was when she was most vulnerable. Tinker was fine but Megan was hearing a dog growling a lot at the moment and she knew trouble was around because of the angels that constantly walked around the house. Not that this worried her at all. She felt honoured, they were all welcome, but something was lurking and trying to get to Megan; she could feel it. Sally decided to have a word with the office when she went into work that night.

Every day Megan had chores to do: putting on the washing, cleaning and cooking. Both children had put on weight; when Megan arrived she had been extremely frail. Her bedwetting had also stopped, which was a great relief all round. The children were blossoming.

The growling was something Megan had got used to; it seemed to bother Sally more than her now. The angels were around, but the grey mists were slowly creeping back. Every now and again, she was catching a glimpse of it from the corner of her eye. She had hoped originally that part of her life was gone but slowly realised that is was, and would be, part of her life, probably always. The thought made her shudder! She also kept hearing a little voice; it made her turn and look but she never saw anyone. It kept saying, "Be on you guard, look out, be aware!" The only thing she could possibly think of was the way Harold looked at her strangely as if he were thinking something. She also caught him looking at Tinker; sometimes it made her spine tingle and she shuddered just thinking about it so she tried to put it to one side.

Sally's job was now pulling on her. Harold, being in senior management, had no pressure at all, but Sally really wanted to be at home more now. She realized just how much she had given of her life to the hospital. Not that she regretted it, no never, but she had a little family now and kept thinking of the children and how with their previous parents they had lived as latch door kids, feeding and looking after themselves. She contrasted this with how nice their life was now and how they very much appreciated it. Megan and Tinker thanked Harold and her nearly every day, not that he needed thanking the lazy bastard, all he did was run them around and pay for things. Sally and Megan did most of the work between them; they had become a great little team and it was working well. Yes, the decision was made: no more night work! She would go to the office the very next day and ask for a change in her employment contract.

Sally was a psychic medium, and a very good one. She was very sensitive and could pass on messages, sense problems and see spirits of the departed but she knew she was nothing like Megan; she was one special little girl whom the universe was trying to protect and nurture. She often thanked the angels who walked around the house for the opportunity of looking after her. They never responded, just looking at her and smiling; but that was enough. She had stopped reading the cards. It was something she loved doing which helped a lot of people and earned her some extra cash but work had taken over and there really was no time now. If she stopped the night shifts she could start reading again and, perhaps, Megan could help? *Oh how exciting that would be*, thought Sally.

"Megan, a word in the kitchen please, darling," called Sally. Megan got up from the floor where she was writing some poetry which Sally had looked at earlier. *Bloody hell, where did that come from?* she had thought. "Megan," said Sally, "how would you like to come to Spiritual Church this Friday night? It would just be you and me. You can meet some of my lovely friends."

"Oh," she replied, "I would love to. What about Tinker?"

"Well," said Sally, "Harold can look after Tinker. We will only be a couple of hours, it's just down the road. I've missed it. I haven't been for about eight months now. It's decided then. You will have to help with dinner on Friday, though, and straight home from school for both of you. We have to be there at 6.45 to get a seat and help Claire and Elaine, who run the church, if they need it. Is that okay?"

"Yep!" Megan replied.

"Right then... Harold!" Sally cried out.

"Yes, dear?" Harold called back.

"Here please in the kitchen!" Sally cried back.

"What?" snorted Harold.

"Don't 'what' me, you bugger," she retorted. "Me and Megan are going out on Friday night to the spiritualist church, so I want you home early, no going out, you will have to babysit Tinker."

"Oh for God's sake," replied Harold, "I was thinking of going out myself."

"Well you can forget it, Harold, I'm bloody fed up of you going out all the

52

time and leaving me here. When was the last time I did a reading; when was the last time I went out with the girls; when was the last time I met up with Claire and Elaine at the church? No sorry, Harold, whatever you are planning will have to wait; I'm going out for a change. Okay?"

Harold just looked up to the ceiling and did his normal snidey look, which always made Sally a bit wobbly, but she got her own way and out on Friday it would be. She picked up the telephone and dialled a number.

"Hello, is that you, Elaine?"

"Hello, stranger!"

"Just checking there is a service on Friday night."

"Yes," said Elaine, "are you coming?"

"Certainly am," Sally said excitedly, "and I am bringing a very special person."

"Who?" asked Elaine.

"My foster daughter," replied Sally.

"Oh my God!" exclaimed Elaine. "How bloody fantastic, Sally! Well done, girl. What does it feel like to be a mum?"

"The best feeling in the world," Sally replied. "Anyway, got to go, Harold's throwing a wobbly as usual!"

"Oh, God, kick him in the nuts," laughed Elaine. "Can't wait to see you Friday and you can tell me all about it. By the way," she asked, "what's her name?"

"Megan," replied Sally.

"Oh!" exclaimed Elaine, "why am I seeing trouble?"

"Oh, no trouble, nothing I can't handle," Sally retorted.

"Well, Sally, be careful, look after you please, you lovely lady, and I will see you

and Megan on Friday. I'll tell everyone our lovely Sally is back!"

"Will do, darling," Sally replied. With that she put the phone down and walked towards the living room, only to bump into two angels having a conversation and looking towards Megan, who was still on the floor writing her poetry. "Sorry," she said. Seeing their faces she realized they were talking about Megan. "Look!" she said, exasperated, "she will be with me and I will look after her. She will be fine. Okay! Come with us if you want." They bowed and smiled at her. *I bet they bloody will,* she thought. "Who are you talking to?" shouted Harold. "Oh shut up for Christ's sake, I was just talking to myself."

Sally's not acting normal, thought Harold. *Bloody dog barking all the time, now she doesn't want to work nights and it's all been since those bloody kids have arrived. Best try and move them on then*, he thought, *get back to normal, to my nice little life*. He grinned and thought wicked thoughts. Sally saw him do just that. *What are you thinking you fucker?* she thought as she sat on the sofa and cuddled Tinker who was watching the television. *Best be on your guard*, she heard a little voice in her head say. *Yes I will do that!* she replied inwardly.

Friday came quickly. When Megan and Tinker got home from school Sally was busy in the kitchen.

"Fish fingers, chips and peas tonight," she called out as Megan and Tinker ran to their bedrooms to get changed. *Oh, God not again,* thought Harold, *we had that last Friday!* "Raspberry and apple crumble for pudding," she called out. "Megan made it last night." Sally popped her head out of the kitchen and called, "Harold! Harold!"

"Yes, dear?" Harold replied. "Is that okay for tea, you never answered?"

"Yes, dear," replied Harold. "Could you lay the table then please?" Sally replied. *Oh sodding hell*, thought Harold. *What else do you bloody want?* "I heard that!" Sally cried, and walked into the lounge where Harold was trying to read his newspaper. "I never said a word! You must be a bloody mind reader!" he said. "You forget; I am!" she retorted. "Now lay the table, please!" *Bitch,* thought Harold. "And I bloody well heard that as well!" retorted Sally, walking out of the front room.

Megan smiled. This constant banter never worried her or Tinker. It was like a game to them really but lately Harold was acting a little different and being slightly more uptight. She had noticed it the other morning when she and Tinker were leaving for school. Sally was at work and Megan overheard him on the telephone trying to make an appointment with someone. He had ended up slamming the phone down and walking out of the house, murmuring under his breath, "Fucking bitch, bitch, bitch!"

The table was quiet. No one spoke as they ate their fish fingers, garden peas and crinkle cut chips. It was lovely but Megan missed the fresh vegetables she had grown up with. Sally was a lovely cook but the lifestyle she and Harold led meant convenience food a lot of the time. When Megan and Tinker were at home fresh vegetables were always available. Their mother was always sending them down to the bottom of the garden to cut cabbage or pick beans and peas. But she thanked the Lord and the angels every day for the wonderful people that now loved them so much. *Perhaps Harold would let us grow some vegetables in the garden? I could teach Sally how to cook them.* Megan planned to ask Sally that very evening.

Sally and Megan washed up the dishes then said goodbye to Tinker and Harold, telling them they would be back in about two hours. With that they got into the car and Sally drove them to the spiritualist church not far down the road from where they lived. On entering the church, a lovely, large, buxom lady grabbed Sally from behind. "Hello, gorgeous lady!" Sally hugged her back. "Long time no see old friend." Elaine screamed with excitement. "Lovely to see you too," said Sally. Elaine turned to the little girl holding Sally's hand.

"Oh, and you must be Megan." Elaine extended a hand to shake Megan's but, in an instant, curtsied. "Oh, God," she said into Sally's ear, "why have you brought her here?"

"Megan, say hello to Elaine, a very good friend of mine and a brilliant psychic."

"Yes, but not to your standard!" Elaine looked at Megan and spoke directly to her. "Welcome, Megan to our very humble church."

"It's not humble," Megan replied, "it's wonderful, you should be very proud." With that she made her way down to the seats at the bottom of the aisle with her spine tingling; it was a wonderful feeling. Then she heard a call, a growling sound. She turned around and her heart

nearly stopped. There, looking right at her, grinning and growling at the same time, was that man with the green eyes, the tall hat, the talons and the big black wings! He could not enter, so he called to her through the doorway. Sally immediately looked up. "Oh, God," she murmured. "Oh for fuck's sake, why did you bring her here? She's a fucking devil!" cried Elaine.

"Oh shame on you," replied Sally. "She's not a devil; half-demon I think and a nice one, really nice. There's not a nasty bone in her body, especially after all she and her siblings have been through.

"Well then," replied Elaine, "let's deal with this bastard who's making all the noise outside."

She walked up the church aisle, looking directly at the demon standing outside and shouted, "No demon suppers available here tonight!" Very unceremoniously she slammed the church door shut and said, "Take a seat ladies."

The service was lovely and afterwards Sally stood on stage and passed on messages to people gathered around the podium, eager to hear from their loved ones. Megan noticed angels of all different shapes, sizes, and beautiful colours coming and going and holding the shoulders of the people they were escorting to the service that evening. She saw this all the time, so nothing was new in this area, but what she did experience was immense sadness. It was almost enough to make her cry. Every time a message was pointed at a particular person their angel would hold on to the shoulder of that person as if to say,

"It's okay, I'm here with you," just to help them accept the messages coming through and, of course, to comfort them in that very special moment. This was heaven for Megan. It felt very normal. She watched and listened, sometimes pointing out a few angels who were lingering and helping Sally to get to the right person while speaking on the podium. *One day I will do this*, Megan thought. *Yes you will, little one*, came a reply. *Perhaps this is what I am meant to do*, she thought, but no answer came. Sally watched her reactions, and every now and again gave her a wink, as if to say, "You got it, girl!"

The evening finished and the public, who had gathered to hear from their loved ones, shuffled out of the church. The helpers gathered together washing up cups and saucers and stacking chairs to be placed along the walls. It had been a good evening: twenty-five attendees at five pounds per head made £125 towards the electricity bill. "Sally!" cried a skinny, red haired lady, standing about 6' in designer clothes.

"Oh, God, Claire!" exclaimed Sally.

"Oh, Sally how good to see you, we have missed you so much. Are you well? Elaine called me and said you were coming tonight. You were brilliant up there; thank you, the same old Sally."

"Yes I am wonderful, thank you, and let me introduce my foster daughter."

"Oh wow!" said Claire. "How wonderful. Congratulations. Who is this?" she asked.

"This is my Megan," Sally beamed.

Claire asked, "What is she?"

"She's half-demon, but a good one," Sally muffled to Claire.

"Oh my fucking God! Sally!" Claire exclaimed. "You really were meant to do this. Please, please bring Megan over to my circle when you have some time."

"Yes of course I will, I would love to. I am just changing my contract with the hospital. I don't want to work nights any more, I need to be with the children, then I am going to start reading again, with the help of Megan." Elaine popped over from the kitchen. "Just what I have been saying to her; we have missed her. It's time to come back and be one of us again." Claire kissed Sally on the cheek, and said in her ear, "Be careful, Sally, I have an awful feeling about you."

"It's nothing I can't handle," replied Sally. "Well then, beautiful lady, you and Megan are welcome at my house any time. We'll sort that bugger out, the one outside. I saw him too and heard the noisy sod!" Sally laughed, "Sorry, he cries every night you know, but we are used to it now."

"Okay then, keep in touch." With that she passed Sally a card. "It's my new number, don't lose it, I don't give it to everyone."

"I won't," said Sally. "Thanks, Claire, I knew you would understand."

"I do," said Claire, "but watch that bugger Harold, you know what I mean don't you?"

Sally nodded. "Yes, yes, I do, but don't worry it's all in hand; this is my time for happiness," and with that Claire vaporised!

"Bloody show off!" shouted Elaine.

"Oh don't worry," said Sally, "you think that's good? You want to see what's going on in my house!"

"Bloody hell, I am worried about Megan," said Elaine.

"Don't be," replied Sally, "she's been pushed to the limit, and God only knows what she's been through already. It's my job to protect her. There are bloody angels everywhere in my house. I even had to ask permission to bring her here tonight!" Sally and Elaine grabbed each other and laughed.

"I'm going to start reading again too," said Sally.

"Oh thank God!" said Elaine. "About bloody time; and what about Harold?"

"Don't know," admitted Sally. "Christ, my senses are really returning, you know. It's a really good feeling and thank you, Lord!" She looked up towards the ceiling and smiled. "I do feel I am going to have more problems with him than the kids but I really don't know."

"Well," said Elaine, "keep in touch, promise?"

"Promise!" said Sally.

"And you know you are both welcome any time; we hope to see more of you on a Friday if you can make it."

"If we can, we will," exclaimed Sally with a big hug. The car ride was a quiet one with neither of them saying much. Within twenty-five minutes they were back to a very quiet flat. Harold and Tinker were apparently in bed when Sally unlocked the door.

"Horlicks or Ovaltine, Megan?" asked Sally. "Which one would you like? You can take it to your bedroom if you want," she said. "A Friday night treat."

"Horlicks please," replied Megan. "Thank you!" Just then a very shaky Harold emerged from Tinker's room. Sally looked over, concerned, and asked,

"Everything all right, Harold?"

"Yes, just settling Tinker down. He's been upset about his mum and dad not being in contact; he's fine now." Then he quickly went into the bathroom and locked the door behind him, which was unusual as the family rule for the bathroom was if the door was shut someone was in there so 'no entry'.

Sally suddenly went cold. "Wait here, Megan, love," she said and made her way to Tinker's room. "Just checking on Tinker," she called back. "Watch your milk or it will boil over." It seemed an age, but Sally finally returned, agitated. "Come on let's make your Horlicks and get you to bed." Her tone of voice had completely changed and her face was very red; not a usual sight unless she was upset. Megan quickly poured the hot milk into a jug, added three large teaspoons of Horlicks and stirred until it was thick and creamy, just the way she liked it. Never sugar; Megan hated sugar. "I'll just pop in and say goodnight to Tinker," she called out on her way to the bathroom.

"No!" replied Sally in a very forceful manner. "I've just settled him down and you can clean your teeth in the morning. Megan knew instantly that something was wrong and that it would be another bad night. The sound of her little brother softly crying next door and the growling from outside of her window woke her; she must have drifted off. An angel stood in the corner of her room, just looking at her as she stared at the closed curtains where the growling was coming from. "Thank you for being here and looking after me and my brother," she said to the angel. "Is anyone looking after my other brother and sister and my mum?"

"Always, dear Megan. Don't worry; you have yourself and your brother to look after." He smiled again, opened his massive gold and navy blue sparkling wings and left.

Still hearing Tinker crying, Megan put on the lamp, found her slippers at the end of the bed and quietly slipped out of her room into Tinker's. She found him still crying. "What's the matter?" she asked. "Nothing," replied a startled Tinker.

"Of course there is, you never cry. What's the matter?" she asked again. "Nothing, can't say," he replied. "Why?" she asked back. "Sally said."

"It would be okay now."

"Do you miss mum and dad and everyone?" he asked. "Of course I do," she replied.

"Shall I get in with you?" asked Megan.

"Okay," replied Tinker. So she got in and cuddled her brother in his bed until they both fell into a deep, peaceful sleep, watched over by an angel in the corner of the room until morning.

Megan woke to the sound of Sally's voice calling frantically.

"Megan, Megan where are you?" Megan shook Tinker and sat up in bed. Sally burst through the door and a beautiful sight met her eyes: both of them sat up together in bed, like two little peas in a pod. "Oh goodness! Megan, please don't do that to me again. All right, Tinker?" she asked. "Come on you two let's get some breakfast." *Thank you, God! I thought I'd lost them*, she thought.

Breakfast was delicious: real back bacon fried crispy with a fried egg, freshly grilled tomato, mushrooms and fried potatoes, all washed down with strong, hot, sweet tea. They ate with relish. Tinker was in good spirits, laughing and teasing his little sister. *What a beautiful pair of children*, Sally wondered at the sight in front of her and then said, "Surprise!"

Harold was nowhere to be seen. She had got him up early and sent him out on errands; she would keep him bloody busy today!

"I have a treat for you both today. Harold is taking us all out for the day, on him!" She winked excitedly at them both, making them chuckle and laugh even louder. "Yes, we are all going to the zoo and then to your favourite Little Chef diner for tea. I will make sure that he buys you your favourite pancakes with cherries and ice cream for pudding. How about that; how does that sound?" she asked. Megan and Tinker looked at each other and screamed with joy. "Okay then," said Sally, "let's get our little chores done first, then shower, teeth and dressed then we will be ready, okay? 11 o'clock we are aiming at, okay?"

"Okay!" they shouted back excitedly.

It was a brilliant day. Bristol Zoo was fantastic; in fact so interesting that they went around three times. Megan and Tinker wanted to visit every animal and say hello to it. They took pictures on the little Kodak camera that Sally had managed to find. Best of all were the penguins who were diving and flying underwater, then jumping out at great speed and landing on the rocks perfectly. All the children there screamed with delight at the sight. The giraffes with their long, blue tongues made Megan scream when one tried to lick her while Tinker loved the monkeys and their antics, especially as Megan said he looked like one. The massive, silver back gorilla was intriguing; he just lay there eating a large bunch of bananas, peeling each one with absolute precision before gently placing the whole thing into his mouth.

The children screamed with delight and Tinker shouted, "Can Harold get a whole banana in his mouth?" This made Sally shiver. "Come on now, kids, I think we have had enough. It's nearly 6 o'clock, and you have only had ice creams and fizzy pop this afternoon, time for some real food. Harold, get your wallet out," called Sally. "We are off to the Little Chef for dinner."

Dinner at the local Little Chef was a real treat for the family, with Sally telling them to order whatever they wanted. A very glum looking Harold looked on, thinking of his bank balance and nothing more. After mountains of burgers, chips and relishes they finished off with their favourite pancakes with cherries and ice cream. This really was a wonderland of food for them; eating out never happened at home. Their mother always cooked because there really was never enough spare to go out. That would have taken the sherry away from Patsy so she had become a brilliant cook and that's all they ever knew. They both fell asleep in the car coming home and were carried in and put to bed by Sally. Safe for another night at least.

Rows between Sally and Harold became more frequent. Sally always seemed to win, but not really. She was trying to change her shifts at work in the hospital and was asking for her contract to be changed so she would no longer have to work the night shift which started at 10pm and lasted until 7pm. In the mornings the children needed her more than ever and she wanted to be there; either to see them off to school or to be there when they came home.

This was not popular with Harold. Stopping working nights meant a drop in salary and a reduced pension. Rows about money were frequent but Sally was adamant: no more night

shifts. The hospital was not happy either; they stood to lose one of their most trusted and professional nurses, for whom everyone had the utmost respect. Sally was one of the most trusted nurses to run a very busy ward at night because if anyone was going to die, or if any problems arose, you could bet your bottom dollar it would be on the night shift so they really needed the very best staff.

Eventually, after much contract changing and negotiation with HR, she got a new contract signed and Sally got her way. *No more night shifts, thank you, Lord,* she thought as she came out of the office with her new contract that sunny day. The new shifts suited Sally and the children down to the ground; she felt happier and more in control. Harold got grumpier. She started booking psychic readings in the afternoons when she got home early from work. Word of mouth spread and, once again, the diary began to fill and the money to flow. Twenty pounds for a half hour reading was quite pricy back then but she was helping really needy people; giving advice and generally sorting out their lives. She was worth every penny and it was topping up her income. So what she lost by not doing night shifts, which were paid at double time, she was managing to put away in a little savings account that Harold knew nothing about. This made her feel really good and gave her more confidence. *Just right for a rainy day*, she would tell herself.

They had a great little system going. As soon as Megan got home from school she would get trays of cups and saucers ready with little homemade cakes on doylies ready to give out. The doorbell would ring; if it was customers she made them feel welcome, smiling at them, and making them a cup of tea. Then she sat them down to wait until it was their turn. When a customer left Megan would show them to the door then go back to Sally and tell her who was next. "It's Mrs. Norris and her dad's here with her. There's trouble in the family; the angels said it's her boy Dixon who needs sorting." Or, "It's Rose Dawson, hubby's just died, wants to know where he's hidden all the money. It's in the garage, wrapped up in newspaper in a large metal box on the shelf at the back," she would say and it would always be right. They became a brilliant little double act and Sally thanked the Lord every day for being able to cut out the night shifts. It was making all the difference to them as a family; bringing in extra cash and making family life really comfortable, especially as she couldn't ask Harold for extra money for the children's things. This was heaven; heaven, for everyone.

Until a phone call one Friday night...

"Hello, Sally, it's Brenda, Brenda McCullick from the hospital. Sally, we have a problem; Sister Linda Blewins has been killed in a car accident and we have no nurses, or head staff, available for the night shift on Horfield and Blagdon wards. The agency has also let us down.

I know it's asking a lot, what with the children and everything, but is there any way you could help us for the next couple of nights until we can get ourselves sorted?" Sally's stomach suddenly lurched; she really had a very bad feeling about this. "Well," said Sally, "not really, I have the children you see..."

"I know that, Sally," said Brenda, "but we are in trouble and need help. We have no one else to ask; your patients need you. It's only for a few nights; I'll pay you double time, triple time if needs be, just think of all the times I have accommodated you when you needed time off and I have been here myself with no one."

"Yes," said Sally, "and I have given you twenty-five years of my life. I've been totally dedicated and jumped through hoops for you as well!"

"Sally, please, I really don't have anyone else. It's just for a couple of nights that's it, I promise." Sally felt very sick. Megan came in through the door saw Sally's face and her heart skipped a beat. She felt sick too. "Okay," said Sally, "but two nights only, that's it and no more. My children come first now."

"I understand and thank you, Sally," said Linda. Sally suddenly realised that she had probably just made the biggest mistake of her life. "Oh, God help me and be with me," she said aloud and looking up to the big blue and gold angel walking through the hallway. "Please get me through these next two days and I will be yours, Lord, forever and ever amen."

"Megan!" she called out. Megan had walked back into the living room, realising there was a problem looming. She had heard the telephone conversation and knew that she and Tinker were being left alone for two nights with Harold; she suddenly felt fear. It rose once again in and around her, something she had not felt since moving in with Sally and Harold. She could tell that Sally felt it too. It was not a feeling she liked; there was always trouble when this feeling arose. Sally came into the front room. "Megan," she called again. "Come into the kitchen, love," she said. "Right, my girl, this is not a problem. I have to go and help, they need me. It's just two nights, that's all." She looked into Megan's eyes. "Okay? Then it will be back to normal." Tears started to well up in little Megan's eyes. Somehow she knew this would be the end, not really knowing why, but she knew the end was coming. *Why am I so bloody weak?* Sally screamed to herself inside when she saw that little face. *I should have said no, no! Sod 'em, I've given them twenty-five bloody years of my life and filled in for every bugger else when they wanted time off for God's sake! What's wrong with me, Lord?* Anyway it was done. She called Tinker into the kitchen, made them both tea, got them ready for bed, prepared breakfast and called all the appointments for readings she had planned to do that evening to rebook. She even made sandwiches for lunch, just in case Harold was not around, and gave them five shillings each for emergencies. She would be leaving for work at around 9.30pm and would be home by 7.30 in the morning. It would be a long shift without sleep and filled with worry. She decided she would ring Harold in the night just to make sure the children were okay and safe.

It was Harold's work's skittle evening. He played in the team every Friday night in the Winter League and he was always home by 9pm in the evening. Sally was sat dressed in her crisply ironed Sister's nurse uniform with a beautiful Victorian silver buckle adorning the belt at the front of her dress. Harold had bought it for her as a present for passing her Sister's exams and getting promotion. It was the only thing he had ever bought her which she truly cherished and she wore it with pride. She sat waiting, her stomach churning and her head hurting already. The children were in bed and she had decided she definitely would phone to check on them. She never normally did but, after that little episode with Tinker, she had to protect these children; it was her job. Harold always got himself something to eat on a Friday but she had left some egg mayonnaise and smoked salmon sandwiches, his favourite, covered in foil in the fridge. She was due on shift at 10pm and it took fifteen minutes to get to the hospital but Sally, ever the professional, always liked to be early. She took preparation seriously, it was the way she was trained: the old way, the best way, not this modern nursing training that now took place on the wards. Good old fashioned care with back rubs, bed-panning the patients every hour and staying to feed them rather than just leaving food on trays so they didn't eat because they felt too ill to try. She was absolutely brilliant at it; could run a ward or two standing on her fingertips and could always get the very best from her nursing staff by telling them off if they were wrong and then encouraging them to improve. Sally was a master at this and could bring the best out of anyone. She had proved it time after time over the years and the hospital knew how good she was at her job.

Tonight, though, she felt dreadful. *What on earth was it; why was she feeling like this?* It was 9.40 and Harold was late for a start. *Where the bloody hell was he?* She had two wards to takeover in fifteen minutes. At last the key went into the door and a very drunk Harold fell in through it. He wasn't a bit surprised to see her standing there in her nurse's uniform waiting to go to work and suddenly a massive chill went up her spine. "Evening, darling," slurred Harold, "going somewhere?"

"Yes actually," replied Sally. "I have to do two night shifts, tonight and tomorrow. Linda Blewins has died in a car crash and they have no one, not even the agency."

"Well," said Harold, "how unfortunate for her and fortunate for our finances. Double time I hope?"

"Yes," said Sally. "The children are in bed. I will be home early in the morning to see them off to Saturday School. I've made some sandwiches for you but the state you are in, I doubt whether you will manage to eat them. Everything is done, Harold, go to bed, and sleep it off."

"Oh don't worry about me, dear; I have lots of ways of amusing myself." He looked at her in a nasty, sneering way which always worked by tying her tummy in knots and making her feel quite sick. "Off you go little nursie, nursie," he mocked.

"Harold," she called out as he was walking towards the bathroom, "touch one bloody hair on those kids' heads while I'm not here and I will bloody castrate you myself. Understand?"

"Oh don't worry, Mummy," said a very nasty and slurred Harold, "they are safe with me tonight."

"They had bloody well better be," said Sally. With that she walked out to the car and slammed the front door as hard as she possibly could.

All in a night's plan, thought Harold as she left.

The Cat's Away

That had been a terrible night shift and the end did not come quick enough. She had worked on these two wards for the last 25 years, and when her contract was eventually changed, she had moved to the Outpatients Department, dealing mostly with patients suffering from Dementia, Alzheimer's, and other specialty diseases like Parkinson's, which affected the geriatric patients in the town. This suited Sally down to the ground as she had dealt with these diseases on the wards for the last 25 years. She was a loyal nurse. Being an only child like Harold, she had an ordinary upbringing. Her father was a bus conductor, and her mother worked in a local pub as a very popular barmaid. She attended a very ordinary secondary school and got very average grades, and all in all, she was a very average student. But Sally always thought that she was missing out on something. She was interested in nursing, but had not attained enough GCSE'S to apply to train as a nurse. Thankfully the local hospital had a scheme where you could train as an Auxiliary Nurse, starting at the very bottom of the ranks, but over a period of time, you could have in-house training, and make your way to the very top of the profession if you so wished. Her parents were so proud when she was accepted into the scheme, as they had never really aspired to do much with their ordinary mundane lives, which really in all honestly, suited them both down to the ground. But Sally was different; she wanted to be different, and to make a difference in people's lives, and so the die was cast.

Some 25 years later, and here she was, a senior Nursing Sister, back on a night shift, helping out again on the same two wards she had left months ago so she could be with her precious children. Both wards were in crisis, with a shortage of staff, and what staff they did have, in her opinion, were very badly trained, and to be absolutely honest, not really interested in the job.

Both wards were built in the 1900's as part of a cottage hospital, serving the local community. It had a small Accident and Emergency unit, Day and

Outpatients departments, and the usual X-ray and A&E department, 4 elderly bedded wards, a Maternity ward, and of course an overnight stay ward for the A&E. So all in all what started off as a little community hospital had grown over the years, as the growing population in the town demanded the attention they needed from the professionals that provided the all important health care.

Now, Sally was a professional, trained to the highest rank in the old school ways. Good old fashioned nursing was all she ever knew, and all she wanted to teach, not these bloody silly no touch nursing techniques they were teaching today, that do absolutely nothing for the patients. After all, that's why they were there, to nurse and attend the sick people that needed their caring and reassuring touches in their hour of need, and especially in their final hours. She ran her wards with precision. Cleanliness was of the utmost importance. So was the need to dispense good old fashioned back rubs, which get the circulation going, most important for bedridden patients so open to bedsores, when the circulation was poor after lying still in bed for so long. This also got the staff interacting with the patients, creating a bond of trust, which is so essential, and very much missing today, and best of all, she knew her regime worked. She used it all the time, and no one could match her for recovery rates, and success with bedsores. She just seemed to have the knack, and of course the other benefit she had was that she was a physic medium, and could interact with her patients, and handle distraught family members. For those who had no one, which was quite often the case, she could help them pass over peacefully, and fully aware that even though no one from the family was there with them, she was, and she also let them know that their spirit family would be coming to collect them when they went into the light, and so a peaceful passing for them would occur. She also passed on messages to relatives and loved ones, and the two wards were almost a place of magic, a place where everyone who worked there, really wanted to be there, wanted to do the best, be the best, and the staff sickness and absenteeism was the lowest in the whole hospital. The two wards were known for their superior nursing, and a place very sick people wanted to be if they could choose so.

That was until Sally left! The greatest shock for her was walking back onto the wards to find distressed patients, two of whom she had nursed before she left. They were up to their necks in urine and both wards smelled terrible. Some of the staff were just standing around chatting, looking at magazines and generally looking totally uninterested, whilst there were patients calling out and being ignored, who were hungry and thirsty.

She took over the night shift, listened to the handover report, and let the late shift staff go, then called the new staff into the office. "Right then," said Sally. No one looked up or acknowledged her, and some even carried on chatting. "Right then, you bunch of slovenly fuckers, listen up," she bellowed, grabbing their attention and making them all sit bolt upright and take notice of this small blonde haired blue eyed Nursing Sister who was taking charge of the shift that night. "You will work your bloody asses off tonight getting this place back to shipshape order, just like it was when I left. You will clean the wards top to bottom, change every single bed, feed and drink everyone, then dispense back rubs, empty catheters and then the sluice room will be scrubbed till it bloody shines. There will be no smoking or phone breaks, and you will report any problems to me. We have here two wards of very ill patients, and they need our attention, all of it, understand, and if you don't fucking well like it, fuck off! I can't be bothered with staff who don't give a toss about the work here; we can always replace you with people who want a job, care about what they do, and what people think of them, and have the pleasure of being paid double time for the privilege of doing so, get me?" she finished sternly, giving them all her strict and foreboding Sally look. And with that, in double quick time, the two teams were assembled and directed their work for the night. Sally oversaw it all, but she was so engrossed with all the problems she had to solve that night that she totally forgot to ring Harold.

By 6 that morning, both wards were totally transformed: the nasty smell that hung in the air had gone, the sluice rooms sparkled, every patient was in a lovely clean bed, all medications were given and they were all bathed and sat up having a lovely cup of tea before breakfast. In Sally's eyes the situation had returned to normal, and the team worked brilliantly. Both the nursing stations were cleaned and in an orderly manner, and ready for the new shift to take over. A really good job had been done by all, just in one ten hour night shift. Sally sat back in her chair and grinned. Good, she thought, just as I'd left it, back to normal, real nursing. As always, all through the night she had been teaching, talking to and advising the newly recruited staff, on how to run a ward successfully, and the do's and don'ts of nursing life.

There were also two deaths to deal with that night, both thankfully expected, and with the help of Sally they were very peaceful. Both bodies were dressed and dispatched to the morgue with the utmost dignity, just how Sally had always done it and the relatives had been informed and the paperwork completed. She sat back in her chair and was delighted with what they had all achieved that night, and thought to herself, Yes both wards are now back on track. And how good did that make her feel inside? Totally and utterly wonderful!

Oh, God, oh, God, she suddenly thought, with all the problems that her and her staff had encountered that night, she had not one single moment to even thing about Megan and Tinker, let alone think of ringing Harold. "Oh please, Lord let them all be okay," she prayed out loud to herself as she handed over the wards to Brenda McCullick at 8 that morning, telling her what a wonderful team she had recruited, and how they had managed to transform the two wards in one night, something the last teams had failed to do in the last six months. Brenda was open-mouthed with shock. "Now, Brenda," said Sally, "you have a great new team here, who I am looking forward to working with tonight, but I have to leave now and go and get the children off to Saturday School. I don't know who you had working here, but the wards were a disgrace to the nursing profession, and the NHS, and really, I don't know who I should report this to, but between us let's make sure the relatives of the deceased are looked after today when they arrive, and I will see you tonight, my last night!" Brenda looked at her agape, and muttered a meagre, "Thank you, Sally."

Sally got home in double time, running through a red traffic light, and constantly looking behind for the police car that she was sure was following her. It was with absolute and utter relief when she put the key into the door and walked in to find Megan and Tinker happily chattering away at the breakfast table, chomping on toast with honey and hot sweet tea. Sally ran to them and hugged them with so much love, relief pouring from her heart. "Where's Harold?" she asked.

"Don't know," they both replied.

Strange, thought Sally, but smiled at them and made herself a quick cup of tea. She then got them off to Saturday School trying not to make them late, eventually dropping them outside. "See you later, enjoy!" she called as she drove away back home.

Now last evening was Harold's skittle evening, and he was dropped off by one of his work colleagues as he had consumed far too much alcohol to drive home. Harold and Sally did not really have a sex life as normal couples do. From day one of their relationship he had always been upfront with Sally that there were particular things he needed from a woman, which he could not possibly ask his wife to do for him, so it was better for him to go to a professional aide, a woman, a professional prostitute who could fulfil that side of his needs. He had used one already since he was 18 years old. He did not love her, he made that quite clear, she just satiated his unusual sexual needs, and her name was Veronica. This was the only demand from Harold that was put on the table when discussing marriage. He had needs, which only Veronica could meet. An affliction his mother called it. "Fucking weakness, you silly boy," she would often scream at him when finding out he had indeed once again visited this secret lady of the night. "It will take you to your grave, you little wanker." That was his last memory of his mother screaming at him before she died.

Sally managed a little sleep that day, just napping really. She felt terribly uneasy; it was all around her this unusual silent and foreboding atmosphere, making the hairs on the back of her neck stand up. "Just one more night, one more night," she kept repeating to herself as she busied around the house, putting on the washing, and sorting out the school uniforms for Monday. She decided to make spaghetti bolognaise for tea, with warm garlic bread. This was Megan's and Tinker's favourite midweek meal, but it was Saturday, and she needed something easy to make and serve for tonight. She browned the meat and chopped the onion, just like Megan had taught her so confidently, trying at the same time not to cry. Then whilst she was adding chopped carrot and a little chopped celery for the flavour base, and singing to herself and trying to relax, the phone suddenly rang. "Sally, it's me Harold."

"Hello, Harold, where the bloody hell are you?" she asked him loudly.

"Had to go out and pick up the car, as I left it at the club last night. I won't be home until 9 tonight. I have to go into work now, and after that I have an appointment with Veronica."

Sally retorted viciously, "Fine," and slammed her eyes up to heaven, and shrugged her shoulders at the same time. "Your tea will be in the oven on a low, so don't be late. I will have the children in bed so they won't disturb you," and with that she put the telephone down.

The spaghetti was well made and delicious, and ready for eating by the time the children got back from Saturday School. This was a once a month treat, 10 until 4, where the school opened especially for students to try out new subjects like German, or new sports like Rugby and Roller Hockey, which were not the norm of the school curriculum for everyone. It turned out to be another lovely day for both of them, and by the time that they got home, they were both ravenous, and demolished the spaghetti under a mound of grated cheddar cheese, which they ate with the soft warm garlic bread

"My goodness you two, you must have worms," Sally commented, after seeing how fast the meal had disappeared into the happy smiling children, which immediately made the both of them scream out with laughter.

"No," cried out Tinker, "snakes," and with that last comment, they all fell about the floor laughing until their bellies ached.

"Right, that's enough now or I will never get anything done," said Sally wiping the funny tears from her eyes, and smiling at them. "There's chocolate mousse in the fridge, and when you have finished that, homework!" she said to them sternly, but with a smile. "And then you can watch TV for a couple of hours, but I want you both in bed by 9, before Harold gets home, okay you two?" she asked.

"Okay," they replied back in unison, heads down tucking into their chocolate treat.

Sally suddenly lost her appetite; she had just realised what she had said. She realised that with her not around to protect them, the children may well be in danger. "Oh my god!" The alarm bells rang out in her head, and she suddenly felt very sick and heaved. What on earth was she doing going to work tonight, putting her little angels in danger?

The phone rang and Sally jumped up with fright. "What?" she cried out loud.

"Sally, it's Brenda."

"Oh, God, what it is now, Brenda?" she asked distressed and loudly, her head spinning with fear.

"Is there any chance you could come into work earlier tonight, say 9 not 10?"

"Not possible," replied a now nervous and sweaty Sally before Brenda could even finish. "Harold's working until late and will not be home until 9.30," she replied, pinching herself as she lied, "and I can't leave the children on their own, but I will be in as soon as I can, okay?" she replied firmly holding her head in one hand as she responded.

"Yes, yes thank you, Sally," replied a very sheepish and quite disturbed Brenda, thinking this was not the usual person on the end of the line. "See you later," she quietly replied and put the phone down.

Megan had not heard any growling lately, actually possibly for as long as two weeks, which was having a very positive effect on her. She was feeling

70

better, sleeping well and doing wonderfully at the new school. Yes all was going well, that was until tonight. The demon had been very quiet, running from his older female, Patsy to Megan. Night after night he would check on them both. But Megan was very well protected in Sally's house, so it was easier for him to feed from her mother Patsy, still causing problems and trouble for her while the two children were away. But he had recently sensed a chink in the armour. He sensed an evilness which quite excited him. He could smell and taste it in the air; it would be the downfall of the heavenly and very protected Sally. One day he decided to follow her male, Harold, and after only a few hours, cloaked from the daylight, and sat in the corner of his office watching him closely listening to the string of phone calls from all his contacts, realised he was right.

Megan was sat in the bedroom on her brightly coloured bedspread, when she suddenly heard the very noise that she dreaded the most, and it sent a terrible chill and tingle down her spine. She jumped up and pulled the curtains closed, but his call carried on. Her stomach lurched, and she wanted to cry and be sick at the same time. Trouble tonight, she thought and ran up the hall into the kitchen where Sally was making fairy cakes for tomorrow. She was crying and praying quietly to herself, and Megan guessed that she had heard it too. "Do you have to go to work tonight?" asked a very frightened and worried Megan, knowing that Sally knew this was a time of trouble brewing.

"Yes, yes I am sorry, I really am, I have tried to get out of it, but it is just for this one last night, and that's it, okay? One more night, I promise," Sally replied hugging her.

"He's back," said Megan now shaking inside and realizing she was once again very vulnerable. "He's growling outside my window."

Sally grabbed her by both hands, and looked deep into the crying small face, her tears falling like raindrops. She pulled Megan over to the kitchen table, and put her up on top, so she could be on the same level as her. Wiping the tears from her eyes, and holding Megan's face in her hands she said, "Right then, m'girl, listen to me. Megan, it's not the dead you have to worry about, it's always the living. The dead can't hurt you, unless you let them. He can't get in here nor anywhere unless you invite him in, do you understand that? You are safe here with me, in fact, my little darling, you will always be in my life, even if you do go back to your original family… the Lord has seen to it that I will always be here to protect you, do you understand that?" she asked even more firmly this time, and Megan nodded her head, tears streaming from both eyes. Sally cuddled her trying to hide the tears on her cheek as well.

At 9pm on the dot the sound of the key in the door made Sally jump up from the chair she was sitting in, waiting in the kitchen for Harold to arrive. Her uniform was pressed and clean, and her big silver ornate buckle on the front of her belt shone with pride. But something inside her was making her feel so bad, making her feel sick with worry. What on earth was it, she kept asking herself? She was ready for her last night shift in the hospital, even mulling over In her head if she could afford to give the job up for good, just to be home with the children all the time, and her head was spinning when the door opened. Harold's evening meal was on low in the oven.

"Is that you, Harold?" she called out, now shaking inside.

"Who the bloody hell do you think it is?" he replied.

Oh, God, something's wrong, she sensed, immediately feeling a chill go right down her spine. Harold sauntered into the kitchen after throwing his briefcase and coat over the hall chair. Oh, God not again, she thought. She could smell alcohol on his breath. "Bad day or evening?" she quizzed.

"If you must know, both," he bellowed back at her.

"Oh," said Sally, "sorry."

"No you're not, you're never bloody sorry," he roared back at her.

"Your dinner is ready in the oven if you want to eat it."

"Later," he replied nastily. "I've lost my appetite," he said as he poured himself a very large whisky.

Oh, God, thought Sally at that very moment, I should ring in sick.

"Go on to work, little nursie, leave everything to me, see you in the morning. I will be here as always," he said with a very menacing look, which made Sally shudder right through to her core.

"Harold what's wrong, love?" she asked. "I know you are not right, what is it, love?" she said softly and walking towards him.

"Nothing, nursie," he replied with a venom in his voice. Then he turned and walked into the lounge, sat down and turned on his precious television set.

Sally was in a daze, not really knowing at that particular moment what she was actually doing. She put on her coat and left for work… quietly closing the door as she left, trying to get up the courage not to go, but to stay, but the call of duty and her honour for work and to the hospital she had served in for so long, got the better of her, and just for a second before she got into the car, she heard him. A cry, almost painful, growling around Megan's window. Absolutely livid and shredded with shame in the fact she was going to work, she screamed out in response into the dark night air, "And you can fuck off, you demon, she's safe with me now, you will never get her." She slammed the car door so hard, a couple of her neighbours' kitchen lights went on, and nets were pulled back, but when they realised that it was just Sally getting into her car and probably going to work, they relaxed.

The growling instantly stopped. It was dark for some reason. The street lamps were out, and the dense blackness hung in the air like fog. She heard nothing at all. She opened the car window and tried to listen just for a moment, but there was still nothing. In the distance, just by the side of Megan's bedroom window was a pair of green demon eyes looking directly at her. "Huh!" she retorted loudly. She turned on the engine and drove to work, and cried all the way there!

When she arrived on the ward that evening, her new team was waiting for her, all ready and eager to start their shift, all looking to their leader to give them duties and directions. They had all received so many compliments and thanks for the total renovation of the two wards last night, they were all eager for more, ready to prove that the hospital made the right choice choosing them for their jobs, so a very busy night it would be.

Good, thought Sally, it will keep my mind busy. "Right then, staff, let's get busy. Team 1 here's your rota, team 2, here's yours. You know what you have to do, so let's get busy and get to it," Sally firmly directed them, and with that the night shift started.

Back at home Harold was still unsettled and on his third large glass of whisky.

Good job I have another bottle under the stairs, he suddenly remembered. "Bitch, bitch bitch," he muttered aggressively to himself, now grabbing his erect member and rubbing it hard. "Fucking bitch!" he cried out again, now deciding to read some porn to try and ease his pent-up and fast growing frustration. In fact that very evening, Veronica, at the very last minute, whilst Harold was sat outside of her house in the car waiting for his appointment slot, had rung him on his very new and large mobile phone and cancelled, telling him she had just received some bad news. "What!" screamed Harold. "What about me? What about what I need now?" he again bellowed at her down the phone.

"Well," replied Veronica, "my mother has just had a massive heart attack and might not make it through the night, and I was advised by the consultant who has kindly rung me, to go to the hospital immediately, so therefore I will not be keeping the appointment with you Harold."

"When then?" he screamed back at her, now foaming at the corners of his mouth, and acting very animated in the car.

"I will ring and let you know," she replied with utmost dignity of the situation, and then put the phone down.

Harold went wild. "Bitch, bitch, bitch. Fucking bitch!" He was screaming out so loud that the whole of the street could have heard him. Well that was all he needed after the day he had just endured. He sat in the car screaming and shouting obscenities for at least two minutes until one of the neighbours who lived next door to Veronica heard this noise coming from outside his house and decided to investigate. He ran up to the car, and saw Harold behaving like a gorilla on heat, ranting and raving like a mad man inside.

"What are you on, man? Shut the fuck up, my kids are in bed just here, do you want me to shut you up?" he roared at him through the car window, trying not to attract any attention to them both. Frustrated that Harold did not stop screaming profanities from inside the car, he smashed his fist down as hard as he could onto the bonnet of his car, peering menacingly at him to try and get his attention.

It worked and Harold instantly came back to normal life, and on seeing this thug through the windows of his car, shouted back at him, "Fuck off, you cunt, I need a drink." He started the engine, and drove off down the road like a mad man, his wheels spinning and gearbox crunching as he sped out of view.

Sally's night on the other hand was going really well. Both wards were sparkling clean, all meds were done, all beds changed, and all the necessary bed baths completed. Now it was time to do the real nursing. Nightly turning and back rubbing began. She was really proud of this team, they all worked so well together, and the biggest thing of all, was they listened. Sally was now teaching and directing a young man called Stuart. He was in his early 30's, and was already designated as the new Matron of the ward, and very good he was too. He accepted the position with great humility and understanding of what was needed, and was sucking in all the information that Sally was giving him of how the wards needed to be to operate successfully, and efficiently. He also loved the old fashioned nursing practices, which he took straight to his heart, and promised Sally he would never give up in favour of this new silly tish tosh that was being taught now in the nursing schools. She also talked to him about the staff, how to get the better of them, and how to get the best from them, which was so important. How to get them to give their all, because that was what they really needed in a place like this. "Kick 'em, and kiss 'em," Sally had told him. They were both laughing over a cup of tea. "Tell them off for doing wrong, but bloody praise them to the high heaven when they've done well," she told him as they giggled and discussed the ward and the staff. Yes it was all going really well, and the night was passing all the quicker. Stuart would take the reins and carry on where Sally had left off, and this gave her a good feeling in her heart. Twenty-five years on, she'd done her bit, now it was time for someone else to carry on. Yes Brenda would be pleased with her handover of this team in the morning; they were ready to take over. Thank God, she inwardly thought.

It was now 2am and Harold on the other hand was getting even more drunk. He was already on his second bottle of whisky, and he decided to have another. The second bottle was now half empty. He decided to try again to read more porn, this time choosing something completely different, which should satiate him. My god, he had so much stuff stashed away in his secret cupboard under the stairs. He had acquired it from a local head master who ran a primary school not too far away; in fact it was the very school that Megan and her brothers and sister attended. He was also a discreet businessman, and head of the secret porn circle. He got it cheap from one of his associates who was a mason, and of course, it was all very hush hush you know, which made it easy for people in the know, and with the right connections to get hold of the precious material they all needed to fulfill their own special sexual needs. And it was only recently when he attended a dinner invitation at the Masonic lodge,

where he picked up his blessed package, that he overheard his friends and associates discussing the demonic ancestry of the masons. He heard them talking about demons, and devils and how they should be respected, and not to be dismissed as mythical creatures, as they had been mentioned highly in the Bible and often in the world as we know it now! Much proof abounded about these frightening and worrying creatures that could cause so much havoc to people today. They were also discussing how strong they were, how they fed on fear, and how they would die to protect their chosen one, which made them in the eyes of some to be most admired.

Something clicked in Harold's head. It all made sense now; it was that little evil bitch Megan. She was one, he knew it, he always sensed something unusual about that girl, that's what all the trouble had been about, she was protected, and his Sally was bloody well protecting her, over him! All that bloody howling and screeching every night and the bloody scratches on the wall outside her bedroom window, which he had covered over with paint twice now, was all making sense. That was it; he decided there and then to get rid of that devil child the nastiest way he possibly could, that would make him feel so much better!

Harold took another magazine from his newly acquired package and started to think again about the conversation he had witnessed in the lodge, making his head spin, but he had drunk so much, he passed out lying prostrate on the very large sofa with his tackle hanging out for all to see, an empty whisky bottle at his side. What an awful sight he made. If Sally came in now and saw him like this, she would probably kill him herself. But! While he was asleep, Megan and Tinker were safe.

The demon sat on the roof of the house. He had been watching Harold with interest, peeping through the large gap in the curtains in the living room that Harold had accidently pulled open as he stumbled around in his drunken state. This was one beautiful outrageous, nasty and disgustingly evil man. He loved him! The demon loved evil, of course he would, he was himself pure evil! And he always fed well on evil deeds, and nasty foul play, it made him even stronger. Especially fear, which was good, he loved fear, and there would be lots of it this evening. Fear was good and growing; he could feel it, making him lick his lips with anticipation of the unfolding evil events. This was his food, his energy and there would be much fear and feeding for him tonight. What was bothering him though, was his young female was inside. She was his, his female, and if he could get into the house, he would fight to the death for her. He needed her unspoilt and unmated. That would be his job, to spawn a new demon son, which they usually were. But panic was slightly getting to him. This was a safe house; three Archangels of the highest order and a spiritual woman resided here. Suddenly realising what was about to unfold he became increasingly agitated, and started to scratch and claw at the bricks outside the bedroom window, again taking off the paint that Harold had repainted not so long ago. He was worried and growling loudly now, so much so, that the neighbour's lights started going on; he could be heard some quarter of a mile away, so loud was his resounding call.

Harold suddenly woke; it was about 5am, and he had the biggest stonking erection his body had given him for months. He was crying with joy as he smeared Sally's expensive French butter with salt crystals onto his massively enlarged member. "Ohhhhh, my beauty you are back," he cried to himself with exuberant jubilation of this wondrous gift from above. The demon on seeing Harold awake started howling louder and louder, now slapping the window pane with his tail, the noise thundering around the room. "Fuck off, devil! I know you are there, Harold's now going to have some fun and you can just stay outside and watch," he laughed with a high-pitched evil sneering laugh.

Back at the hospital, Stuart, who really had the utmost respect for Sally said to her, "Look, it's 5.15, knock off early, I know you have been worrying about your foster kids, I can do the handover."

"That's really kind of you, Stuart," said Sally, "but Brenda won't have that."

"She'll never know," he replied smiling. "All these years you have given to this hospital, you could be collecting meds from the pharmacy while I do the handover, what do you think?" he queried her.

"Thank you, Stuart, I will do one last round, and if I am satisfied, yes thank you I would love to finish early."

Harold was now very drunk, and stumbling around the flat, happy and delighted with the new found stiffness which he craved for, but it was now so hard, it started to hurt. "Oh, God." He suddenly sucked in a breath, "Gonna have to relieve you soon, my beauty," he said looking down and admiring his throbbing stiffness. "Oh yes, it's playtime, and I have many toys to play with," he said out loud, spitting at the large window pane and seeing a pair of red eyes boring directly back at him. He walked out of the living room, licking his foam encrusted lips in anticipation and padding as quietly as possible towards Tinker's room. He gently pushed his door open and crept slowly and stealthily towards a sleeping Tinker. "Wake up, wake up, Tinker, Harold's got a present for you. It's all ready, and it's a nice present." He spoke quietly in anticipation of the gratifying events that would unfold to satiate him, but two very large Archangels appeared on the other side of Tinker's bed with their swords drawn, and pointing them directly at him. "Oh piss off, you can't touch me," he slurred at them, telling them both of the new found information he had acquired from the lodge. Did they and Sally think he was so stupid? He had always seen these celestial beings that suddenly arrived with the two children, but he had always disregarded them as ooky spooky beings he might or might not have been seeing, always trying to ignore their irritating occupation of his house.

Tinker suddenly woke with a start, and Harold grabbed him hard, screaming and struggling from his bed. Harold was now very animated and started screaming profanities of delight into the silent and malevolent atmosphere of the house.

"Don't hurt him," screamed out Megan who suddenly woke hearing Tinker's screams in the other room. She ran into the living room to see Harold in a completely depraved state, trying to force Tinker onto his stiff body, but to no avail. Tinker was biting him, screaming and kicking as hard as he could, which unfortunately just made Harold even more frustrated and nasty. Pure evil now flowed in and around his face, creeping into his aura, seeming to make him stronger, and on seeing Megan in her pyjamas in the doorway, his face lit up. The demon outside who had been watching Harold was now going berserk, making the walls of the house actually shake like thunder. He was also thrashing the window with his tail, so much so, it was as though they would smash any minute. Harold was about to harm his young female, he had to get in and protect her!

Harold threw the screaming and thrashing Tinker across the room. He landed with a thud, temporarily knocking him out, but coming around quite quickly on hearing Megan screaming, as a naked and ominous Harold was dragging her around the room by her hair, in full view of the window pane, where the demon was looking in on this revolting demented man. Harder and harder he shook the house, almost taking the roof off at one point, his rage and venom exploding on seeing the events playing out in front of him, now making him feel so helpless.

"Leave her alone, leave her alone," Tinker screamed as he hit Harold hard on the back with his tennis racket which he had picked up from the bedroom floor. "Where are you Mum and Dad when we both need you?" Tinker was screaming out and crying at the same time.

"Well, you little bastard, they're not here are they, I am. Ha ha ha ha ha ha ha," he venomously screamed out. Once again his strength seemed to come from nowhere, and picking up Tinker like he was a dolly he threw him across the room knocking him out cold, and leaving him in a crumpled state.

Now that he was out of the way, Harold could again concentrate on Megan, and the delights he had planned she would give him. He pulled her against his ridged body. His grasp was so strong and his strength unbelievable, it was sucking the life out of her. He was still screaming at the top of his voice, "Come on, you devil, I'm here, I'm here." He was laughing out loud, feeling like the devil himself inviting the demon watching to come in and fight for her. He was dancing around the room in a euphoric state like a demented monster, Megan's body dangling in his grip, her being ebbing slowly away. She was in a dreamlike state, unable to breathe or move. So hard was his grip around her neck that she felt she was dying. Harold grabbed a bottle of brandy from the side of the cabinet; it was half full. Pulling the cork out with his teeth, he poured a large slug into his whisky glass. Sally would use the brandy for sauce on a Saturday night when she cooked duck. "Sod the duck," he exclaimed downing half the pour in one go, but Megan was fading and the two Archangels were screaming at her to wake up, looking up above for help.

"Wake up, wake up!" they repeatedly screamed to no avail. They were now screaming up to the Lord himself to help with this desperate dying situation. It came. A flash of light came down and struck Megan hard, bringing her suddenly back to life, and a chance to fight for life, and with all the strength she could muster in her little body, she bit down hard.

Harold's wail could be heard halfway down the street, he was totally in shock. Pain ran through his depraved and abusing body, blood pouring all around him. He was now desperate, slapping and grabbing at Megan's neck, feeling suddenly faint, and out of control.

Megan was free, and she was heaving violently, releasing the disgusting evilness she was forced to consume, her breath coming in big hard gasps, blood and bile covering her little face. She struggled to bring the life-giving breath back into her body, which it had been deprived of for so long.

Harold on the other hand was running around the flat screaming, "I'll kill you, you little bitch." He was covered in blood and a terrible sight to see.

It was 5.40am as Sally pulled up outside the flat wanting to rush in and pick up and cuddle both of the kids she loved so much. She felt relieved, that was it, the last shift, they could all be a real family together, something she had always dreamed of, and prayed very hard for.

Immediately she got out of the car she knew there was trouble; angels were everywhere outside and probably inside as well. A few neighbours were peeking out of their curtains, listening to the screaming and howling that was coming from inside the flat. The demon was also going demented, screaming and howling like she had never heard before. Oh, God, Megan's in trouble, she immediately thought. "God and angels please help me, I need you now, please come and help me with this situation," she called out running to the door with the key in her hand. The door opened, and the scene that confronted her was nothing short of a scene from a horror film. Angels were everywhere, Tinker was unconscious on the floor, Harold was screaming and running around the flat, blood pumping everywhere from his lower body. He was holding a hand towel over it, but the blood was still pouring out, and little Megan was heaving, and being sick on the floor, covered in Harold's filthy blood which was all down the front of her pyjamas.

"Harold," screamed a shocked and bewildered Sally, "what have you done?"

"It was her," he wailed back at her pointing to little Megan who was still fighting for breath, "she's bewitched, a demon girl, she made me do it, asked for it!"

God, thought Sally, he really is out of his head.

"Call me a bloody ambulance, you bitch," he screamed at her.

"Harold, you bastard," screamed Sally back.

"Get a fucking ambulance," he screamed at her even louder this time.

With that, Sally went over and picked up the struggling Megan. "All right, love, I'm here now," she said wiping the blood from her face.

Harold suddenly lost it completely; he ran across the room and hit Sally hard across the head, nearly making her drop Megan. Sally stopped, gently laid Megan on the sofa, stood up and with all the might she could muster, whacked him back, right on the chin. "Get a fucking ambulance yourself, you perverted bastard," she screamed back at him. Harold tripped backwards, and fell, drink getting the better of him, and he could not control the fall, and cracked his head on the corner of his very expensive and beloved coffee table.

Sally sat cuddling with the two children, and called the police, and then an ambulance. Harold was pronounced dead at the scene when the police and the ambulance men arrived. He had died of severe blood loss from hitting his head on the coffee table, and what a pitiful sight all three made cuddling together on the very sofa which Harold had tried to stop Sally so hard from buying. It would have melted any heart. Even the on looking angels were in shock, and the demon still looked in through the window unable to roar. Harold's body was splayed out on the floor and there was blood everywhere.

"God," said the sergeant when he arrived, "what the bloody hell has gone on here?" No one said anything; everyone went about their duties not saying a word. What could one say? You just had to look around and drink it all in to realise what had gone on here, it was in fact, total carnage.

Social Services arrived thirty minutes later. Sally was still holding Megan and Tinker, whilst being interviewed by the police. Her trusted neighbours came in, cleaned up, and bathed the children, while Sally, Susan and Norman talked. They would allow them all to stay together that night whilst the investigations were carried out, and they would talk again the next day.

"We'll see you in the morning," said Susan. "Do try and get some sleep," she told Sally and with that she and Norman were gone.

All three of them slept in the same bed that night. The hotel staff were really kind to them, bringing extra tea, milk and cheese and tomato sandwiches, which the children ate very slowly, and very quietly, no one really saying anything, just fearing what the next day would bring.

The next morning, Sergeant Evans and PC Wilkinson arrived at the hotel to see Sally. They told her no further action would be taken, as they were quite convinced that Harold had died in accidental circumstances. His alcohol blood limit was eight times over the driving limit and, during the whole day, he must have consumed at least four bottles of whisky. Obviously, this contributed to him tripping and hitting his head on the coffee table, which had caused a brain haemorrhage and killed him. Sally was numb: frozen and very unresponsive.

That evil bastard had taken away Sally's only chance of having a loving family life with two of the most beautiful, and deserving children she had ever met. Now it was over.

"I'll spit on that bastard's grave," she said, looking directly into Sergeant Evans's eyes.

"There is something else," said Sergeant Evans. "You very quickly need to get some advice from a good solicitor. It appears that Harold was sacked from the council yesterday; they found pornographic images of young children at his work. He was part of a larger circle that has been under investigation for some time and it only came to light when a cleaner found some photographs which Harold had hidden. She reported it the next day. You need to know where you stand moneywise with his pension etc. There is also the attack by Harold on the two children; you will need some help, especially if the parents were to take this any further. I can recommend someone." It turned out that Harold's own solicitor was part of the circle himself.

"Leave the children, Sergeant Evans, they don't need this after all they have been through. Don't you think they have been through enough already? I will be speaking with Social Services today, they will be back later and we need to work out what will be best for them. Then, if we need you, we will call you; okay?"

"Okay, Sally, if that's how you want it, fine... but if the Murphy family decides to bring charges, we will have to speak with the children, no matter how painful it is to you or them."

Sally smiled and said,

"Thank you, Sergeant Evans, good day." Under her breath she muttered to herself, "They will never know if I can help it, anyway their mum couldn't care less."

That afternoon was painful for all three of them. Sally, Megan and Tinker were all in tears when Angie Wells from Social Services told the children that their mother was better and responding to treatment so they could both go home. They pleaded with her to stay with Sally but, as she was now a single parent, this did not conform to the guidelines laid down for fostering so the children would have to go back to the family. There wasn't another family available or a hostel that could take them. Megan and Tinker begged Sally to adopt them; anything, anything at all, just to stay together as their little unit but Angie Wells was having none of it. Once again, exactly as they had been removed from the family home, they were removed from the care of Sally: screaming, kicking and crying. Both were dragged off into the back of a waiting car with Sally following them in tears and screaming that she loved them and would always be there for them.

It seemed the whole car park was growling and very noisy; even Angie looked around to see where the noise was coming from but she was hardened to this, it was her job: removing children at risk to safe houses and, hopefully, loving parents who could never have children of their own. Today's decision, though made her feel sick inside. She knew these kids were going back to a house of hell and a very nasty and deranged mother. Although she had not actually told Sally, Angie had pleaded with her boss for the children to stay where they were. They were having none of it because of the police involvement and the fact that the newspapers had gotten wind of Harold's paedophilia. It was easier all round to send the children back; they would intervene, be there for them and support the family as necessary. A mental health nurse was appointed to call three times a week and Angie would call every other day for the first month to monitor the situation and report back to the office so they could plan a good cover story. *Bastards*, thought Angie as she drove the screaming kids away back to their house; this was just asking for trouble.

Meanwhile, Sally was trying to make some sense of it all. The flat had been cleared and cleaned by the local council and it was the only place she had to go. So, with the heaviest of heavy hearts, she put the key in the door and entered. It was as if nothing had happened. She walked over to the hall chair, took off her coat, put down her bag and walked into the kitchen.

"Oh my God!" she screamed. There in her kitchen sat Claire and Elaine.

"Hello, darling," they said together, then got up and cuddled her at the same time.

"How did you know I would be back?" she asked.

"My angels have been keeping an eye on you and the children since you came to church. I knew there would be trouble so we've come to help," Claire said kindly.

"How can you help?" replied Sally with a tear. "I've lost them."

"No, Sally, you haven't," replied Claire. "You will always be in Megan's life; she absolutely can't live without your support. It is going to be nasty for her for a while but she will be back. She will come looking for you, maybe not for a little while, but she will be back, I promise."

"Promise?" replied a very tearful Sally.

"Oh yes, darling, I always keep my word; so does our Lord and the spirit world. You, of all people, should know that. Now come on, a cup of tea is needed. Elaine, put the kettle on, nice and strong. Now then, Sally, let me tell you all about Michael, Megan's big angel, and his plan." Sally smiled at Claire and realised that this was just the beginning of a new and very long story.

Back Home Again

There was no nice warm welcome home for the children; only a note for Megan to do the school uniforms and make soda bread for her brothers and sisters. The babysitter answered the door to let them in and said,

"Patsy said I could go when you all arrived. She told me to tell Megan to make up the two beds. *Nothing bloody changes,* thought Angie. She was surprised that the house was absolutely spotless, if sparse in comparison to the Smiths' flat. It was comfortable there; she always felt funny in this house and often wondered if it was haunted. She could not actually put her finger on it, but it felt terribly oppressive. *Bad vibes,* she concluded and shivers went right up her spine to the top of her head. *I could never live here,* she thought to herself.

"Right then, you go," she said to the babysitter, "and Megan and I will get these beds done. Then we'll have a look in the fridge to see what there is to eat." Megan was already at the top of the stairs, opening the immersion heater cupboard and pulling out thin, brushed nylon sheets and blankets to make up the beds.

The fridge was almost empty. There were just some eggs, old tomatoes, a piece of hard cheese, an old onion, some cold cooked veg and buttermilk for the soda bread. Angie gasped with amazement as, within just a few minutes, Megan made a loaf of soda bread which was now ready to go into the oven. When Angie asked how on earth she was going to feed her brothers and sisters she replied,

"I will make a big oven omelette; it's a type of Spanish omelette. It will be really tasty, don't worry."

So, she whisked the eggs good and hard, added salt and pepper and managed to find the little bottle of precious olive oil, which made Angie grimace.

"Olive oil," she said, "for ear aches?"

"One day everyone will cook with this oil," Megan replied and carried on with her preparation. She greased a large deep flan dish with butter, grated the hard cheese, sliced the tomatoes, onion and old veg and then added them to the flan dish. She covered it all with the beaten egg and topped it off with the grated cheese and a swirl of the olive oil. She placed it in the oven, under the soda bread, to cook for twenty minutes. If she got it right, both would be done together. Angie wondered: *where the bloody hell did you learn to cook like that?*

"My mum and the blue lady," Megan replied.

God, she's reading my mind now, Angie thought.

"That's bloody amazing, Megan!" said Angie, and it had started to smell wonderful. Ten minutes later, the table was laid, the bread was out resting and Megan was checking if the oven omelette was cooked by gently touching it with her forefinger. The aroma filled the kitchen and Megan brought the flan dish out to rest for a few minutes before serving.

"This firms it up a bit, so it won't be sloppy to serve," she said. Angie looked at Megan who was quietly speaking to someone in the corner of the kitchen, by the back door. Of course, there was no one there! Megan smiled.

"What is it?" said Angie. "What are you staring at?"

"Oh, just my lady in blue," she replied.

"What lady in blue?" asked Angie.

"She helped me cook it," replied Megan.

"Is there enough for me to have some?" Angie asked, realising that she had not eaten all day. The beautiful aroma of the food was making her ravenous.

"Yes, of course," replied Megan. "There is always enough to go around. I've already laid a place for you; she said you would be staying for tea." Angie smiled and looked at her.

"Oh, God this is really freaky but I'm starving and it smells wonderful," she said.

"Good," said Megan, "let's eat!"

The feast tasted divine.

"Glad you're back!" said Megan's little sister and brother. "We have missed your cooking!"

"Oh," said Megan, not really wanting to ask any questions in front of the social worker.

"Right then," said Angie. "Thank you; that was more than amazing and I have learned something new tonight. I'll try that myself one night when I get home late. Let's wash up, tidy up, and get everyone to bed, so everything is shipshape for when Mum gets home." *You poor little sods,* she thought.

With the kitchen clean and everything washed, tidied and put away, Megan tidied the front room, putting all the cushions exactly back in their right place. The four kids got into bed, but not before they had all gathered together and said their prayers. The sight of four little children, all praying together, brought an unexpected tear to Angie's eye. She tucked them in, one by one, and kissed them all goodnight. Having told them she would be back next week to see them all, she went downstairs to wait for Patsy to come home.

She sat at the bottom of the stairs, thanking God that she did not have to stay in that house. It was very unnerving; God knows how the children coped but it felt bloody horrendous to her. *What was it in this house?* She looked around the hallway at all the religious pictures of Christ and the Virgin Mary and chuckled at the little font of holy water which was on the wall by the front door. She got up, intrigued to find out if there really was any holy water in it. As she just popped her finger into the font she felt the soft feel of warmish water and, at the same time, heard a key in the door. It made her jump. *God, this house,* she thought to herself.

"Hello, Patsy," said Angie.

"They're home then," replied Patsy.

"Yes," said Angie, "home and safe." Patsy came in and walked into the kitchen, putting down her Fine Fare carrier bags.

"Well?" said Angie.

"Well what?"

"Aren't you going to ask me if they are okay?" Angie replied.

"Why?" said Patsy, "I know they are, or you would have told me. Megan you mean?"

"Yes," replied a very angry Angie, "yes, her." *How bloody pure evil,* she thought. "She came straight in, made your sodding soda bread and fed the kids with the crap you left in the fridge. It was bloody amazing. What's the matter with you? She's wonderful!"

"She's a fucking demon, that's what the matter is!" Patsy replied. "Trouble, always will be."

"My God you don't deserve those children," replied Angie, and thought, *I*

hope to God they are all praying right now for new parents and a better life.
"One more bad report, one more incident and I will have them all taken away
next time. Do you hear?" She pointed at her while she was screaming.

"Fuck off and mind your own business!" Patsy replied. "And you can see
yourself out," she said pointing to the front door. Angie opened it and let
herself out.

"Fucking evil bitch," she spat as she slammed the door.

Behind her, Patsy let out a loud laugh, reached into her shopping bag and
brought out a large bottle of cream sherry.

Megan lay in bed that night, praying to her angels.

"Please protect me, my brothers and sister and my dad wherever he is.
Please don't make Mum hate us all again. Stop the baby crying and the
person who comes up and down the stairs all night trying to get into our room
and please, most of all, let my mum love me!"

It was nearly one in the morning when Megan heard her mother start to
climb the stairs. *She's drunk again,* she thought. *Please go to the bathroom
and get into bed.* She shuddered when she realised that her mother was
heading for her bedroom. The door opened and Megan froze with fear,
pretending to be asleep. Her little sister was tucked into her back for warmth,
sound asleep. Patsy looked at the two sleeping girls, bent down over them
and emitted a low, moaning growl. Megan thought she was going to faint.
Patsy stood back up, grimaced and walked towards the door. At that very
moment, Megan could hear an unusual dragging noise. She peeked through
one eye and looked at her mother going out of their bedroom door. She just
glimpsed what looked like a gold coloured tail behind her!

That night dogs barked, owls hooted and something growled outside her
bedroom window. The baby started crying and there were footsteps up and
down the stairs. The door handle of their room was shaking as if someone
was trying to get in. This went on all night – yes, Megan was home.

Patsy Murphy

Patsy was sat on her stool in the kitchen and had just finished feeding the children. Megan was now organising their baths and bedtime whilst the ironing of the school uniforms had also been done along with the washing up. She was deep in thought and tears were falling steadily. Her mind was in a frenzy, all over the place, and she was already half way through a very large bottle of sweet sherry.

She was lonely, very lonely, with her mother dead, and her sister living miles away, she had no one. She felt alone and very vulnerable, unable to mix with anyone or have any friends. The constant fear of trusting anyone hit her hard. Sometimes she just wanted someone to talk to but the one person she really wanted in her life at this particular time was not there: her man, her man mountain, her love, her passion. She always felt she was nothing without him: naked, afraid, and lost. He had left her for money. This hurt so much. *Why?* She didn't understand why this was more important than being a family, all together and supporting each other. But he was gone; gone for the money to help that bloodsucking lot in Ireland who didn't give a toss about his family in England but would soon bloody shout if the money didn't arrive every week. They had taken him away from her. It was them to blame for all of this misery. Of course he still loved her, she was sure of that. She sat drinking even more, trying to convince herself, trying to blink back the tears, smiling to herself at the memory of when they had first met.

When they first met she was 16, and he was 21. He was her very first and only boyfriend. She was dragged along, very unceremoniously, by her older sister to the weekly Irish dance, which was held at the school rooms at the top of St Michael's hill in Bristol. She was wearing second-hand clothes and very worn shoes. She had begged not to go, but her sister was having none of it. Their mother had said that if Patsy didn't go with her there would be no dance that night. Always safety in numbers, their mother would say. Her mood was lightened when her sister agreed to lend her some of her nice underwear and a new skirt that she had purchased only that day.

She was sat in a quiet, dark corner of the dancehall with a large lemonade on the table in front of her, watching everyone dancing and twirling on the floor. Suddenly, she saw him across the room, dancing with his friends at the bar and showing off in front of all the young ladies gathered in that area waiting to be asked for a dance. She gulped, her skin prickled, her heart started to race, thumping in her chest. Oh God in heaven, she wanted him. Yes him, right there in front of her, she had to have him. She felt sexually aroused just by the thought of him holding her hand. *Oh, God,* she cried out to herself. She watched every move he made, every word he spoke: this sexy, big, strong boy with thick dark hair and a strong jaw line. She wanted those lips on hers, his hands on her waist. She stared intently, mouthing to him in silence, almost in a trance and not caring where her sister was. Patsy wanted to be with *him*. Again she mouthed in silence to him, projecting herself out to him, to get into his mind. *Over here, I'm here, come on, look, I'm waiting for you, over here*! Her eyes now glowed a very beautiful sexy green. She sat transfixed, drooling at this beautiful, handsome young man who could dance, really dance. *Oh, God, could he move.* She was now panting hard, her breath rasping in and out of her lungs with a desire she had never ever felt. God it felt wonderful. Excitement was starting to rise within her. He was to be hers, all hers and no one else's. No one was even allowed to speak to him, she'd kill them all, all of them. Her fangs now dropped.

She got up and walked into the middle of the room. Their eyes met and suddenly, as if in a dream, they were dancing together. All around the room, everyone was looking on and admiring this beautiful couple who had swept onto the floor. This couple who only had eyes for each other, touching intimately as they danced and entwining their bodies almost in a frenzy. *You're mine, all mine.* Again and again she projected this through her mind to him and now she was in his arms. He was totally hooked; mesmerised at this beautiful young, blonde, green eyed girl.

At the end of the dance he walked her home. It was a long walk, about three miles away from the dancehall. They never spoke, just walked holding hands. A light goodnight kiss sealed their union and when he finally got back to his digs in the early hours of the morning, he sat on his bed and put his head in his hands, trying to work out what exactly had happed that evening. Out of nowhere, he now had a woman; a beautiful and sexy one at that with long legs, big green eyes and long, blonde hair. She was a stunner and all he felt was love: an intense and protective all-consuming love. He took a small piece of paper out of the pocket in his jacket with her name and address on and realised he was missing her already. They had arranged to meet again at the same dance next Saturday. God, could he wait that long?

"Oh for God's sake, pull yourself together!" he cried out to himself. Too late, he was hooked and he dammed well knew it.

She was struggling now with her inner demon. "Never let it get a hold," her angels would tell her when she was younger. "Don't listen to it, tell it to go away he can only come in and affect you if you invite him in. When she was much younger she had made a silly mistake on a very busy evening with her grandmother and her customers. They were all sat and gathered around a Ouija board when she made her one fatal mistake.

Patsy's mother, Blodwyn, was a brilliant psychic medium who always helped everyone and anyone who needed angelic assistance. Her mother was born into a family of witches in south Wales who practised the old cult ways: yo-yoing between black and white magic. They were feared by everyone in their village and people would cross the road and bless themselves with the sign of the cross if they even came near them.

It was a whisper in the family that Blodwyn was cursed with the demon essence. Apparently, the essence can skip and Blodwyn's mother did a deal with the devil himself to spare her, which had worked. Unfortunately, the curse would be passed on to the first born daughter and *her* first born daughter after that. The price, it seemed, was not that high at the time but a warning came from one of the wise old witches that, if this deal was accepted, it would bring nothing but suffering and misery to everyone associated with these children unless they could be strong enough to resist the pull of the demon.

Blodwyn's mother was a very high practising priestess, untouchable by most and greatly feared by all of the sect and the village. She, in turn, feared nothing: not even the Devil himself. So, she believed these children that would be born with the passed on essence would be more than strong enough to deal with this menace of a demon. She accepted the Devil's offer without realising the newborns would indeed be angelic and work within the realms. The one thing she had misjudged was that they would be part human and, as we all know, it's the human side that has weaknesses and flaws. Without knowing it, she had just condemned these two children to a living hell! There was no escape for Blodwyn either. Yes, she was spared the curse of the essence, but was destined to live a horrible life; suffering under many, especially her very violent husband. It was a suffering that would linger with her until her dying days. She would eventually greet death with an eagerness to flee the pain, suffering and ridicule she had endured through her short life. She died early in her 46th year from excruciating, untreatable breast cancer.

Patsy had sat with her Great Granny Brunt so many times when practising with the Ouija board. She always made it look very easy and Patsy remembered everything. First form the circle; ask the angels to come in; cloak everyone with protection then thank the angels for working with them at that time and protecting everyone with their love and strength. Then would come prayers of invitation to bring forward the spirits of the departed loved ones so that contact could be made with them before passing on any messages. Finally, thank the spirits for coming to contact their loved ones and gently ask them all to leave before closing the portal through which the spirits have come through and saying a prayer of closure and protection. All done, easy! So she thought.

A circle was arranged in Blodwyn's house; it would be a Ouija session, by invitation only. Blodwyn never liked the Ouija, always choosing cards as the better way to pass messages on to loved ones. She had managed to escape from the village and the sect when she was 18, coming to Bristol with her, also very psychic, grandmother. They would do palm and tea leaf readings to survive and feed themselves. She was good, really good and very accurate. Occasionally, she would hold a Ouija session with trusted people who were trying to contact their dearly departed, often with spectacular results. There was one particular night when a local neighbour discovered where the deeds to her house were. Her husband, Ron, had hidden them before he died, fearing she would leave and divorce him. When he died suddenly her affairs were a mess and she was unable to move on and sell the house.

One day a neighbour just happened to mention that old Mrs. Brunt was holding another Ouija session. The neighbour had already spent over £100 on psychic readings with absolutely no results whatsoever and £100 was an awful lot of money at that time. However, intrigue got the better of her and she found her way by invitation to one of Mrs. Brunt's circles about six weeks later.

She didn't feel nervous when she knocked on the door of number 51 Grey

Street. It was opened by a small girl of about 14 with blonde mousy hair and a very nice smile.

"You must be Mrs. Rita Thomas," she said. "Welcome, we have been waiting for you, please follow me." She followed the young girl up the corridor to a door. "Can I take your hat and coat?" she asked nicely, putting them onto an already bulging coat rack on the wall.

"Thank you, what's your name?" she smiled at the young, blonde haired girl.

"Patsy," the girl replied.

"Well thank you for a lovely welcome."

"Through here," directed Patsy, leading her into the living room, where 5 people already sat around a table with numbers and letters written on it in chalk. The curtains were drawn and only a single lamp lit the semi-darkened room. She noticed the fire burning brightly in the hearth, giving some warmth to all that were attending and throwing flickering flames that made long patterns up and down the plainly painted walls.

"Good evening, and welcome everyone," said Ma Brunt once she had sat and settled herself. "Now we are all here, please relax. We are all well protected. Even if you don't believe in angels, please believe me when I tell you that you have all brought your own angels with you tonight. They are here to protect you and work alongside my angels. Please say nothing unless you are asked to do so. Please also be aware you are totally safe, and hopefully we will be able to get some important answers for some of you tonight. I must add that perhaps not all of your relatives may come through tonight but I will tell you that I have been sending messages out to the universe inviting all those we would love to contact to appear here tonight and communicate with us."

The room went very quiet and everyone was asked to join hands around the table, close their eyes and ask for the person they wished to communicate with to come forward. Patsy, in the meantime, lit all the candles that were placed around the room.

Within a few minutes they were invited to open their eyes. A slight, cold breeze wafted around the room, even though not a door or a window was open, and the fire roared out heat from the hearth. It was eerily silent; you could have heard a pin drop. Mrs. Thomas's skin prickled right up the back of her spine, almost as though someone was kissing it. She suddenly wanted to cry. Old Ma saw the change in the aura around her and asked everyone to place their forefinger, very gently without any pressure, on top of the tumbler which sat in the middle of the table. When they did, it immediately moved, much to the surprise of the guests sat around the table. Gasps of disbelief came from their mouths.

"Quiet please, everyone, we do have some spirits here with us," Ma called out loud. "Do we have anyone here in spirit wishing to contact anyone sat around this table this evening?" The tumbler suddenly went wild, sliding around and around the table frantically in big circles as if trying to decide which one to pick. Everyone was flabbergasted and tried to call out. Suddenly a mist started to fill the room, wafting up from the floor and encircling everyone sat at the table. The temperature suddenly dropped. *A good sign*, thought Ma. *Spirits are here, plenty of them trying to communicate, we'll earn well tonight.*

Ma asked again, "Who would you like to communicate with?" Again and again the tumbler flew around the table. A faint smell of cigars filled the air, coming from nowhere it seemed. The glass suddenly jerked to a stop right in front of Rita Thomas, who screamed out with fright. She was suddenly feeling worried and spooked.

"Don't worry, it's quite normal, everyone please quieten down. The spirit needs all its energy to contact us. Our talking does weaken them. Who are you?" she asked. The glass quivered, shaking as if it was trying to decide where to go, then slowly, amidst gasps of wonder from all around the table, the glass started to spell out words, s-o-r-r-y.

"Right," said Ma, "thank you so much for communicating with us. Do you want to say sorry to Rita?" Again the glass quivered; slowly moving almost it seemed by magic. Ma felt the glass being pulled quite strongly. *Must be a man*, she thought to herself. Again the tumbler quivered and started gliding around the table, stopping to spell y-e-s, this time. It regained its speed and was quickly circling the table, with everyone struggling to keep their fingers placed on the top of the tumbler. It slowed and started to spell s-o-r-r-y. Ma interrupted. "Can we ask you some questions please?" Y-e-s was again spelled out.

"Who are you?" she asked. "What is your name?" The glass started to flow around and around the table, picking up speed, but slowing to spell r-o-n.

"Oh my bloody God, Ron, Ron is that you?" Rita cried out. The glass now went into a frenzy, so much so it flew off the table.

"Everyone calm down now," called out Ma. "It's just the spirit getting very excited because he has made contact." The glass did not break and was quickly placed back on the table by Patsy, who smiled to herself.

"Rita, ask Ron a question, but keep it simple please."

"Ron, Ron my darling. Love and miss you, but I need your help. Where are the deeds to the house please?" she asked in a tearful voice. The glass quivered then started to flow again, round and round the table, picking up speed, slowing to spell s-o-r-r-y. Rita said quietly, almost embarrassed, "Ron, I love and forgive you, now please, please tell me where they are hidden." Tears quietly flowed from the corner of her closed eyes. The glass, once again, quickly picked up speed and made its way around the table.

"Quick, another piece of paper!" Ma instructed Patsy to write down the letters. It spelt b-l-a-c-k b-a-g.

"Oh thank you, thank you, darling," Rita quietly said. "Are you telling me that you put them into a black bag for safe keeping?" Y-e-s came the reply "Oh thank you, you sensible wonderful husband of mine," she said now, not caring about the embarrassment in front of the others gathered around the table. "Darling, where is the black bag?" she asked. The glass hovered, moving side to side as if it was contemplating the answer. "Please, darling, I really need to know," Rita again pleaded. The glass still quivered for a few seconds, and then slowly slid around the table spelling the next word: g-r-e-e-n-h-o-u-s-e. "Oh, Ron, thank you," said a now very heavily distressed and crying Rita. Once again the glass sped around the table four or five times, without stopping, slowing eventually to spell out s-o-r-r-y again. As suddenly as it had started, it stopped.

"Ron has left us now, Rita, are you okay?" asked Ma.

"Yes, thank you so much." *The old bugger*, Rita sat quietly thinking; it was the only place she had not thought to look in.

It had been a good night, all expectations had been surpassed and everyone around the table had connected with their loved ones and all questions had been answered. Hot tea and biscuits were now being passed around the room to everyone but Rita decided to go. She hugged Ma Brunt and thanked Patsy before placing a £20 note in Ma's hand and £5 in Patsy's.

"You have done more tonight for me than all the others I have been to see. I will spread the word."

"That's all we ask," replied Ma, seeing her to the front door.

"Great result tonight, my girl." Ma winked at Patsy who fondled the £5 note, which was a small fortune to her, and pushed it towards her grandmother.

"No, you have that, you deserve it," she smiled back at her. Patsy ran straight upstairs to hide it under her bed in her dolly box, leaving Ma to say goodnight to all the other satisfied customers.

Word had now spread; Rita Thomas had kept her word. She did indeed find the deeds to her house in a black bin liner, buried in the greenhouse, just as her spirit husband had told her in the Ouija session. Three months later she moved to Cornwall to be with her daughter, just as she had wished. There was now a long waiting list to attend these sessions and a basic charge of £10 was levied to all who attended. On a very regular basis some people would leave, walking away to great wealth, without even offering a penny which made Ma a bit disgruntled. The angels very quickly gathered, telling Ma to charge everyone for all her hard work. She worried that a £10 charge would put people off coming, but the angels reassured her that her name was now so famous, it would not. They were right, the list and the waiting time just grew longer but she still stuck to just taking five at the table; with her it made six: a good and lucky number. That meant they would earn £50 each night and it kept them all fed and the rent paid. Bills were now becoming less of a worry; yes, the angels in their wisdom as always, had worked it all out and life was getting better.

Ma only did meetings twice a month on a Saturday night but the pressure and demand was bearing down on her. Letters and knocks at the door were starting to drive them all crazy, so she relented and started to do the meetings every week. All went well at first but she was an elderly lady, well into her 80's. Her health had been declining for some time and, with all the extra pressure, she was finding it sometimes a little too much.

Patsy sat in the kitchen reading the Bible whilst waiting for her grandmother to join her in prayers before the start of the session. This was always their regular routine; she had already got all the teacups and saucers laid out on trays ready and a barrel of biscuits was ready to plate for the guests later that evening. The kettle was full and two big homely teapots with loose tea waited next to it. Her mother suddenly appeared. She was going out to a dance where some of the local GI's were still stationed. Despite the war ending some five years ago, regular dances were put on to entertain them until they were eventually sent home.

"Where's Gran?" Blodwyn asked, walking through the kitchen and adjusting her blouse.

"Upstairs," replied Patsy without looking up from the Holy Bible she read.

"Got many tonight?" Blodwyn asked, not really showing that much interest.

"Five, we are full," Patsy replied.

"This really is too much for her, Patsy. For God's sake don't let her get too tired, it really drains her."

"Don't worry, I can always help out and take the circle," Patsy replied. Blodwyn looked directly at her and in a very loud and firm voice said,

"You must never do the Ouija without Ma, do you understand?" Patsy sat there just looking and saying nothing. "Do you understand?" her mother screamed. "Promise me!" Patsy looked at her mother, tutted and lifted her eyes up to the ceiling. Blodwyn swiftly clipped her across her ear and, before she could even reply, tears stinging in her eyes, her mother bent down and spoke directly into her ear. "Never let yourself be open to the curse, that's the easiest way he can get in. How many times do I have to tell you? Now promise me!" she said, firmly holding Patsy's jaw and staring straight into her glowing, green, angry eyes.

"I promise!" she replied.

"Thank you, that's all I ask," Blodwyn said before walking towards the front door, putting on her coat and letting herself out.

Ma came downstairs some ten minutes later.

"What was all that commotion?" she asked.

Patsy replied,

"Mother, making me promise never to do the Ouija on my own."

"Wise words, but when you are older you will. You will read for people too - probably cards actually - but don't worry about the future now, let's get paid for tonight." There was a knock at the door. "Okay," said Ma, "show time." Patsy proceeded to let the guests in while Ma sat in the living room quietly saying prayers before starting the session.

It was a lovely session that evening but just as the last person was receiving his message; the glass working away merrily, Ma came over very faint and flushed, almost fainting at the table. She also suddenly felt very sick.

"Patsy!" Ma called over to where she was sat writing the messages.

"Yes, Ma," she replied, looking up to see Ma a funny shade of grey.

"You will have to finish up for me, my darling; I have come over not feeling well." Patsy looked quite worried but replied,

"Of course, Ma," sounding as professional as possible under the circumstances and trying not to worry the customers. She reassured them that this was quite normal as Ma was an old lady and this happened a lot.

So, she stood at the table and started the closing ritual. The angels gathered, the portal was closed, everyone was cloaked with protection, the angels were thanked, blessings were done and everyone was safe and sound. Nothing changed, it was normal, just as they had always done. The candles were extinguished and the lights turned on. Ma excused herself and went upstairs to bed. Patsy made the tea and passed it all around to the excited customers who had just witnessed their first Ouija and contacted their dearly departed. Everyone was excited and happy with the night's session and promised to spread the word as they left.

That night Patsy was woken by the sound of a dog howling and a scratching sound which seemed to come from outside her window. She got up and out of bed and noticed Angel Michael standing in the corner of her room with a very large sword. She had been able to see angels ever since she was a small child; she usually bumped into them in and around the house but had never ever seen them in her bedroom. Seeing nothing sinister outside, but having a funny lurch in her tummy, she got back into bed and pulled the blankets up and over her head before settling down to go to sleep.

The next morning Ma was really poorly and unable to get out of bed which was very unusual. There were angels everywhere in the house. Blodwyn was sat on Ma's bed dabbing her sweating brow and looking really concerned.

"Patsy, what happened last night?" she asked.

"Nothing really, Mum. Just at the end, after a really good session, Ma got sick, felt faint and asked me to close."

"Did she leave the table?"

"No, she stayed. I said all the normal prayers, the angels came and everything was normal."

"Well, everything is not normal, recite me your ritual," Blodwyn demanded firmly.

Patsy did as she was asked, going through the whole ritual word by word.

"Correct, I don't understand this, something is very wrong. You said all the angels were in attendance?"

"Yes," replied a now very confused, and worried, Patsy.

"Where did you sit?" Patsy went quiet. Her mother looked up at her and, expressionless, repeated the question. "Where exactly did you sit at the table?" Patsy gulped, really not wanting to reply. "Well?" Blodwyn now raised her voice with anxiety.

"I didn't, I stood," she replied truthfully, now feeling very sick to her stomach.

"What?" cried out Blodwyn. "Were you holding hands with everyone else to keep the circle closed and safe?"

"No, I didn't know I had to. Ma never said anything; she was holding hands in the circle with everyone and I just said the closing prayers to finish the ritual." Ma was now breathing heavily. Her breath was coming in gulps and she was burning up with fever.

"Go and fetch the doctor," Blodwyn shouted at Patsy. "Quickly!"

The doctor arrived and very quickly diagnosed pneumonia. Old Ma would have to go into hospital and her life was in grave danger. She was old and frail but a great fighter and, at the age of 80, had lived well and long.

"They'll do everything they can at the infirmary," the doctor promised them both as the ambulance drove away. Ma was the mainstay of the family, the strength, the glue that held them all together and made them all work as a team. She was really something special, the sort of person every family should have.

"Oh, God, please look after Ma," they both prayed together before leaving the house that evening to go to the hospital in the centre of town.

They were armed with a small bottle of sweet sherry (Ma's favourite), home cooked ham sandwiches, the Evening Post, and a tube of Trebor extra strong mints.

She was sat up in bed with an oxygen mask on her face, sweat pouring from her brow.

"You took your bloody time," she snapped at them both.

"Sorry," said Blodwyn, "it's the earliest we could get away. How are you feeling?"

"Well, I've been better but both of you sit down; we need to talk." Patsy suddenly noticed angels all around and her stomach lurched, making her feel quite sick and uneasy.

"What is it?" asked a very agitated and sick feeling Patsy. Her head was whirling and spinning even before any words had been said.

"Patsy," said Ma, "you were wonderful last night; I thank you with all my heart. You were brave to finish the session. You got straight in there you did, just as I had taught you, never blinking or questioning anything." Big tears were rolling down her face.

"What's wrong?" Patsy cried.

"It's all my fault," Ma sobbed.

"What is it, Ma? You are frightening me," Patsy replied, fear creeping up her already tingling spine.

"When you closed last night, I should have told you to sit at the table and join hands to complete the circle of protection. I am so sorry, my darling, I felt so poorly it just went right out of my mind."

By now Ma was in a real state: crying and wailing into Blodwyn's arms.

"Patsy, you were the only one not cloaked and protected last night. The curse, he's here, he's got in," she cried out even louder. Poor Blodwyn was trying with all her might to quieten and comfort poor Ma and a nurse from the front desk appeared at the side of the bed.

"What on earth is going on here?" she demanded, shooing Blodwyn and Patsy to one side and putting Ma's oxygen mask back on. "Mrs. Brunt needs all her strength, she needs to rest, please leave now," she commanded. Blodwyn and Patsy left the ward under a cloud, neither speaking to each other until they got on the bus that would take them home.

"What does all this mean?" Patsy asked her mother, who was still shell-shocked.

"It means that you are now cursed and your first born daughter will be as well. All this bloody time we have been trying to keep it away, and we could have done. Bloody Ma and that fucking Ouija board."

"It's not Ma's fault, Mum, I wanted to do it as well."

"I know, my darling," Blodwyn replied. "You do have the gift, it's really strong, you are strong, but I should have warned you sooner. I am so sorry."

"What do we do now?" Patsy asked.

"Be really strong, you have the essence of the demon but you must never connect with him. Never let him into your space; never invite him into your aura, your head, in fact anywhere. He will constantly bombard you with songs and words, thrown at you just to confuse you. You will hear him talking in your head, singing to you. In fact he will try absolutely anything he can to get your attention. Don't acknowledge him, ever. Be strong, really strong, stronger than you have ever been in your life. He will always be watching and waiting to connect so he can plant the seed to control you and destroy your life. Your defence is to laugh and be happy: sing, say your prayers, and talk out loud to the Lord. He feeds on fear so if you laugh you make him weak. If you say your prayers and attend mass you will make him even weaker. You will always have to be on your guard." Blodwyn grabbed her daughter's shoulders and looked directly into her glowing green eyes. "You can beat him, you have the gift so you just have to be aware, make no mistakes and be strong, okay?"

"Okay," replied Patsy, turning her head, and looking out of the window as the bus rumbled on towards their estate.

Ma soon came home from hospital, still weak from the pneumonia, but in good spirits and quite spritely in herself. There would be no more circles for the moment, much to the disappointment of the clientele. Blodwyn was, of course, very able to conduct a sitting, having often sat with her mother doing exactly the same as Patsy had been doing with Ma. She was much higher than Ma in the spiritual pecking order and more powerful.

"Oh my God, I wish it was me that had taken the sessions," she admonished herself. "This would never have happened."

"But it has," Angel Michael chirped up suddenly, trying to comfort her. "We need to manage the situation now; he's in the house you know. Patsy must be strong, I will order my angels to keep a watch out over her and I will need you to be alert. I will do as much as I can."

"Thank you, Michael, I will," she replied as he spread his magnificent blue black wings, dotted with little gold dots, and flew up and away out of sight.

*

Over the next three years Patsy, Ma and Blodwyn worked hard, keeping the family together and the demon at bay. Daily prayers were said and a Bible was read from in the house on a daily basis. Much to everyone's relief and delight, twice monthly Ouija sessions recommenced. They were especially careful with cloaking and protection. Blodwyn made sure that she attended every single session; overseeing the protection of Patsy and Ma and also upping the charge to £20 per person. It didn't make any difference; customers still came and the waiting list got longer. The dog still howled at night and odd things were still happening around the house, but life still went on in a funny way.

Patsy was now 16 and had three other siblings: two brothers and a sister. She became a second little mother, helping with all the chores around the house. Her life became a daily blur. She was helping with all the household chores, going to school, cooking and helping Ma whose health was, by now, really deteriorating. Angels still walked around the house. Every Sunday the family would gather around the radiogram, in front of a roaring fire, to listen to the world news. The Korean War was raging, the Conservative party had just won the election and a brand new government road crossing scheme, designed to cut road deaths, was to be introduced. As soon as the news would finish, they would all settle down to listen to the new play that had just started broadcasting. The Archers quickly became a sensation and turned from a short story play, which would run for just a few months, into a national institution.

Life was returning to normal. Patsy was sensing her demon but definitely managing it well. She had started to grow taller and was becoming a beautiful young woman. Her two brothers now stayed with their Auntie Gwen who lived in Clevedon. Her older sister, Julie, who used to live with Blodwyn's ex GI boyfriend, had now come to live with them. Patsy and Julie hit it off immediately. Julie was very interested in boys and Blodwyn had her work cut out dealing with this one but she loved her curvy girl with big brown eyes and coffee coloured skin: she really was a stunner. Patsy's father was in the army. She had actually never met him, as Blodwyn chose to visit on a monthly basis at his barracks in Wiltshire. She wanted to keep him away from the family. He was not a very nice man and could be handy with his fists. That way the kids were safe, was what she always told herself. Ma, though, was struggling. Her aura was now changing on a daily basis. Blodwyn decided not to go to the barracks this month as she was really worried about Ma. *He'll have to go without this month,* she thought to herself while helping Ma to get comfy on the sofa.

Ma had taken a turn for the worse. She had been in bed now for three weeks and the district nurses were calling in on a daily basis.

"I'm dying, the curse is killing me," she would cry out in her delirious moments. The district nurses put it down to the medication.

"Morphine can play with the brain," they would say to Blodwyn and Patsy, but they both knew better. The demon was in the house and Ma was old and weak so he was draining her. The tell-tale signs were now becoming more apparent; black rings around the eyes were absolutely typical. Blodwyn had been brave and written to her mother in the sect in the little Welsh village, asking for advice. No one replied and she had never felt so alone. Her beloved grandmother was now, she had accepted, dying. Little Patsy, she knew, would soon succumb to the demon and she herself was feeling unwell. A very large boil on her breast kept weeping. She was bathing it regularly and kept a plaster over the hole that was releasing a foul smelling green liquid. It hurt like buggery and the pain went right down her arm, into her hand. She would have to go to the doctors at some point, she kept telling herself.

Old Ma lasted another three weeks, dying a terrible demon death. She ended up skin and bones and her body was almost unrecognisable as the person she was. It was explained by the doctors as advanced malnutrition caused by old age dementia. This was the cause of death written on the death certificate. The funeral was a meagre affair. She was cremated at Arnos Vale crematorium and the wake was organised to be held in the house. Patsy didn't attend, preferring to stay at home and make the food that would feed the hungry mourners. Anyway, she had already said her goodbye to Ma some weeks before she actually died because, in her mind, she was already dead then. She put on a real feast as her contribution.

It was a mournful day, over 150 gathered to say goodbye to Ma. Fifty were invited back to the house, as that was as many as they could cope with; after all, it was only a small house. She was a well loved and respected lady and the mainstay of the family. Now she was gone, Blodwyn would need Patsy's and Julie's help, especially as she found herself with child again. *Oh, God,* she thought to herself, *this will take some explaining.*

Just as the funeral wake had finished, there was a knock at the front door. Patsy called out,

"I'll get it." Running down the hall she opened the door and there, on the front step, stood a tall man in a very smart and important looking army uniform adorned with four silver medals that hung from a silver bar covered with ribbons of all colours. It reminded her of a Christmas tree.

"Hello," he said, looking right at her and making her stomach lurch, "is your mother in?" He was trying to look past her down into the hall.

"Who shall I say is calling?" Patsy asked.

"Your father," he replied. He was looking her up and down as if she were a piece of meat. She slammed the door and ran back to the kitchen where her mother was trying to encourage Jonny and Timmy, her brothers, to eat up all the leftovers.

"Mum!" screamed Patsy.

"What?" Blodwyn screamed back at her in frustration and annoyance that

Jonny and Timmy were giving her a hard time over the food.

"There's a man outside in army uniform, he says he's my dad." Blodwyn stopped, the blood draining from her face.

"Right everyone, stand in a line, it's your father. I know you have never met him; I tried to divorce him if I am honest but he must have heard of Ma's death and he is here. He is still my husband and he is your father."

"I don't like him, Mum, he's nasty."

"Stop that, Patsy," she cried at her, glaring her big blue eyes as if to say, *shut up.*

"Now all of you; stay there and I will go and let your father in."

"No need," said a voice from behind her making her jump. "I'm here, came in through the back door, which was left unlocked. That won't happen again." The children felt the menace in his voice and saw the terrified look on their mother's face. Big trouble had just walked into their lovely homely home and it all felt bad, very bad.

"Right, who do we have here then?" he asked, inspecting them all just like a sergeant major would. They introduced themselves one by one to the father they had never met. Each child was conceived and born off the barracks, their mother visiting him once a month for conjugal rights. Choosing to live away, she regretted the day she ever married him. When escaping from the sect in Wales, she had stopped over for a couple of nights in a little town called Chepstow. She had stayed in a small hotel in the town centre. Arthur was billeted then at barracks on the outskirts of Chepstow and one night they met in the bar of a local pub. He had stayed with her that night and, true to form, they were married six weeks later. She soon found that he was a very strict authoritarian and also very handy with his fists if things were not done his way. Dinner on the table at 1pm prompt, not a minute late, house to always be totally immaculate, and everything in its place. Order, tidiness and obedience were his expectations and he made sure that they were implemented into his marriage with absolutely no compromise whatsoever. Do it, or take the consequences. This was the main reason that Blodwyn did not want him around her children; it didn't matter if he hit her, she could take it, but she didn't want him around them.

"Oh, dear God, he's here now, this means only one thing," she said to herself, shuddering at the thought of him harming any one of them, "trouble." She wasn't wrong.

No one slept that night; the children were confused about this man who had appeared from nowhere right into their lives. The sounds from their mother's bedroom distressed them all: cries, moans and then screams could be heard. The last thing she had said to them when she put them to bed was that they must all stay in their rooms, whatever, she would be fine and see them all in the morning. She tenderly kissed them all goodnight, knowing what was coming.

Arthur, their newly found father, greeted them in the kitchen next morning, dressed in a collar and tie and very smartly pressed trousers. The table was laid, a pot of tea was brewing and breakfast was cooking.

"Porridge, toast, scrambled eggs and sausages," he called out to them as they made their way to the kitchen.

"Right you lot, have you all washed and cleaned your teeth?" he bellowed out loudly. "If you haven't, back upstairs now!"

Some bloody welcome, Patsy thought. They all ran back upstairs like lightning, bumping into one another and trying to be the first into the bathroom.

"And don't come back down until you have, clear?" he screamed like thunder up the stairs. Even the next door neighbour must have heard through the thin walls. Patsy relented and let the boys and her sister be first to go and clean their teeth. She sat on her bed and waited for them all to finish. She hated that man already and didn't really know why; she just sensed something really not right about him, almost evil.

"Always trust your instinct," Ma would tell her, "it tells the truth." She was sure it wasn't lying to her now; angels had appeared all around the house, which was not a good sign. She would go and ask Mum, she would know what to do. Slipping past the three squabbling siblings she made her way to her mother's room and quietly snuck in to wake her gently sleeping mother who was on her side.

"Mum!" she called quietly.

"Patsy, get out, love, go and have breakfast, go on go!" She talked in a very low voice. Patsy nearly fainted at the sight of her mother's beautiful face. She had a black eye and a split lip. There was bruising all over her face, arms, and around her neck. "Go!" she shouted at her. Patsy ran out of her room and straight into the bathroom. She brushed her teeth and had a quick wash before returning to the kitchen. Anger was burning in her now.

He's a nasty man, she told herself. Michael the angel appeared.

"Quiet, child, be strong, we are here to help."

"Then help my mum," she replied.

"Patsy!" her father called her from the kitchen.

"Go, child." Michael encouraged her to move so she went downstairs slowly and deliberately, walking into the kitchen in a very defiant mood. Her brothers and sister were hungrily eating their toast and sausages.

"Not much left, m'girl, you have to be on time in this house now," he said with an almost comically nasty look on his face.

"Not hungry," she replied, looking directly into his eyes which, in her opinion, glowed with pure evil.

I'm going to have trouble with this one, he thought to himself. *I will enjoy breaking her, just like all the others.*

No you bloody won't, thought Patsy with an inner grin.

He realised she could read his thoughts. *Shit,* he thought, feeling a sudden bolt of consciousness go right through him, *I'll have to leave this one alone for the moment.*

"Sit down, girl!" he ordered her, pointing to the empty chair. She duly obeyed and sat down, not for one moment leaving his eyes. A voice welled up in her head,

"You can kill this evil man if you want to and release your mother from her pain. Go on, you can do it!"

Yes, I could, she thought as he placed a bowl of porridge and a mug of sweet tea in front of her.

Evil, evil, evil, was running through her mind as she sat there quietly sipping her tea and eating her porridge. She watched his every move.

School that day dragged. Patsy knew that her mother was unwell and now that man was here and he had already hurt her. He was evil, pure evil, she could feel it. How on earth did her wonderful mother get together with that brute of a man? It must be the Devil's revenge, she decided.

She made her way very slowly home, stopping and talking to everyone she could. Trouble was here now, loud and clear. How was she going to handle it? Michael suddenly appeared at her side.

"Home, child, you are needed; run!" Acknowledging his wisdom, she ran as fast as she could, almost screaming inside with fear. Now the yellow, green eyes appeared in her brain.

"Kill him, child, save everyone," it said. She ran faster, now certain there was trouble at home.

The house appeared empty. It was eerily quiet as she entered.

"Mum," she called out. There was no answer. It was cold and none of the fires had been lit. She ran upstairs and checked all the bedrooms, but found no one.

"What the hell?" she called out. Her bedroom was a complete mess, the dressing table had been overturned and clothes, books and her precious nick-nacks were all over the floor. Gasping for breath now with fear and anger, she ran back downstairs and checked every room.

"Oh God in heaven, what has happened here?" she called out loud to the angels. Again she was met with silence. "Angels!" she screamed, again, absolutely nothing. In sheer frustration, she ran back upstairs into her bedroom, immediately putting the dressing table right and tidying the room. *Where is Julie?* she suddenly thought. Shivering with cold, back downstairs again she ran. She checked the larder; she could make some food tonight, and went to the freestanding stove in the middle of the kitchen which was out.

"Right, let's get some heat into this house," she said to herself out loud, clearing the warm ashes from the bottom and putting them into the ashes bucket. With both fires laid, she gently lit the stove first, encouraging the flames to take hold by adding more kindling wood. When that was furiously burning away, she lit the fire in the living room. Within ten minutes of lighting both fires, warmth started to spread around in the house, turning it into a home.

She checked the larder again: potatoes, carrots, corned beef, flour, butter and eggs.

"Right then, corned beef hash," she said to herself. But before she could start, she knew she needed more wood and coal from the dreaded coal shed. She hated that shed, spiders as big as saucers lived in there. She had already been bitten by a massive house spider when she was small and the fear of those nasty, eight legged monsters stayed with her, sometimes even keeping her away from the coal shed. Her mother would laugh, picking them up to show her how friendly they actually were and making fun of her.

"There's worse than that to be afraid of," she would say to her but, no matter what, Patsy was convinced that they were always out to get her and now, alone in the house, with two fires to see to, she would have to go to that bloody shed alone.

Picking up the bucket, she took in the warmth of the two fires, now burning brightly and throwing shadows up and down the walls. She suddenly noticed the silence, which was strange and eerie. There was not a single angel, nothing. They had told her to get home, run in fact, and yet no one was here; a tingle went up her spine and a dog howled somewhere in the distance.

"Oh crap, let's get that bloody coal and wood in," she thought to herself, opening the back door with a lit oil lamp in her hand to show her the way. The shed door opened easily.

That's funny, she thought. It was usually on the latch, but tonight the door was slightly ajar. She placed the oil lamp on the side of the mound of coal and started to pick up some smaller pieces that would be needed to coax the fire to set in and burn nicely before the larger pieces could be placed on top to bed the fire in for the night.

Just as she picked up the lamp in the coal shed, relieved not to have bumped into any eight legged monsters that evening, she heard a noise. Her heart missed a beat and her nerves started to jangle. She stopped and again she heard it; this time a moan, almost a cry which sounded to her very human.

"Hello," she called out quietly, "hello, anyone there?" This time she heard a soft sniffle.

"Who's there?" she called out loudly, lifting the lamp up to spread the light out so she could see more. There, in the corner of the shed, wrapped only in a sheet, eyes swollen, mouth bloodied and hair in a tangled mess was her sister, Julie.

"Oh my God, Julie!"

"Help me," Julie cried out. Patsy jumped over the mound of coal and grabbed her with both hands. She was freezing, almost hypothermic, and naked apart from the sheet.

"Oh God, Julie, let's get you inside," she said, taking the oil lamp in one hand, while helping Julie with the other. The two girls helped each other back into the house; Patsy making sure to bolt the back door from the inside behind them.

Placing Julie beside the fire, she ran upstairs to run a hot bath and grab a spare blanket from the airing cupboard. With the bath run and the kettle boiled, she made a large mug of hot, sweet tea. Patsy sat with Julie in front of the roaring fire. Julie was shaking from head to toe and holding her hot tea with tears streaming down her battered face.

"Come on, I've run a bath for you," Patsy said, pulling Julie to her feet and helping her up the stairs. She watched as Julie gingerly got into the steaming tub. Her face said it all; it was bruised and now very swollen. Her body was bruised and there was a large smear of blood on her inner thigh.

"Did he do this to you?" Patsy asked in a quiet but firm voice. Saying nothing but nodding in reply, Julie held on to her sister. Patsy vowed that he would never do this to anyone ever again; she would make sure of that.

She reassured Julie she would only be in the kitchen and left her to soak in the bath. Downstairs in the kitchen, she quickly assembled the vegetables and started cooking, before taking up a hot mug of Bovril so that Julie could have something at least to line her belly. Patsy had warmed Julie's pyjamas and took them up to the steamy bathroom, also placing a fizzy pop bottle, filled with hot water and wrapped in a towel into her bed to warm it up for her. Managing to push a little hot food into her, she coaxed her into her warm bed. Patsy kissed her gently, tucked her in and told her she was there, just downstairs in the kitchen.

"Just call me if you need me," she told her, leaving her crying and sobbing gently into her pillow.

Patsy was unable to stomach any food that night, feeling physically sick at the thought of what that evil man had done to her beautiful and gentle sister. He had only been here for one day and already the family was suffering.

"Oh God, Ma, I miss you," she said out loud to herself. She decided to bank the fire up and sit in her mother's chair by the fire. She saw the large bottle of sweet sherry in the larder which her mother always drank at night.

"A little tipple before bed does you good," she would always say. "Keeps the doctor away." Perhaps she would try one. She sat by the fire, sipping the sweet liquid. It burned her throat as she swallowed, but made her feel warm and relaxed. In just a few minutes she had finished the glass and returned to the larder for another.

The house was quiet; her sister had cried herself to sleep. Patsy sat downstairs with only the fire as a friend. Another glass of sherry went down easily and her mind was now wandering. The flames were making shapes which seemed to wander up and down the walls, reflecting a warm light all around the room. She heard a growl; it seemed to be behind her. She didn't move; something growled again and was right behind her now.

"Child," it called.

"Yes," she replied. He walked from behind and stood to the side of her. He was almost touching the ceiling: an older man, dressed in antique style clothes with sharp talons, very long fangs and a big pair of black wings fluttering behind him and fanning the flames of the fire into a ball of light so that it spewed out little embers onto the hearth. His big golden tail flapped around his feet like a snake waiting to pounce.

"You can get him you know, I'll help you to hurt him just like he hurt your mother and your sister. I can make you strong so you can stand up to him. Would you like that?" he asked, flicking his tail in excitement and licking his lips. "I can make you really strong," he repeated. "Would you like that?"

The sherry had started to hit the spot. She got up and walked right past him to the larder and poured another. She was really hungry now but the sherry went down better. She walked back past him and sat back down in her mother's chair. She noticed a funny smell and looked at him directly into his big yellow green eyes which were now glowing with anticipation.

"Help me?" she asked.

"The pleasure is all mine," he replied. His fangs dropped further and his talons extended out even more. With a swish of his tail, and his wings opening and almost filling the room, he encased her inside them, wrapping them around her while she still sat in the chair with a glass of sherry in her hand. They connected, mind to mind. The whole house shook; she was in a kaleidoscope where everything was whirling. She was calling, growling, barking and twisting; everything was revolving around her faster and faster until complete stillness took her.

When she awoke, she was laid out in the middle of the living room with the embers of the long finished fire glowing around the edges, still trying to hold on to life. The house was quiet. She got up and looked around. *Was this all a dream?* she asked herself. It was four in the morning but she wasn't tired so she quickly relit both fires and sat back in her mother's chair. Her cold, stiff body greedily absorbed the life giving heat. It would be her chair now, she decided.

"Let that bastard start again and I'll finish him," she smiled to herself before downing another glass of the sweet liquid.

Finally, she made her way quietly upstairs and, on entering her now tidied bedroom, checked on Julie who was sleeping soundly. She pulled the blankets up to cover her completely, tucking her back in and placing a kiss on the top of her head. Feeling quite wobbly now and very, very tired, she quickly slipped into her warmed bed and snuggled down to get comfy. Hugging her warm bottle, the heat slowly sped through her cold bones. Sleep came quickly to her and it was very deep.

"Patsy, Patsy!" Blodwyn was shaking her.

"Oh, Mum," Patsy cried out, sitting up in bed and feeling absolutely awful.

"Come on, get up!" she called to her.

"What time is it?" asked a very sleepy Patsy.

"One in the afternoon," Blodwyn replied.

"Oh, God, sorry, Mum," Patsy cried out, looking at her mother pulling the sheets off of Julie's bed to wash.

"Don't worry, your dad's gone off to meet up with some old army mates of his and we have work to do m'girl."

"Where's Julie?" asked Patsy.

"I've sent her off to stay with Auntie Gwen for a bit and don't worry, I know the fucking bastard! He'll get his comeuppance, trust me," Blodwyn said firmly. Patsy looked at her beautiful mother who was not bothered it seemed, by her black eye and split lip. Her bruises were now turning black. There was also something else: she knew her mother was with child.

"Mum."

"What?" replied her mother. "Come on, love we have work to do."

"It's not his is it?" she asked tearfully, worrying for her mother.

"Now don't you go worrying about me, lass, it'll all be sorted soon, you hear me?" She looked Patsy in the face. "Oh, God, you've connected."

"Sorry," Patsy replied.

"I knew this would happen, Ma predicted it. I should have divorced the bastard while I had the chance, but I was weak, I believed him. He lied to me, I trusted him and he let me down. All this is my own fault, Patsy, and the Lord, believe me when I say this, is punishing me now!"

"Oh, Mum, please don't say that sort of thing. I love you, no one is punishing you," Patsy cried, hugging her mother.

"Patsy, believe me when I say that absolutely nothing in this world is free. Everybody, and everything, has its price. Everything has to be paid for and I am now paying the price of being free from the curse. The trouble is he's making me suffer in other ways. Oh believe me I am being made to pay," she sobbed.

Patsy and her mother worked continually for the rest of the day: washing, ironing, cleaning and pressing. The floors were scrubbed and all the rooms cleaned.

"Now, m'girl," Blodwyn spoke gently to Patsy looking directly at her, "as

110

long as I am alive, and when I am dead, please, please promise me that you will always have pride in your home. You may never be a millionaire, but always have pride in cleanliness and tidiness. Fresh clean beds every week; clean, well fed children, and good, cooked food, not the rubbish they serve up now, real food. If you do this you will never go wrong, now promise me." She looked deep into her lovely daughter's eyes, seeing the demon's mark which gave her a little wobble.

"I promise," she replied and she meant it; it would be her standard. Blodwyn looked with pity on her daughter.

"Oh dear God in heaven please, please go easy on her. She doesn't deserve the pain you are just about to put her through," she prayed as she started washing the final lot of bedding.

Dealing with Arthur

Blodwyn was now working part time at the local pub and was also holding a weekly Ouija session on a Saturday night, charging £15 per person. The money was paying the rent, feeding and clothing them all and, at last, covering all the bills. Blodwyn wanted some new crockery. She was fed up with odd cups and saucers which must have looked so out of place, whilst they were trying to be so professional. She dragged Patsy, who was actually full of a cold and very miserable, down to Woolworth's in Bedminster where she had recently spied some lovely, highly decorated and funny shaped wares.

"Oh, God, that's naff!" Patsy exclaimed, looking at the bright orange and green funny shaped crockery that Blodwyn was handling.

"Be quiet, girl, it's lovely and I am going to have it all," she smiled, carrying the boxes to the till. Patsy was still protesting loudly and struggling with the quantity her mother had given her to carry.

"Are these the special offer boxes?" Blodwyn asked the shop assistant.

"Yes, last one I think. Ooh, I think it's lovely. 120 pieces for £16, what a bargain!"

"I know," replied a very happy Blodwyn, eying up the purchases.

"I've got some special carrier bags just for these," said the assistant, placing the boxes in the specially made extra-large bags. Patsy was still moaning; she didn't like this set. The pale blue one was better in her opinion.

"Well so what? You can bloody well buy your own when you are married, but I like this one, okay? Lump it," Blodwyn tersely told Patsy.

"Okay!" Patsy shouted at her, sniffing miserably, wiping her nose, and dabbing her running eyes.

They walked out heavily laden with their heavy dinner service in large carrier bags, emblazoned with the name 'Woolworths' for all to see. They made their way to the bus stop some 50 yards down the road and waited with

112

about ten other people for the number 10, which would take them home.

"Hello, Blodwyn." A voice from further up the line carried down to where Blodwyn and Patsy stood. "Been shopping?" The question came from the Mr. Nosey of Grey Street. He watched all the comings and goings of the whole street and if you wanted to know anything about anybody - their life story, or anything anyone had hidden in the closet, this was the person to ask; always over a cup of very strong tea.

"Yes," replied a very flushed Blodwyn as she pretended to look in her purse for the bus fare.

"Well?" he asked her.

"Well what?" she snapped, annoyed that he was questioning her in front of the other people in the line.

"What have you been buying?" he asked again.

"A bloody Clarice Cliff dinner and tea service if you must know," she blurted back.

"Bloody hell, girl, your Ouija sessions must be going well. That's the stuff everyone is talking about. You know it's the Welsh girl that's designing it especially for Woolworths."

"I know," Blodwyn angrily retorted. *Oh thank God,* she thought as she saw the number 10 bus approaching.

"I'll have to call round for a cuppa and a Ouija session," he called out just as he was getting on the bus in front of the others. The woman standing in front of them turned around and softly spoke to them.

"Are you the woman that does readings?" she asked with wide eyes.

"Why do you ask?" Blodwyn replied.

"I need some help, can I have your address?" she asked. Blodwyn took a slip of paper from her pocket with her name and address already written on it.

"If you would like to put your name on the waiting list, give me your details and we will contact you," Blodwyn explained just before boarding.

"Thank you," she replied, looking into Blodwyn's eyes. "Get yourself to the doctor," she told her. Blodwyn shook inside.

"Yes, I must," she agreed, nodding to her.

They walked wearily up the road to their house, stopping just for a second and seeing the living room light on. The boys were with their Aunt Gwen and Julie was on a sleepover after a birthday party. They had left both fires banked right up, so they would still be lit, and the house was warm when they got home.

"Oh, God, he's back," Blodwyn said turning to look at Patsy.

Bastard! Patsy thought, almost screaming it out loud but just managing to keep it in for the sake of her mother.

"Stop it now!" Blodwyn screamed at Patsy. "Project pink and love to him. Put a ball of pink all around him and a golden ball of protection around you and me," she instructed her, whilst starting to shake herself. "Love and good things, love and good things," she started to chant out loud.

"Love and good things, love and good things," repeated Patsy as they opened the front door and walked through the hall straight into the kitchen.

They were just putting their bags down, and reaching for the kettle, when a voice behind them asked,

"Been shopping, girls, bought anything nice for me?" Arthur's bitter sounding voice resounded around the kitchen, suddenly making Patsy feel rather sick. *Bastard,* she thought, as she filled the sink with water to wash the newly acquired Clarice Cliff, crocus pattern dinner and tea service.

"No, nothing for you, Arthur," replied Blodwyn, looking straight at him. He was stood in the doorway, smartly dressed in a collar and tie with crisp, pressed trousers. He held a bottle of Cutty Sark whisky in one hand and a tumbler half filled with the amber liquid in the other.

"What have you bought then?" he asked in a very aggressive tone.

"New cups, saucers and dinner plates; I am sick to death of all the odds and ends and nothing matching, so all the old stuff is going out and we can all enjoy the new set, where everything matches for a change."

"Is that all?" he asked, curling his lip as he eyed the pair of them working in unison to wash and dry the new crockery. "Don't you want to know where I've been?" he asked looking directly at Blodwyn. *God she looks good,* he thought to himself, feeling a stirring in his loins. "Not really, but do go on and tell, as you have not even bothered to contact us for the last two weeks. You just show up and expect us to get all excited about seeing you again, what have you brought for us?" she asked calmly, knowing this would really stir him up. "Fucking witches!" he screamed, throwing his tumbler of whisky directly at her; it just missed her face by a whisker before smashing into the wall. "Look what you have made me do now!" he screamed at them both. Blodwyn lunged forward and grabbed him by the arm. "Arthur, go and sit down, you've enough whisky in you. I will make some tea and we will talk later, go on now." She gently pushed him back into the living room then came back and grabbed a tumbler, half filled it with cold water and went

114

back into the living room, pouring a little more whisky into it and then placing it into his hand. Noticing two more bottles of whisky on the sideboard, she shuddered inside.

"Tea won't be long," she said and, walking back into the kitchen where Patsy was stacking all the new plates into the larder, looking very worried and wide eyed.

"Don't worry I can handle him," said Blodwyn to Patsy trying to reassure her. Patsy knew better and was trying not to connect with her demon. Yes, he was here in the house, he let her know it all the time but she was happy with her mother. She sang, laughed and worked with her but her father had come again to spoil everything. *He had better not hurt her again,* she thought to herself.

"I'm here if you want and need me!" The demon's voice rattled through her. Blodwyn stopped and looked at her.

"No, don't let him in. I can deal with this myself. Promise me!" she said in a very low and firm voice.

"Try to," replied Patsy.

"Well, try fucking hard, girl! We don't want any attention brought to this house, understand?" This time she was shaking and angry with Patsy. *What the bloody hell did she have to do to get it through that bloody stubborn thick head of hers?*

"Okay," Patsy replied, without meeting her mother's eyes.

Tea was beef stew they had made that morning and reheated with herby dumplings which fluffed up and floated on top of the boiling thick, brown aromatic liquid. The three of them sat around the newly acquired table. Patsy ignored them both and was working out where the letters of the alphabet, numbers, and yes and no for the Ouija would be positioned. The table was very shiny; a lovely thick layer of varnish covered the top, which was just right for the tumbler to flow around in the Ouji session. To look after the table top, a new table cloth and placemats adorned it and protected the precious surface. Patsy often thought that the tumbler sometimes flew off the old table because it had become unstable, and the surface rough. She ate her tea in silence, thinking about the next session and ignoring her now warring parents.

"I'm going to the pub," Arthur growled as he threw his cutlery with force into the kitchen sink. "See you later, witches."

Fucking bastard, Patsy thought, feeling her mother's eyes boring into her.

"Trouble tonight with him!" Patsy said, looking directly at her mother.

"Nothing I can't handle; leave him to me and don't get involved," she replied sadly, almost shaking inside as if she knew what was coming that night. "Come on then, let's tidy up and get cosy in front of the fire," she said, carrying the empty plates to the kitchen.

Blodwyn and Patsy sat cuddled in front of the fire. They both had new Clarice Cliff teacups and were sipping sweet sherry from them.

"He'll never know you have a little tipple, my darling," Blodwyn said lovingly, pulling Patsy close and giving her a big cuddle. "I knew I should have divorced him but never had the guts."

"Oh, Mum don't look back, look forward," Patsy said, cuddling Blodwyn back and feeling the comforting warmth of her body through her thin blouse and cardigan to reassure her that her mother was actually still there with her. They sat and drank, finishing the bottle. All the while, the world news was audible in the background on the radio. Blodwyn got up and went to the kitchen, taking the empty bottle with her.

"Time for one more, then both of us to bed, m'girl," she said, quite squiffy now. It would help her get through tonight, she told herself. She felt her breast which was now weeping and excruciatingly painful to the touch. She got up, went upstairs to the bathroom and took off the old plaster, squeezing more of the foul liquid out of her very swollen breast. It nearly made her throw up, the pain was so bad. Seeing the hole had got a lot bigger in the last few days, she cut a slightly bigger piece of plaster. She wiped away the smelly green substance, and sprayed some rose water all round her body and in her hair. She knew in her heart that this really was not a boil but something more sinister and that her fate was sealed. She decided she had to make a plan. Ma had foretold her illness. It looked like a little cauliflower trying to bulge out of the hole in her breast. She would talk to the doctor as soon as possible and have a chat with her angels. She would pray hard, she decided, and set it all in motion but first she would have to get through tonight.

"Please, God, be merciful with me tonight. I am not a bad girl, just a mother wishing the best for my children and asking for protection from that nasty bastard," she cried out loud, hitting her head on the mirror which hung over the sink. Michael appeared instantly behind her. She turned to talk to him but he was gone as quickly as he had appeared. The house was quiet; perhaps the Lord was listening, she hoped.

*

An hour later, Arthur returned from the pub. Both Blodwyn and Patsy had fallen asleep on the sofa in front of the fire, the sherry getting the better of them. He punched the back door open in rage.

Oh fucking hell, I forgot to bolt the back door, Blodwyn thought.

"Who forgot to bolt the bloody door?" he screamed out, falling into the kitchen very drunk and aggressive.

"Sorry," shouted Blodwyn, jumping up from the sofa. Her heart was pounding and her nerves jangling. Patsy was befuddled and didn't realise what was happening.

"Sleep," Blodwyn ordered her, turning quickly towards the kitchen door. Patsy feigned sleep instantly.

"You left the fucking door unlocked," he screamed at her.

"It was for you, love, you left your keys in the little tray in the lounge," she replied, thinking on her feet and noting that they were actually there.

"Lies, all lies," he screamed at the top of his voice. "Fucking witches that's what you are, all witches in this house!" *God, they'll hear this in the bloody pub, half a mile down the bloody road,* Blodwyn thought to herself. Panic was now starting to set in. He wobbled into the living room.

"I lost a bloody job today because of you. Everyone is talking about this fucking house and the bloody goings on in it and that bloody brat of yours, down the pub. Lost a job I did because I am connected to you. Everyone is frightened of you."

"Well, leave then, go on, bloody leave. Make your own way; leave us in peace and divorce me," Blodwyn blurted out, not really knowing where that came from, or where the strength to say it did either.

"Divorce you? You evil witch, I'll never divorce you but what I will do is make you bloody suffer you evil cow!" He sounded like the devil himself, evil and twisted. His eyes were the size of saucers and he was drooling spittle from the corner of his mouth.

"Yes, you will suffer, you witch. Think you can make me look foolish in front of everyone? Me, an army officer, having to come home to a bunch of evil witches! Upstairs!" he screamed, this time grabbing her by the hair and dragging her, step by bumping step, up to the bedroom. Before he went, he turned and looked at the prostrate and heavily sleeping Patsy lying on the sofa in front of the fire. "And I will deal with you later," he said to himself grinning, as he gripped Blodwyn's hair harder, making her cry out with pain.

117

Patsy sat up on the sofa, hearing her mother screaming upstairs.

"I'm here, child," said the demon, crawling out of the corner in the living room. His eyes were a bright yellow tinged with green and flashing like a torch. "Revenge, that's what you want..." Patsy laughed at him and he suddenly recoiled, almost as if in pain.

"I'll deal with him myself, I don't need you," she said, feeling her neck thicken. Her demon eyes were now glowing a fluorescent green. "I'd better have a glass of sherry," she said to herself, pouring from the now near empty bottle. The sweet liquid burned the back of her throat and she could hear her mother whimpering; a sad, sad sound for anyone to hear. She could hear him hovering at the top of the stairs, almost as though he was trying to make his mind up whether he should come down. "Come on you bastard, I'm here," she quietly spoke out loud, still sipping her precious liquid amber. Another mighty slap and again her mother screamed. Patsy's anger was now growing. She felt her fangs form and her talons lengthen. She was trying not to react for the moment, keeping it all under control and doing exactly as she had promised her mother. She giggled and the demon once again backed off, cowering back into the corner of the room. Feeling her anger rising even more when another slap echoed out upstairs, the new Clarice Cliff cup disintegrated in her hand, sending raindrops of precious sherry all over her clothes. Her hands grew bigger and three bumps now appeared on the back of her neck, but still she sat and waited. The bedroom door slammed and she could hear him coming down the stairs, slowly and stealthily, trying to be quiet. This was the surprise element. Everything he had trained for in the army he would try to use on her tonight, she knew.

He avoided the living room door and she heard him sneak into the kitchen. Her stomach lurched and her spine tingled. She held her breath, not daring to move, as if any indication she was awake would spoil the oncoming attack. The only noise she could hear was the rattle of the cutlery tray: metal on metal, a metallic chinking that you hear when you are rooting through trying to find the exact implement you need. She was still sat, looking directly at the kitchen door, sweat now trickling down her back and little pearls of perspiration gliding down the side of her forehead. Her spine was now tingling constantly, a buzz running up and down it keeping her alert. Her tail thrashed, sending a plume of embers up the chimney which made her realise that the light of the fire was dying. As quiet as a mouse, still hearing the tinkle of the cutlery tray, she quickly put logs and coal onto the fire in the hearth which instantly burst into flames, giving much needed light which would help her deal with the situation which was about to unfold. The air was electric and she suddenly felt very sick; bile rising to her throat. She had to swallow it back and the bitterness bounced up to her brain, waking up her dull senses. Now she heard him, slowly, just like a cat, crawling up through the hallway. He was going to come in behind her; it was too late to move the position of the sofa, he would hear her. Michael appeared.

"Be brave, child, do nothing, your time will come." *Oh thanks,* she replied in her head, as he disappeared. She held her breath as the living room door just started to open, inch by inch, a very slight creak giving him away. Stealth-trained by the army, he might have been in his 50's but he still knew how to operate. He worked out she would still be asleep; he wanted it to be a surprise attack, just like all the ones he had trained for. *I'll sort that green eyed bitch out once and for all, give it to her real good, just like our little Julie, but better,* he thought to himself, grinning at the thought of what he was about to do.

He swooped silently, his hand going straight to her throat. In the other hand was a two pronged meat carving fork, sharp and menacing, which he pushed straight into the side of her cheek. Blood immediately trickled down like a little red river onto her blouse.

"Gotcha you bitch, just like your fucking mother: trouble, always trouble. Well I'm going to give you trouble now and make you beg for mercy. I'll make you beg at the end, just like your mother just did," he said, squeezing her throat even harder which made her breath come in rasps. She could smell the whisky on his breath as he licked the side of her face with his disgusting furry tongue. He stank of sex and whisky and she wanted to be sick. The rage was now building, her strength growing by the second. He moved his hand from her throat down to her breasts, all the while pressing the carving fork into the side of her face.

"Umm nice and firm and oh so young, just how I like them. Good riding young flesh," he drooled as he explored under her bra. Saliva crept down from the corners of his twisting mouth as his hand started to massage her breasts. He threw the meat fork down on the floor and Patsy could feel the strength in his hands. She never moved or made a sound but just sat very still, looking directly into his face, totally expressionless. Her eyes glowed bright green and her neck thickened yet more. He was waiting for the right time to move. The demon was watching and waiting in the corner. He had a front row seat and was dying to be part of the ongoing proceedings but he had to sit and wait.

Arthur was now starting to try and rip her clothes off. Frustrated that everything was buttoned up tight, he started tearing at her skirt and cardigan, wanting frantically to get to the pure, untouched skin which lay below. The look in his eyes now was evil and murderous. It was frustrating for him that she hadn't even tried to resist or fight back and it was making him angrier. Suddenly, the hand that was holding her throat whipped up and slapped her viciously across her face, knocking her off of the sofa. This was the opening she was waiting for. She released her demon, jumping up and suddenly towering at least two feet above Arthur's gangly but muscular frame. He gasped, wide eyed.

"You're a fucking devil, girl!" he screamed at the top of his voice.

"Demon actually, you piece of rapist shit," she quietly replied to him, as he was screaming and wriggling, trying to get out of her grip. She had him by the throat, at least three feet off the ground. His face was turning blue and he was thumping her chest with all his might, trying to beat her to release him. She slowly brought him up to her eye level and looked directly at him. He was trying to scream but nothing was coming out.

"Now then, Arthur, is it okay to call you Arthur? Thank you. Now then, Arthur, I am going to make sure you never hurt another woman, or anyone for that matter ever again, do you hear me?" she asked. He was flailing around, slapping and beating her in absolute terror. She spied the two bottles of Cutty Sark Whisky on the sideboard. Whilst holding him up in the air by the throat with one hand, she popped the cork of the whisky bottle with the other, it came out easily. "Drink, Arthur?" she asked him, yanking his head back, forcing the bottle down his throat, breaking his front teeth and nearly choking him. She had him at such an angle all he could do was swallow. "I bet you like whisky, Arthur, don't you?" she asked, ramming the bottle further into his mouth and slightly relieving the pressure on his throat so the fiery liquid would go down his gullet without resistance. He was gagging now, trying to scream and be sick at the same time but still she kept the pressure on. "All gone? Good boy, have some more," she said, picking up the other bottle and popping the cork.

"I'll kill you, I'll fucking kill you he screamed," now flailing around at the end of her arm. She rammed the next full bottle of whisky down his throat, only harder this time. He had to drink or he would drown.

"Nice is it?" she asked, pushing the bottle deeper into his throat. He was gagging, almost drowning in bile, whisky, blood and teeth shards. "Good boy, drink it all up," she said, pushing the bottle harder into his mouth. He blacked out, hanging like a rag dolly in her hand. She dropped him on the floor and the demon instantly came out of his corner. She laughed at him.

"I already told you, I can do this myself, I don't need you." She laughed out loud, looking down at a prostrate Arthur who was now covered in blood, bile, sick, and broken teeth. "Oh, Arthur, look at your messy clothes! Tsk, tsk, this won't do, will it? Not up to your army standards now!" She spoke to him as though he was awake and actually listening to her. She bent down and picked up an arm, held his wrist tightly and broke it by spiralling it around until the bone snapped. It popped out from under the skin, bringing fresh blood in little spurts shooting up the sleeve of his shirt. She picked up the other arm and snapped that wrist in exactly the same way. The bones in his arms splintered like match wood. She then lifted a leg and proceeded to break his ankle; twisting it around until the bone snapped. The sound of the bone breaking echoed through the whole house. His foot was eventually pointing the wrong way behind him.

"Better look all the same," she said to him, breaking the other ankle. "That's better. Come on, let's get you upstairs to bed," she said, dragging his broken and bloodied body to the staircase. She looked around and spotted the trail of blood that followed them, then laid him down, found a mop in the kitchen and quickly mopped it up. Her demon was retracting but the sight of Arthur, the bloody rapist and wife beater, brought it straight back out. She could hear Blodwyn crying and whimpering softly, so she picked up the mangled body and headed up the stairs. He was like a rag doll: limp and broken. His eyes rolled around his head and blood, sick and whisky trailed out of the corner of his mouth. She felt bile rising again in her throat and anger at the sad sounds coming from her mother's room. She looked down on this broken, slobbering piece of shit of a man who had hurt so many people and opened her hand, releasing her grip.

"Oops," she said watching the lifeless body tumble down the stairs landing face down right next to his whisky bottle.

She tried to retract her demon before she entered her mother's room but was unable to do so quickly enough so her mother saw her daughter for the first time as a full demon. Funnily enough, Blodwyn wasn't afraid. Patsy grabbed a towel and wrapped it around her bloodied body. He had raped and beaten her to within an inch of her life. The breast with the abscess was split in two: blood, pus, and funny looking white twigs seemed to grow out of the shattered breast. All her front teeth were gone, her wrist was broken, both her eyes were blacked and there were bite marks all over her body. She was now struggling to breathe.

"I will have to get you to the hospital," Patsy said to her mother, rage and disgust making her demon even bigger and stronger. She heard a car starting next door. "It's Mr Dwyer, hang on, Mum," she said, running down the stairs and jumping over Arthur's prostrate, but still breathing, body. She headed out of the back door and down the steps into the street, calling out to Mr. Dwyer their next door neighbour. He had just received a call from the police station; he was needed to come into work immediately.

"Mr Dwyer," she called out to him.

"Patsy, what on earth are you doing up, running around this time of the morning?" he asked.

"Oh, Mr. Dwyer, I have to get Mum to the hospital, Dad's given her a hiding and she's in a bad way."

"Oh, God, of course, love, no worries I can drop you both off on the way; go and fetch her," he said, not thinking that she might need some help. Patsy ran back into the house and back up the stairs. Gathering up her bloodied and battered mother into a large warm blanket, they both gingerly made their way down the stairs. Patsy had to hold her mother up. Blodwyn ignored her prostrate husband at the bottom of the stairs. She noticed his feet sticking the wrong way round at a funny angle. She let a little, painful smile cross her face.

"Don't worry about him, Mum, he's not dead."

"Wish he was, love," was all she could mutter.

Mr. Dwyer could not believe the sight of Blodwyn Russell. It was almost like she had been in a boxing match and lost heavily.

"Where's Arthur?" he asked Patsy who was now cuddling her mother in the back of his car. "Don't know and don't care. Last time I saw him, he was running around the front room with a whisky bottle down his throat."

"Oh, God, not the bloody whisky again?" he sighed. "I'm going to have to report this you know," he said to them gently.

"Please do," replied Patsy.

"Once we've got you to the hospital, I'll send some of my officers round to bring him in. He can't be allowed to get away with this," he stated as if in deep thought.

"Thank you," said a very tired and worried Patsy as they drove on in silence. John Dwyer was driving as fast as possible but trying not to break the speed limits.

"Oh sod it," he said to himself, "I am a bloody police sergeant." With that he pressed the accelerator, pushing the car on and flying down the road as fast as he was able to drive.

*

Sergeant Dwyer had called the local hospital's A&E department, telling them to expect an urgent case - a woman in her early 40's, badly beaten, bleeding and almost unconscious. Immediate emergency treatment would be needed. They were waiting for them outside the department with a trolley when they arrived. A doctor and a nurse helped Blodwyn onto the trolley and she was pushed inside. John Dwyer pulled Patsy away.

"Come on now, lass; let them see to your mother. Let's go and get a cup of tea," he said, walking alongside her to the tea machines which were placed at the end of the long corridor. While they sat waiting to hear how Blodwyn was, he called the station to report the incident, asking officers to attend the scene and bring Arthur Russell into the station for questioning.

An hour later a doctor appeared in the waiting room.

"Patsy Russell?" he asked.

"Yes," said Patsy, standing up to greet him.

"I am Dr. Stone. I have been looking after your Mum and, as you know, Mum's really not very well. She's had the stuffing knocked out of her, literally. She has two broken front teeth, three broken ribs, a punctured lung and a broken left wrist. She was punched so hard in her left breast that it exploded. She's in surgery now having a mastectomy. She will recover from this but the bad news is she had a tumour the size of a cauliflower in that breast. It must have been excruciatingly painful. We don't know how far the cancer has spread; it's a very rare sort of cancer, we don't see it very often. It's a fungating cancer, which rises up and out of the skin."

"She thought it was an abscess," jumped in Patsy.

"Yes, I can understand why," he replied. "We will have to keep her in for a couple of weeks, run some tests and generally look after her to get her strength up. Also," he took a deep breath, "she is about five months pregnant."

"Oh dear God," said Mr Dwyer. "I'll nail the bastard. Sorry, Patsy."

"Have you anyone to look after you?" he asked, looking concerned for this young girl and noticing the blood on her blouse and the puncture marks on the side of her face.

"Don't worry, I have an older sister, she's 18. My brothers can stay with their aunt," she replied, already trying to sort this situation.

"I would not advise you to visit yet, leave it for about a week, she will be in a lot of pain and will need complete rest and quiet," the doctor said gently.

"That's okay, Doctor, I live next door. I'll be keeping an eye on them and making sure that they are safe. If they need anything, I'll be right there. I can also let them know how Mum is," the policeman said, feeling quite responsible for Patsy now.

"What about the man who did this to her, I take it, it was your father?" Dr. Stone asked Patsy.

"Don't worry about him, Doctor, I am going to be having a rather long chat with him. He won't be giving this family any more trouble; I can promise you that."

"Okay then," said Doctor Stone, "now I am satisfied you and your sister will be safe, see you in five to six days. She will be on ward E in the old building. It's nice and quiet there and she will get good nursing. Are you okay, Patsy, your mother was very concerned about you?" He touched the puncture wounds on the side of her face. "Sure you are not injured?" She brushed his hand away, feeling the wound for herself.

"It's nothing really," she replied.

"How did this happen?" he asked, handing her a clean tissue out of his pocket to wipe away the blood.

"Don't know," she said, lying and seeing the events unfold again in her head.

The doctor, Patsy and Mr. Dwyer were just finishing their second cup of tea out of the machine when Dwyer's radio signalled him. He got up and walked into the adjoining room to take the call. He emerged, stony faced, some ten minutes later.

"Sorry, Patsy, it seems your father was drunker than you thought, he's fallen down the stairs. He is in a bad way and they are taking him to hospital now as we speak." Patsy jumped up, crying out,

"Oh, God, they are not bringing him here are they?" tears falling down her face as she reacted to his news

"No, no don't worry, I have explained the situation and they are taking him to Winford Hospital. It seems he did some damage to his ankles and wrists when he fell down the stairs; a typical spiral fracture you get when falling from a great height. Unfortunately he will be in hospital for some time. It seems that our little chat will have to wait. Now, come on, let's get you home," he said, walking with her to his car.

The only thing on Patsy's mind when she got home was to clean the house thoroughly and erase all the memories of the events that took place that night. It was now eight in the morning. John Dwyer called in on his way back to work to let her know that her mother was out of surgery and comfortable. She thanked him and set about dealing with the house: cleaning, scrubbing and washing like a demented demon. Realising she and Julie would have to survive on their own for two weeks, she checked out the larder. There was enough food for a couple of days so she went outside to the coal shed and opened the door to see how much coal there was.

"Plenty, we'll be fine," she said to herself out loud. It was piled high and glistened in the daylight. She filled the coal scuttle and went in to relight both the stove in the kitchen and the fire in the living room.

Upstairs she went next, heading for her mother's bedroom. She had already changed the bedding and tidied and rearranged the room, hoping this would stop reminding her mother of him attacking her that night. Walking around the room, she spied a brown leather suitcase.

This must be Arthur's, she thought to herself, so she pulled it out from under the bed, released the brown leather belt that secured it, flipped the two locks open and peered inside.

There was a bundle of letters with a blue ribbon wrapped around them. She picked them up and started reading them, going through them one by one. None were from her mother. There were pictures of children but none of her, Julie and the boys. Patsy sat on the floor transfixed. It seems her father had several other children, all by different ladies. In particular, there were two sisters. Their photographs had 'Dizzy' and 'Myra' written on the back. Patsy was struck by how they resembled her and hoped she could meet them one day.

"Oh my bloody God, here's the proof you need to divorce him, Mum," she said excitedly. She found bank statements showing a very healthy bank balance and proof of an army pension which, in itself, would keep them all for years without having to work or claim any benefits. Best of all there was £200 in cash, wrapped in brown paper. She carefully gathered everything together and wrapped it all in a towel. Then, putting it inside a waterproof

125

coat and wrapping it all, she hid it in the dreaded coal shed, under a heap of coal, right at the back, amidst the dreaded eight legged warriors, whom she decided now needed to bite anyone who messed with it, except her. She decided she would speak to them nicely, with the help of the angels.

She had placed the stash right at the back of the shed; carefully covering the coal with a coal bag, then coal and then some odd shaped logs that were not usually put onto the fire.

Great, nice and safe, she thought to herself, spying a pair of yellow eyes in the corner of the shed and hearing a low growl.

"Time to get out," she laughed out loud, scrambling down the coal mound and locking the door behind her as she ran into the house.

The next ten days flew by. Julie and Patsy got on really well together, supporting each other, and travelling together every day on the bus to visit their mother who was still in hospital. Her swollen, black eyes were now almost normal. There was still a little bruising but she was looking so much better. Her wrist was in a cast and mending well, her ribs were bandaged still but her breathing had improved and the wound from the mastectomy was all but healed, if still a little red. The doctors had arranged for a dentist from the dental hospital to visit her on the ward and he was going to replace her two front teeth with a bridge. She had indeed had the very best of treatment and care: the best the NHS could offer. She prayed and thanked the Lord and her angels every day for making it out of that situation alive.

Blodwyn smiled to see her two beautiful daughters walking down the ward towards her bed.

"Hey!" she called out to them, waving.

"God, Mum's in good form," said Julie as they approached the bed. They both kissed her, trying not to squeeze her too hard and affect those healing broken ribs.

"I'm coming home!" she shouted with delight to them as they all cuddled.

"When?" both the girls asked at once.

"Saturday, two days' time; the ambulance will pick me up here at four in the afternoon and I will be home by five."

"Hooray!" both girls cried out. They all cuddled together and celebrated her homecoming.

Patsy and Julie doted on their sick mother when she was delivered home from the hospital. Every day they saw an improvement in her health and mobility, but she was still frail and had lost the child she was carrying at the time of the attack. The doctor told her it was God's way of saving her; she would have died giving birth to the infant. *Bloody funny way of showing how much you love me, Lord,* she thought, on hearing the news. He also told her the cancer was a very rare one which grew slowly. She must have had it for some time for it to have got to the advanced stage of protruding through the skin. It had spread to a small area of her lung and also into her spine. When she asked how long she had left to live he replied,

"How long is a piece of string?" He just didn't know. The good news was they could give her radiotherapy while she was in hospital to slow it down.

"Oh please, Lord, give me enough time to see my little Patsy wed," she prayed that night. Of all her children, she was the one she worried about the most; the one that needed protecting from that bloody demon. She accepted that she had let it in, but she was strong, really strong and God only knows she needed to be.

She hadn't asked Patsy about Arthur that night but she knew he was out to get her; just like he had got her beautiful Julie. When she saw her in full demon form, she wasn't in the least shocked. *Oh thank the Lord she isn't a nasty demon. God help us all mind if she ever changes,* she had thought to herself. Ma had predicted everything, the wise old cow. Bloody hell she really missed her. She often wondered about her own mother and father and why they never responded to her letter. But why should they? It was she who ran away straight out of the frying pan into the fire. She was reminiscing as the girls were busying around her and making her comfy; looking back at her life. She was now 43 and about to be divorced with four children. What a mess she had made of everything. She was not bitter or twisted about anything: even that bastard, Arthur. It was her own fault and she always admitted that to herself and her angels who said that she was forgiven and had to make the best of everything from now on. She owed that much to them all, including herself.

The Dance

Julie, Patsy's sister was a big girl in every way. Blodwyn looked at her and smiled: 6ft tall, with feet as big as ships. Size 9 she was with long black hair, big brown eyes, a large ample bosom and a curvy bottom. The boys loved her; she was like a magnet to them and totally different in every way to Patsy. She was loud and sometimes outspoken but bright and diligent. She was born when Blodwyn had thought Arthur had been killed abroad. She received a telegram telling her he was missing and sought the comfort of an American GI. She fell pregnant and the GI returned to America, begging Blodwyn to go with him, but she refused. She couldn't leave Ma and the rest of her family. The shock and horror started after Julie was born when Arthur suddenly appeared out of nowhere after two years. He had been lost in a jungle and finally found, so she was told. Once again he had beaten her senseless but claimed to have forgiven her. In reality, he would make her pay for the rest of their married life.

Julie had just been given her first job, working in a local supermarket on the checkout tills. She had actually applied for a shelf stacking job but the interviewer liked the way she could handle herself and the way she conversed with the public. She passed the little written exam with flying colours. One of the checkout girls had left to have a baby recently, leaving a hole in his team. He thought that Julie would be a great replacement and offered her the job on the day of her interview.

She gave her mother one pound per week of her wages for her keep, leaving her one pound and sixteen shillings. She had never felt so rich and diligently saved ten shillings per week with the Trustee Savings Bank, for a rainy day. The rest was used for clothes and treats like make-up and new shoes. Her job bought her freedom and a newly found self-confidence that she could be like anyone else working in that supermarket. Her supermarket uniform meant that she never had to worry about what to wear to work each day and that in itself gave her confidence, as everyone looked the same. Of course, some wore it better than others but she knew she looked good in the uniform and the amount of admiring glances she received told her so.

Mr Rowell, who owned the shop, was always keeping a close eye on his team; wanting to provide the best service possible. There were lots of new supermarkets popping up all over the area, so competition was keen. He kept his prices as low as possible and had a very wide choice of goods.

The mix of staff made him smile. It was Friday: pay day. He knew everyone's name, where they lived, all about their family and made sure he remembered all their birthdays. He treated them with real respect, always thanking them for all their hard work and support for his business. It was he, every week, who would greet them all in the wages office and hand over their pay packets.

"Julie Russell," came over the Tannoy. It was her turn to walk to the wages office to pick up her weekly pay. She was washing her hands after finishing helping out at the busy meat counter. When she arrived she knocked at the door.

"Come in," a voice shouted out. Mr. Rowell stood at the desk, her brown pay packet in his hand. "Ah, Julie, good, good! Still enjoying the job?" he asked, smiling at her.

"Yes, of course, Mr. Rowell. I love working here."

"Well that's good to hear. I know you have still got two months to go on your probation period but I would like you, as of this moment, to consider it done. I have raised your wages to three pounds per week, as agreed, and I would like to say, thank you so much for being a great new member of our team."

"Thank you so much!" she screamed with delight. "I won't let you down, ever."

"Now, don't you go spending that all at once, will you? I bet you'll be going to the dance tonight," he said - looking at her and admiring her curves.

"Dance?" queried Julie.

"You mean to say no one here has asked you to the weekly dance at St Michael's Hill yet? My goodness, girl, if I was younger I'd take you myself!" he said, winking at her and thinking, *Oh, God if only!*

"I will go and ask the girls," she said, smiling back at him as she signed the wages sheet. He watched her walk down the corridor towards the shop. He loved the way her bottom moved when she walked; she had a wiggle all of her own and he could quite honestly watch her behind for hours. Without her knowing it, he often did on the surveillance cameras that were placed all around the shop.

If only, he thought again, seeing her disappear through the double swing doors.

"Dance, what dance?" Blodwyn cried out, looking directly at Julie.

"Oh, Mum, it's a weekly one, in the school hall at the top of St Michael's Hill. It's only 7 till 10.30 and the bloody bus stops right outside."

"Who else is going?" she asked.

"Most of my workmates; we are all meeting up in the Rose and Crown next door at 6.30, then into the dancehall for 7. Oh please, Mum, say yes." Blodwyn looked at this beautiful girl of hers, with her ample bosom and very curvy hips. She was nearly 19 years old and had a good job. Who was she to refuse her? She was a woman now. What made her wobble, and feel very sick with worry, was that it was at this age that she had made her mistake with Arthur. She had been young, free, single and very sexy on the night she met with Arthur. She had just fled her beloved village in Wales and what she thought were the evil clutches of the sect. Now she wished she could have reconnected with it and found her mother and father to make everything right. She stopped herself and thought for a moment; who was she to stop Julie going out with her friends?

"Right then, take Patsy with you," she said, looking at her daughter whose face now went into spasms.

"Patsy!" she screamed back at her. "But she's only just 16."

"Safety in numbers," Blodwyn countered. "Take it or leave it."

"I'll take it, I suppose," Julie mumbled at her mother, absolutely disgusted that she had to take her little sister along to the dance. She stomped upstairs to her room to sulk. Patsy threw a wobbler. She definitely did not want to go to the dance with Julie to be her chaperone. She wanted to stay home and look after her mother. She would be quite happy cuddling up on the sofa, covered with their cream blanket and sipping sweet sherry. However, after a lot of persuasion and the offer of borrowing a new skirt, which Julie pointed out she had not even worn yet, she did agree to go.

They seemed to take hours to get ready; both of them bathed and pressed their clothes carefully. Patsy was really not interested in going out and was only going because her mother had asked her to.

"Safety in numbers," she kept saying to them, making them promise to look after one another. She repeated this to both of them until, in the end, a very fed up Julie piped up,

"Mum, please, we are only going to a dance!"

"I know, but remember the last bus is 10.40; you will have to leave on time to catch it."

"We will," they replied to her in unison.

"Try some of this," Julie said to Patsy, rubbing a little rouge onto her cheeks.

"Nice!" she said, holding a mirror up for her to see. Both of them had put their hair up into beehives. This was the style of the moment and it really suited them both, making them look a little older than their years. Next a little lippy and then some black Max Factor block brush mascara was applied to their eyebrows and lashes. Patsy suddenly caught sight of herself in the long bedroom mirror.

"My God," said Julie as she walked into the room and saw Patsy looking at herself in the mirror. "That skirt looks great on you, you look about 19-20, wow, what a transformation," she exclaimed excitedly.

"The shoes are tired though," replied Patsy.

"It's not your bloody shoes they'll be looking at, silly, and you look absolutely ravishing."

"So do you," replied Patsy, seeing Julie in a whole new outfit that complemented her curvy figure beautifully.

"Come on, hurry up, the bus will be leaving in half an hour, get a move on," Julie ordered as she walked out of the bedroom and downstairs into the living room. Patsy finished applying more hair lacquer to keep her hairstyle in place and then went down to join them.

"Oh goodness, Patsy!" exclaimed her mother.

"What?" Patsy replied.

"You look lovely, really lovely. I have just realised how much like my mother you look," she said smiling and wiping a tear from the corner of her eye. Wrapped in scarves and heavy coats to keep the cold out they kissed their mother goodbye and headed outside to walk down to the bus stop, which was just down the road from their house.

"Hello, Julie," said two female voices in unison.

"Hi," she replied. It was two of her workmates, Jeannette and Angela who were twins.

"Who is this then?" they asked, again in unison, nodding and looking in Patsy's direction.

"Patsy, these are my friends, the terrible twins. Don't worry; they always speak together, even in work."

"Jeannette and Angela, this is my little sister Patsy."

"Hello, Patsy," they both called out.

"Hi," said Patsy back.

"Looking forward to the dance?" they asked her. "The Irish boys should be there tonight, so handsome," they giggled at each other. Patsy was annoyed.

"I'm not interested in men; I am only here because my mum said I had to keep an eye on Julie." They all burst into fits of laughter.

"That's what our mum said as well," screeched the twins.

"Bus coming!" shouted Julie. When it arrived, they all jumped on the number 9, finding seats easily.

"Not so busy tonight," Patsy said.

Ding, ding went the bell: the conductor's sign to the driver that all were aboard and he could pull away.

"And where are you lovely ladies off to tonight?" he asked, looking admiringly at the four well dressed and made up young ladies.

"St Michael's Hill dance," they all replied together.

"Well, what a lucky bunch of lads, seeing you all here now makes me want to come along." He smiled and his eyes fixed on Julie. "Getting the bus back tonight?" he asked tentatively.

"Yes," they all called out together in chorus.

"Well, I'd better make sure Fred and me are taking the 10.40 back." He winked at them all. "No need for money tonight, girls, this ride is on me and Fred."

"Thank you!" they again all responded together.

"Of course there are other ways you could thank me," he said very suggestively.

"Oooh, you are naughty," they all screamed out, now belly laughing. It was a good bloody job there was no one else on the bus. It was a lovely way to start the evening and everyone was now in high spirits with nice company and a few extra pennies to spend on lemonade at the dance.

"Oh well," said Patsy to herself, "I suppose I might just enjoy it tonight." It was lovely to be part of a happy crowd. God only knows, she'd had enough sadness and fear in her life lately.

The four of them got off the bus when it reached St Michael's Hill. A loud wolf whistle from the bus conductor followed them as they piled into the Rose and Crown pub. It was packed full of dancers waiting for the doors to the dance hall to open. It was a regular thing, they would all gather in the pub, having half of something but choosing to spend the majority of their money on drinks in the dancehall, where the prices were really keen. It was a funny pub, comfy and cosy, and very small. A lovely fire roared in the hearth, which made Patsy smile. The room was full of small, round, very shiny wooden tables with cast iron legs and table tops which were immaculately polished.

Hmmm, bit small for a Ouija table, she was thinking to herself, while waiting for a drink. Small wooden seats were scattered all around the room making it look untidy, she thought. *They should be placed at a table.* Again her brain was going into overtime. All she could hear was the drone of the chatter from everyone in the room; it really was hard to distinguish any particular sound, until the shutters of the bar started going up and down. She noticed that when people were standing at the bar, the shutter would go up, the order for the drinks would be placed, money paid, and then the shutter would go back down. Two minutes later, the shutter would go up and all the drinks ordered would be sat there, ready to be taken away. Then the shutter would go back down and the next person would wait there until the shutter would go back up again. She giggled, it seemed so silly, but that was the way it was done there.

With high spirits all around, the supermarket staff all gathered by the side of the fire, some had drinks, others were just smoking. A thick foggy tobacco smoke filled the air. Julie was already sipping a port and lemonade with a slice of lemon floating in it.

"Want some?" she asked, offering her glass of red liquid towards Patsy.

"No thanks, I'll wait until we get inside," she replied.

"Okay," said Julie, turning around and joining back into the conversation that was taking centre stage within the group. *Bet it's about bloody shopping!* Patsy thought to herself, smiling and humming a little melody while looking around the room.

"Doors open!" called the barman.

"Wait," said the twins, looking towards Patsy and Julie. "Let everyone go on in first; it's a mad rush, we are better here for a few minutes." Exactly as they had foretold, the pub emptied quite suddenly with just a few regular drinkers now sat at the bar and scattered around the room. Very relieved that the crowd had gone, they could all now get back to their boring conversations on the economy and some serious drinking. The pub looked like a bomb had hit it. Barmaids were frantically running around the tables, collecting empty and half empty glasses. There were empty crisp packets strewn all around the floor and a whole, large jar of pickled eggs was empty and abandoned on the bar.

"Come on then," a chap called Eddie called to them all, "let's go!" Julie strode out in front with her workmates, leaving Patsy trailing at the rear.

"Come on!" called the twins, grabbing her arms, one each side, so they could walk in a threesome along to the hall.

There was a small queue outside the hall, lights were flashing out of the windows and a hum of music could be heard faintly in the distance. As they approached the music got louder and expectation heightened. Everyone was excited to be out for the evening to dance, have fun and experience whatever the night had to offer them.

"Tuppence please!" called the man at the entrance, collecting the entrance money and handing out the tickets. "Keep this if you want to hand your coat in," he said, talking to everyone he could see making their way into the hall. He would earn well tonight and was already counting the money in his head. It needed good attendance, though, because if no one came, none of the staff would be paid. Tonight it was stuffed to the gunnels and some staff bonuses may even be possible he thought, as he was filling yet another money bag.

The hall was massive. A large open bar took up the whole of the back of the room which was, of course, the dinner ladies' serving area for the schoolchildren in what was really a school dining hall. Once a week, on a Saturday night, one of the local publicans would rent the hall and put on a dance with a bar and stock his own alcohol to provide a well-deserved treat for the local people. Starting from nothing, when only 30 – 40 people would attend, the word spread and now it was the place to be on a Saturday night in the middle of Bristol. Crowds poured into the hall, bringing good profits for all involved. Even the school benefited from it but what it did for one man, in particular, was prove to him that a dancehall was desperately needed in this emerging and rebuilding city. Fred Locarno, decided to look into having a dancehall all of his own. "The Locarno," he smiled to himself as he decided what he would call his dancehall. In years to come it would mean that Bristol had the finest dance hall in the south west of England and his name would be famous. That decision would make him a multi-millionaire. He didn't know it yet, of course, but what he did notice, as he was smiling to all the incoming clientele, was the long legged, green eyed beauty arriving with that bunch from Rowell's Supermarket. A nice lot, he decided, never any trouble, drank and spent well, always welcome and never loitered like some he had to throw out at the end of the night.

The happy bunch entered the hall to the sounds of Glen Miller. The track that was playing, through very large loud speakers and filling the air with heavenly music was 'In the Mood'. It certainly looked like everyone was in the mood; the floor was packed with people dancing, the drinks were flowing from the bar, pints of beer and glasses were being passed over heads to thirsty dancers who could not even get near to the bar and had to rely on friends to pass it all back. A large sparkling ball on a long chain turned above the dance floor, throwing little sparkling, reflected shapes all around the room and lighting up the dark corners every ten seconds or so. The workmates very quickly split up. Julie was already dancing with Eddie from the supermarket and the twins were talking to two young lads who offered to buy them drinks. Patsy had quickly asked for a lemonade when Julie and Eddie were at the front of the bar. She made her way around the edge of the dancehall, keeping to the darker corners. The central dance floor was well lit, so she could watch the ongoing show and listen with ease to the beautiful, melodic music thumping all around from those large loud speakers. She found a corner with an empty table and a great view of the dance floor and bar. Throngs of people were coming and going; some were laughing and all were swaying with the music. The air was filled with love, gaiety and so many expectations.

She was watching Julie and Eddie; the twins were dancing away to 'String of Pearls'. Glen Miller certainly was popular; Patsy loved his music as he was one of her mother's favourites. She was miles away, soaking in the atmosphere and sipping her lemonade, when a group of about 10 young men entered the club in a noisy manner. One, in particular, caught her attention. He was built like a house and must have been at least 6' 8" and full of glorious muscles. He had dark hair with a strong jaw line; really, really handsome. She heard someone call out,

"The Irish boys are here." A cheer went up in the crowd and they all headed for the bar. Some were showing off their dancing skills to the young ladies standing around waiting to be asked to dance. Whilst waiting at the bar, Patsy's heart started to pound; she was mesmerised. The rest of the night became a blur: a very, very pleasant one!

*

Blodwyn woke suddenly. She was tired and not sleeping properly that night, knowing her two girls were out. She had sat in front of the fire, sipping sherry as usual, from her beloved Clarice Cliff cup; she didn't know why but it tasted so much better than out of a glass. The house was locked up but both girls had a key, just in case they were separated. Her angels were wandering all around the house like worried parents. *That's nice*, she thought.

"Thank you," she called out loud as she sat there in contemplation of what was coming in her now to be very short life.

Her wrist ached and she still had a small, irritable cough which pained her because her ribs had still not properly healed and they gave her short stabs, reminding her to take it easy. She had taken herself to bed with a couple of aspirin; sleep wasn't easy. Her mind was racing and trying to make plans for the time now left to her. She turned and turned, finally finding a position that was pain free. Sleep eventually crept up, slowly and deeply.

Giggling from outside and the soft croon of an Irish accent singing a lullaby encouraged her to get out of bed and go to the window.

"Oh, Ma thank you," she called out, lovingly putting her hand over her heart. Right there, standing under the lamppost outside the house, was a giggling Patsy. Her eyes were glowing a beautiful, sexy green and she was with a giant of a young man with the voice of an angel.

"Oh, Patsy, you found him!" she cried out in a low voice, so only she could hear. "Now keep him, girl, he was sent to help you." Tears fell from the corners of her eyes as she peeped out of the bedroom window. She stood, watching and listening as they playfully kissed, cuddled and teased each other. All the while the young man was singing softly to Patsy. Blodwyn could make out the song; it gave her goose bumps and her head was spinning with memories. The song was 'The Girl from Clare'; she knew it well, her mother used to sing it to her when she was a small child. Although it was an Irish song, many Irish had migrated to south Wales and it soon became a favourite, sung in pubs and clubs and around camp fires, as well as at home. Hearing it took her back to her childhood. Blodwyn didn't have many good memories; she hated the witchcraft, it always made her feel uncomfortable, but she remembered one particular night when she must have been 5 or 6. She had a fever, a really bad one which lasted for days. She came through it after about ten days but there was one particular night that all feared she would lose her life. Her mother had sat by the fire rocking her whilst her father held her hand and sat next to them praying. All she could hear was this beautiful melody of the song, 'The Girl from Clare'. She had sunk into oblivion but awoke five days later to everyone's amazement. She was sure in some angelic way that song had saved her life and here it was again, taking her back to memories of a life lived many years before. *Surely this was a sign?*

"Ma said I would know; this must be it." She spoke quietly to herself looking around her bedroom at the ticking clock. God, it was now 2.30 in the morning. She looked out of the window and rapped the pane. Patsy immediately acknowledged her mother and said,

"Got to go now."

"Really?" he said to her. "I was just getting to know you." He took her hand and planted a kiss onto the back of it. Blodwyn knocked again, harder this time. She had noted a few lights had turned on in the street, especially John Dwyer's, the friendly police sergeant. She didn't want him to think that there was any more trouble.

"Got to go!" Patsy said firmly, placing a small piece of paper into his hand with her name and address.

"When will I see you again?" he asked with a worried look on his face.

"Next week at the dance, I'll be there."

"So will I," he replied, pulling her into his big strong arms and embracing her as if she was a precious doll.

"Don't forget me now," she said, wagging her forefinger at him in a teacherly manner.

"Impossible, I love you already," he said. *Christ, where the bloody hell did that come from?* he asked himself.

"I love you too," she replied, those big green eyes glowing at him as her heart pounded like a drum in her chest. She was really struggling to hold back her demon at this moment. She wanted to possess him right now, grab him, taste him, feel his beautiful body and make him all hers. Her cheeks flushed, she could feel her talons protruding and her fangs dropping. It was a good job he couldn't see the tail which was swishing all around like a fly swatter. Her mother could though.

"Oh, Patsy, not yet!" she gasped. This time she banged even harder on the window.

"Oh, Lord, it's my mother, I have got to go," she said, kissing him hard on the lips before turning and running up the steps. She let herself in through the front door, stopping and turning to wave goodbye. She watched him walk down the road; his hands in his pockets and his head up his ass, totally and utterly in love. He was whistling while he walked and the air was turning colder so he turned up his jacket collar and buttoned his jacket.

"It'll be a cold walk home," he said to himself in between whistling his favourite tune. He was so in love, he never even noticed the two hour walk in the freezing weather.

The next morning, Patsy and Julie sat with their mother at the breakfast table, neither of them uttering a word. Eggs on toast and hot tea were eaten by all in silence.

"What are you both up to today?" Blodwyn asked.

"Oh, I'm seeing Eddie," chirped up Julie.

"Nothing," replied Patsy.

"Great, well then, Patsy, after Julie has helped us strip the beds, do the washing and clean the house."

"Oh, Mum," butted in Julie.

"Just as I was saying, when all the chores are done, Julie can go and see Eddie and you and me, Patsy, will go shopping. Okay?"

"Okay," they both responded together. Julie flew around the house in a flurry to finish her chores. Her mother giggled to herself; she loved Julie, she was really proud of her: good job, money coming in. *Good for her*, she thought, but she could be a little lazy at times when it suited her to be. Since coming out of hospital, she had left Patsy to do most of the work, which she always did without question, so she decided today she would treat Patsy to some new clothes of her own. Now she had a boyfriend she would need them.

The next six months were a blur. Blodwyn had recovered well and had also received good news about her cancer; she was in remission. Julie and Eddie were engaged which, quite honestly, no one really was surprised at as they were inseparable. A year later, with a child on the way, they were married. It was a quiet wedding held at the local White Friars registry office to save money. Patsy helped Blodwyn with the food for the wedding reception, which was held in their house. Thirty guests were invited to a delicious finger buffet. Tea, coffee, sherry and beer were on offer and it turned out to be a great day. The bride looked absolutely radiant and the groom slightly worried. He now had a child on the way and his own council flat. Rent would have to be paid every week and Julie would have to give up her well paid job when the child arrived. They would make it, he decided finally, smiling and forgetting all his worries as they both cut the wedding cake which Blodwyn had made and iced despite her delicate state.

It was just Patsy and Blodwyn now that the wedding had ended. The happy couple were sent off for a honeymoon weekend at the Royal Grosvenor Hotel in Temple Meads, just off the centre of Bristol. Everything was paid for jointly by both families so they could enjoy a lovely weekend and start the process of learning to live together as husband and wife. Neither family could be happier: it was a good match and both families got on really well. Patsy and her mother sat on the sofa in front of the fire with their Clarice Cliff cups filled with sherry. The wedding was over; they had washed and cleared everything away and any food left over was wrapped in silver foil and sent home with the grateful guests. It was now their treat to sit under the blanket and reminisce with a big bottle of sweet sherry warming on the hearth for their next drink.

"So when am I going to be introduced to your man?" Blodwyn asked Patsy quietly. Patsy went rigid, saying nothing, and looking down into her cup of sherry.

"Well?" her mother pressed. "Look, if you are serious about him, you know you are going to have to tell him," she said. Still there was no reply from Patsy. "Patsy!" her mother now cried out, grabbing her face, bringing it up to hers and looking directly at her.

"Oh, Mum, I love him so much, he's wonderful but if I tell he'll leave me," she blurted out with tears falling uncontrollably like rain.

"No he won't!" Blodwyn replied loudly. "Love always finds a way and if he loves you as much as you love him you will make it. He'll help you be strong and keep the demon at bay. Remember, say your prayers, laugh, sing; be happy."

"I am happy when I'm with him, it's just..." she stuttered.

"What? Spit it out, girl for goodness sake."

"I'm jealous."

"Of what, girl?" her concerned mother asked.

"Of anyone and everything. I have to have him for me, only me. If he talks to anyone, or looks at another girl, I get nasty, angry and I feel that I am going to do something terrible."

"Oh my darling Patsy." Her mother grabbed her face again but with both hands this time. "You can handle this you know. This is the demon's work. You have to remember in real life he will have to look at other women and speak to them too but not because he's interested in them, silly, it's life. It's the same for him when all the men look at you and, believe me; I see many taking an interest because you really are very beautiful. I've heard the wolf whistles; nothing gets past your old mum. It must drive him crazy as well when he's with you; try and think about that when you are just about to throw a wobbler. Remember it's you he loves; you and only you, so trust him! You have no reason not to; you were meant to meet him and he's here to protect and help you, just as Ma predicted. Come on, girl, you just have to be strong!" Blodwyn cuddled her distraught daughter and noticed the yellow eyes in the corner of the room. "You can bloody well piss off you bloody demon eedgit!" she screamed out before bursting into laughter, followed by Patsy. The room filled with wonderful, loving, funny screams and the demon immediately disappeared.

They spent the night cuddling and chatting on the sofa in front of the warm and relaxing fire. They woke in the early hours as the embers glowed and the coldness embraced the empty, quiet house. Patsy banked both the living room fire and the kitchen stove, making sure it would be warm when they finally got up. She helped her frail mother upstairs, making her way to her bedroom, looking at Julie's empty bed and saying a quick prayer of protection for her and her mother. She also enjoyed some naughty thoughts of her beautiful man mountain who would, sooner than expected, be her husband.

The following Sunday, Tom was invited to Sunday lunch. Blodwyn and Patsy made slow roast shoulder of lamb, homemade mint sauce, roast potatoes, parsnip mash, roasted carrots and onions with sage and onion stuffing and, of course, cabbage, all served up with the most wonderful lamb gravy. The food blew him away. His mother was a brilliant cook and always had to make a silk purse out of a sow's ear, quite literally, but this food was fantastic. Tom and Blodwyn hit it off immediately. Patsy's mother noticed her eyes glowing green a couple of times when she and Tom were deep in gloriously funny conversation. She pinched her hard.

"Stop it, young lady, learn to control it. It's you he loves, not a silly old woman with one tit like me!" Patsy burst out laughing; Blodwyn had got used to her mastectomy now and often made fun of herself. Julie and Patsy would always laugh along with her.

"That's better, lass, now go and give him a kiss while I get the apple pie out of the oven." It was a wonderful day and they both stood at the doorstep waving this huge, beautiful, handsome man, goodbye that evening. They heard him whistle all the way to the bus stop and, a few minutes later, he was gone.

"Oh, God, he's such a good catch!" Blodwyn declared, wrapping her arms around Patsy and kissing her on the top of her head. They went back into the living room where the fire roared in the hearth and a warm blanket awaited them on the sofa. Two Clarice Cliff cups were waiting on the sideboard, next to a bottle of cream sherry, which would end the evening beautifully.

They were soon engaged. Patsy had managed to get a job as a chamber maid at the Grosvenor Hotel where Julie had spent her honeymoon. She had overheard the staff talking about how much they were in need of some new good reliable staff so Patsy applied a week later and was instantly employed. Her attention to detail was very quickly noticed and, within six months, she was promoted to head housekeeper, outshining the existing staff easily. She was able to deal with grumbling, unhappy, and sometimes drunk and disorderly guests which was a real advantage. (Little did they know who they had dealing with them, sometimes having the essence of a demon can have its little rewards!) She soon settled in as the new 'wonder girl' and, goodness, was she happy; only having to use the essence every now and again when she needed to. She gained the respect of regular guests and management and, most of all, her mother.

Just like Ma said, Blodwyn would think as she sat by the fire sipping her sherry. *At last, thank you, Lord, oh and you, Ma, wherever you are.* She would raise her cup into the air and relax back into the sofa for comfort.

Patsy had changed her religion from Church of England to Catholic, much to the delight of her new Catholic family, so she would be having a full Catholic Mass at her wedding. Her mother encouraged it as it would help her keep that bloody demon under control. She underwent three months of Catholic night school with the parish priest and the local nuns. She learned about the religion, what it stood for, how they all helped each other, how to worship the Lord, and most of all, how to respect the Church. She was instructed about giving regular contributions so the church could survive. The big subject, as always, was contraception, which made Patsy feel very uneasy, especially as the priest asked her if she had already had relations with her fiancé. She felt her demon rise instantly; it was as much as she could do to keep it under control. She actually wanted to scream out to him, *"Mind your own fucking business you wanker of a pervert!"* but she congratulated herself as she left replying, "No, Father," trying to act all meek and mild. "Just wait until I tell mum about this," she giggled to herself as she made her journey home on the bus.

Blodwyn and Tom had spent some time talking about the curse and how it affected Patsy. Blodwyn also went into some details of her family history and how the curse would affect their first born daughter. She told him of how she ran away and met Arthur on the rebound. She was very truthful about Arthur's attack on the two girls and how she had divorced him with the help of Patsy finding the letters and photos. She also told him that she was in a position to help financially, if they were to wed, but she would only allow them to get married if he promised, with all his heart, to love, protect and nurture both Patsy and the first born daughter. She also made him promise to keep totally silent about the curse. She told him that the Church would know about Patsy. They monitor demon activity and many of the parish priests were actually angels or psychics working alongside the Catholic faith so they would always know where a demon would be. She told him that they always reported back to the Vatican, where there was a map of the world which was dotted with little red pins that indicated where a paranormal person or event would be. If it was likely to interfere with the dominance of their faith they would likely find her and his family and, especially, the new daughter. It was something he must take into consideration and think about. Could he live with this secret; could he protect Patsy and the vulnerable new daughter? Surely he would have to talk about it with his family; it was a lot to take in. She asked him to leave early and go home to think about everything. It was a massive decision, one not to be taken lightly because, if he married Patsy, it would definitely be difficult living in the shadow of the Catholic Church. But, as she quietly said to him,

"Love always finds a way." Tom kissed Patsy and hugged Blodwyn.

"Thank you," he said, turning to Patsy as she opened the door to let him leave. "I will be in touch," he said, smiling and closing the door behind him.

"Dear God in heaven, if you are there, please, please make sure that he does," prayed Blodwyn as she and Patsy made their way into the living room and their sherry.

She was a beautiful and radiant bride; only just though. The whole Russell family went into meltdown the night before the wedding when a very happy and squiffy Julie lost track of time and over-processed Patsy's perm. Instead of shining curls, she had an afro effect style which threw Patsy into a rage. Blodwyn had to step in, calming everything down and sending Julie and Eddie home. She reversed the perm, saving the day. A quick visit in the morning to the local florist produced a beautiful floral head ring, which looked absolutely exquisite with the new hairstyle.

The wedding and the mass went beautifully, without a hitch. All the bridesmaids behaved themselves, both families got on well and, by the end of the day, became one big family. They sent Patsy and Tom off on honeymoon for a week in a little bed and breakfast in Dublin so they could go to Gorey on their way home to stay with Margaret, Tom's mother. It was here he decided that he would talk to his mother to clear the air and also get some advice. His mother adored Patsy and always told him what a wonderful girl he had chosen and how well she would fit into the family.

"Oh, Lord, thank you for looking after my son," she would call out in her quiet moments.

They arrived from Dublin, walking the two miles from the train station to his mother's house. Tom called for his mother from the gate,

"Mam! Mam!" he called. Margaret emerged from the cottage with a cabbage and a knife in her hands; she had been preparing vegetables for the evening meal.

"Oh Jesus, Mary and Joseph, come in, come in!" she cried, dropping the cabbage and the knife and running towards them with her arms open wide, so excited to see them both.

"Oh God bless the two of you!" she exclaimed with tears welling up in her old crinkly eyes. The cottage was warm and welcoming. A fire roared in the hearth and a big black cauldron of stew was bubbling away on it. She pointed to the black pot.

"That's tea, beef stew. Uncle Johnny is coming later to take you to the pub for a celebration drink but I'd love to come if you don't mind," she said, cuddling Patsy and reminding her that she was now her daughter-in-law. Then she embraced her son and reminded him that he was now a married man with a lovely wife before saying another prayer out loud to thank the Lord.

"Did you have a good time in Dublin?" she asked them. They both smiled, and replied,

"Wonderful."

"Your wedding was wonderful, did you enjoy the Mass, Patsy?" she asked.

"Oh yes it was amazing, so emotional," she replied, looking over at her beloved husband.

"Right then, let's get you settled in," she said, pointing to a doorway across the room. "It's all ready for you, go and make yourselves comfortable."

A freshly made brass bed awaited them with a beautiful, brightly coloured patchwork throw on top over the covers.

"It's yours to take with you, a wedding present from Aunt Bryony from Donegal; it's a wedding gift." Margaret smiled at them before closing the door and walking back to the bubbling cauldron.

Right on time, Johnny arrived in his big fancy tractor, pulling a trailer with straw bales atop to be used as seats.

"Come on," he shouted to them as he reversed the trailer into the cottage driveway. Once all three were aboard, the tractor chugged towards town. They were headed for O'Malley's bar. He served a great pint of Guinness, brewed his own beer and made his own cider which, locals said, was the best in the area. It was situated a bit out of the way as he had built a pub in one of his barns which had quickly become a favourite with the locals. They met up with more of the family, picking them up on the way and, when they arrived at the bar, the rest of the family were waiting to greet them. What a celebration this would be!

There were huge platters of steaming mussels cooked in cider and platters of fresh oysters and cockles from the bay; large slabs of soda bread and butter adorned the tables. What a treat, all laid on by O'Malley himself to welcome the newlyweds to the family: the Irish family!

The next morning, Tom, Patsy and Margaret sat at the table in silence. It had been a great party and all three had fuzzy heads from far too much cider and Guinness. Johnny had nearly put the tractor and trailer into the ditch on the way home.

"I wonder how Johnny is this morning," Margaret commented. All three burst into laughter at the same time.

"Blodwyn had a word with me at the wedding," Margaret said, not looking up from her porridge. Both Tom and Patsy froze with fright.

"I was going to tell you, Mam," he blurted out as Patsy almost fainted in shame.

"It's all right you know, nothing to be ashamed of. Far worse things than this happen in the world but you are going to have to be strong, both of you and beat this together. You're stronger together than one trying on their own." She looked into her big son's eyes which were misty as he tried to fight back tears.

"We can do it, Mam," he said, taking Patsy's hand and kissing it. "I love her so much," he said looking at his new beautiful wife with a tear just trickling out of the corner of his eye.

"It won't be easy, son," she said. "It's not a game, and we have to make sure we keep this away from the Church. You can't trust anyone, even family. Do you hear?" They both nodded in dumb shock. "Are you planning to have children?" she asked, looking directly at Patsy.

"If the Lord allows us," Patsy replied sheepishly.

"But what if it's a girl?" Margaret asked firmly. Silence. "Well?" asked Margaret again. "Speak up; we have to talk about it. What if it's a girl?"

"We'll have her adopted," Patsy replied in a very quiet voice.

"No you bloody well won't, you will bring her here to me. We'll look after her; we always look after our own." She spoke very firmly pointing her finger and banging the table top.

"It might not come to that, Mam. We've no plans to start a family straight away and, anyway, if it's a boy we are fine," he said stubbornly.

"Yes I do understand that, Tom," she said, "but you both must promise me that if you do have a girl child then she comes to me here; at least for the first five or six years until she can start school. It'll be the best all round for everyone, understand?" Tom and Patsy looked at each other and then back at Margaret.

"We promise," they both said together.

"Good, now that's all that will be said until the time arises."

"If it arises," Tom retorted.

"It bloody well will, son," she said to herself, sipping her tea and hearing a dog howling somewhere in the distance.

They returned to England the very next day. Both of them now had good secure jobs to return to, a new flat to decorate and a new life to live together. As sure as eggs were eggs, Patsy found herself with child some 5 months later and, in due course, they became proud parents to a beautiful baby boy who weighed in at 9lbs 5 ounces. It was almost perfect. Blodwyn was on hand to help out and Julie, who now already had her second child, lived nearby and was always popping in to see if she could help out in any little way. The child was christened immediately. They named him: Tinker John Murphy. He couldn't have been more loved. A beautiful, bright and happy child made Patsy feel good about herself. She was a mother, a good one who kept the house spotless and orderly, washed, cleaned and cooked: keeping them all happy and sated. She was now even managing her demon: attending mass regularly, reading the Bible and laughing with little Tinker kept the bugger away, for the moment anyway.

Life was good for them all. Tom was earning good money working for a marble company in Bristol. They managed to pay the rent, bills and eat well with a little left over at the end of the month to save for a rainy day. They didn't want another child at the moment, particularly a girl, so Patsy decided to visit her local family planning clinic, just to have a chat of course, as Catholic girls could never take contraception. The family planning clinics were a confidential service which dealt with this type of problem all the time and were keen to help large, poor families who just did not need more mouths to feed. The Catholic Church, on the other hand, would preach that if you really did not want more children, then total abstinence from any sexual activity it had to be: separate beds! The priest would tell you that this was fine in the eyes of the Lord. Well now, Tom was a red blooded male and he adored his beautiful, sexy, wife so that really was out of the question. Patsy quietly slipped into the family planning clinic one cold Monday morning to have a very discreet chat with them and she emerged two hours later a lot happier and protected from another pregnancy; not to mention the terrible thought of bringing another demon child into the world.

Six months later, in absolute shock, Patsy found herself with child. Her new contraceptive coil had failed her and she was far too long gone to abort the child. Her mother tried her best to placate her and calm her down but her health was failing, unbeknownst to Patsy and Julie. The cancer had returned, spreading to her liver and the other breast, so time was not on her side.

"Oh, Lord, please let me live to see this child into the world and help protect her," she prayed every day. Ma's predictions were all coming into play now; everything she had predicted was coming true.

"Oh, Ma, I wish you were here now," she would often say out loud when she was alone, hoping the Lord and the angels were listening.

Little Megan was eventually born after a labour lasting over three days. Tom was informed by the doctor that the child could possibly be dead, as no

146

heartbeat could be detected. Patsy was distraught and exhausted. Two midwives had sat with her all the way in the final two days of the labour, fearing they would lose both mother and baby to blood loss if they attempted to get her to hospital. A drip was set up in the bedroom and the doctor called every three hours.

Then, as if by magic, after three days, out she popped into the world. Both Blodwyn and Tom's mother Margaret were there to welcome this beautiful little bundle: nine pounds of black haired, soft skinned, beauty. Patsy, though, refused to even look at her, not wanting to hold her or breast-feed her. She hated this child; the devil child, the one that nearly killed her. Tom, on the other hand, adored her, immediately cooing and kissing her tiny fingers and toes. He adored them all, much to the absolute disgust of Patsy. She kept asking herself, *how could he love this devil child, evil child, nothing but trouble child?* It would be a thorn in Patsy's side always from now on. She would have to share his affections with her, and she didn't want to.

Megan amazed even the doctor.

"How this child survived I'll never know," he said to them both while examining her. "Yes all there, every finger and toe. She's exhausted, like the mother, but she will do fine," he said, handing her back to Blodwyn. She and Margaret had realised that she would actually be born and live when the angels started arriving in the bedroom. This made Patsy even madder, screaming at them to leave but, eventually, Megan made it out into this world and that was it. Margaret immediately told Patsy that, as soon as was possible, she'd have the child to live with her in Ireland, just as they had discussed on their honeymoon. Blodwyn, on the other hand, could never part with any child and would try her best to make Patsy love her and keep her there; but it was not to be, and she knew it.

Margaret returned and spread the news of the new arrival. She decided to tell everyone that Patsy was poorly and that little Megan would quite soon be coming to stay with her and her son Jim, who now lived with her after his wife had died. This left a very poorly Blodwyn to change and feed little Megan as Patsy had absolutely no interest in the child at all. Tom was really worried about her and not able to comprehend her behaviour. He had a word with the visiting midwife who, in turn, had a word with the doctor when he visited to check Patsy's blood pressure.

He sat and chatted to her for some time, eventually diagnosing Post Natal Depression.

"Don't worry, Mrs. Murphy, Post Natal Depression is quite common after a traumatic birth like yours. I will prescribe some Valium to help; you'll be back on form in no time. I will call again in two weeks to see how you are doing." He was concerned at her total lack of love for the child. Patsy had not bonded with it at all; it seemed very strange, she would not hold or feed her, or even look at her. He made a note to himself to have a chat with a local psychiatrist who specialised in PND. Perhaps a visit to him might help, he decided as he made his way out of the front door, hearing a dog howl somewhere in the distance. He felt uneasy. Looking around he could see nothing but his spine tingled. He decided that the atmosphere in the house was strange, very strange. Just every now and again he would call in to see a patient and have a funny feeling about the house. His wife always told him that he was psychic and that he was picking up on the energy being given off. He always dismissed her nonsense but today, for the very first time, he thought to himself she could be right.

*

Megan was deposited in Ireland at the tender age of 9 months. Tom was anguished and felt totally devastated at having to leave his baby girl. In his heart he knew it was the best thing, especially as Patsy was already with child again and her health was quite unstable. She was now under the local psychiatrist who had confirmed her Post Natal Depression. She was only just able to deal with Tinker and now, with Blodwyn very poorly and unable to help with Megan, there seemed no other choice but to leave Megan in Ireland with his mother and Jim; but something inside irked him. He hated Patsy for being so willing to get rid of this child so easily. He often asked himself,

"How could she not even look at her own child?" He knew that, but for Blodwyn's loving help and assistance, Megan would spend all day in the cot without one ounce of attention, only being fed and changed when necessary.

Margaret, on the other hand, was absolutely delighted to have Megan to live with her. As soon as they arrived she noticed the beautiful angels that suddenly appeared around the house. A cot was put into her room, next to her bed, and the rest of the family had contributed most of the baby items that she would need, including clothes and a pram. She had even arranged for her to be christened Megan Anne Murphy, as Patsy still refused to acknowledge her. When Tom, Patsy and Tinker eventually left to go back to England, Margaret was able to give this little bundle the constant love and attention that she so desperately needed.

Tom cried quiet tears all the way home to England, vowing to himself to visit at much as possible and to bring his daughter back when it was time for her to go to school. Patsy's mental state and health improved remarkably as soon as they returned home, much to Tom's annoyance. At least the house was clean, Tinker was well looked after and they were all well fed. Since Megan had gone, she had started smiling and laughing again. It was as if the whole weight of the world had been lifted from her shoulders. The only other problem they had to face, along with the next new child, was Patsy's mother Blodwyn who was now bedridden. The cancer had taken a hold and Blodwyn was now in the last stages of her life. Patsy visited every day, spending hours sitting by the side of her bed, reading passages from the Bible and giving her little sips of her beloved sherry. The doctor had insisted that she could have anything she wanted, anything at all, as she didn't have much time left, so her sherry would be one of her final comforts.

One afternoon, when Patsy was sat next to her mother and Tinker was playing happily at the bottom of her bed, there was a knock at the door.

"I'll get that," Patsy said out loud as the district nurse finished attending to her mother. She carefully made her very pregnant way downstairs to the front door.

"Coming!" she called out before finally opening it. A small blonde haired woman in a black cloak, with a shiny purple lining and a big hood stood at the front door.

"Is Blodwyn Russell here?" she asked, her big, blue eyes boring into Patsy. *God where do I know this woman from?*

"I'm your grandmother," she replied, which shook Patsy as she realised this woman had heard her thoughts.

"Mum's not well," Patsy said meekly to her.

"I know, that's why I am here," she said, pushing past her and going straight up the stairs towards her bedroom.

When Patsy arrived back upstairs with tea, Blodwyn's mother was sat playing with Tinker on her lap. Blodwyn was in tears.

"So you must be Patsy," she said, "my granddaughter, and this little chappie is my great grandson?" She only had eyes for the beautiful baby boy bouncing on her knee.

"Yes," was all Patsy could say.

"Where is the girl child?" she asked quietly while still playing with Tinker.

"Ireland," Patsy replied.

"She has the essence?"

"Yes," said Patsy, now feeling quite sick.

"She's strong, really strong; not weak like you." She spat the words out almost in disgust.

"Mother, please..." Blodwyn coughed as she spoke, a trickle of blood coming from the corner of her mouth. Patsy ran over to her mother, taking the handkerchief from the side of the bed and helping her to wipe her mouth.

"My God, Blod, you really messed up you know," said her mother looking directly at her. "It didn't have to be this way," she said whilst admiring Tinker playing with some toys at the top of the stairs.

"Well it bloody well is, so deal with it won't you?" Blodwyn replied briskly; her mother always drove her crazy.

"The girl child, what's her name?" she asked, sipping her very welcome cup of strong tea. "Megan," said Patsy.

"Nice name," she commented. "She'll be back."

"I don't want her back," cried Patsy, now quite alarmed.

"Well, child, she will be, so deal with it. Gifted too! She'll work."

"Oh, God, Mother, please..."

"Please what? I'm just telling it like it is, so get used to it. You've not got long, lass," she said lovingly to her daughter, "you have the smell of death about you."

"I know, just look after my Patsy for me please, Mum?" she begged her.

"I'm more concerned about you at this time," she replied.

"Look, Blod, there's no pain when you pass. You just drift out of this world into your new one. It's wonderful there, don't fight it, go when you are ready and don't hang on by your fingernails just to protect his one. Ma will be there waiting for you and you can pop back and keep an eye on everyone when you want to. Do something for you for a change," she said.

"I'm not ready yet, still things to sort," Blodwyn replied. "My funeral for one."

"I'll do that, Blod; good at arranging funerals I am. I lost your dad three years ago, been arranging everyone else's for them ever since."

"I don't want anything fancy," Blodwyn said, a tear falling from the corner of one of her eyes. "And keep it cheap. Bloody funerals are a waste of time and money: bloody undertakers and florists, bloody bloodsuckers, that's all they are!" She sat up straighter into her plumped up pillows, her breath now coming short and laboured.

"Well I've brought a bag and I'm here to stay until you don't need me. You can go now," she said to Patsy, who had sat quite still listening to their very personal conversation, "your mother needs her rest." She picked up Tinker, kissing him gently on the cheek and handing him over to Patsy.

"Shame you couldn't love Megan the way you love that little lad; it's another boy by the way," she said, nodding to the swell of her belly.

"Thank you," said Patsy who shook to the core with relief, kissing and cuddling Tinker and taking him over to her mother's bed so he could kiss his granny goodbye before they left.

"Bye, Mum, see you tomorrow," she said, kissing her mother gently. "Is there anything you need?"

"Nothing child, I'm here now," said Blodwyn's mother. "Just get yourself home and look after your family, we'll be here tomorrow. I will make a list of anything we need."

"Okay," Patsy replied, putting her coat on and picking up Tinker. "There's some cooked veg and ham in the larder and a beef stew on top of the stove. Mum needs something later, she's not eaten a lot today," she called out.

"Thank you, Patsy," Blodwyn's mother called back. "See you tomorrow."

"Bye!" called out Patsy as she left the house, pulling the kitchen door closed behind her as she made her way outside into the cold, damp air.

Blodwyn lasted another three weeks, dying eventually in the most indescribable pain. Not even the morphine that the doctor and district nurses administered four times a day could touch it. Her mother stayed at her side, constantly praying and telling her to let go and die, but she clung to life by her fingernails, just as her mother said she would, calling out to Patsy while she slowly drifted in and out of consciousness. Patsy was delirious with grief; watching her beautiful mother die like that was heart breaking and very frightening. She suddenly feared her own death. Would it be like this: painful and nasty? Still, having Tom, Tinker and the new baby made her life bearable and kept her focussed and strong as she dealt with their day to day lives. She only crumbled when she entered her mother's house and saw her lying there, prostrate and near death. The angels were gathering in the house and she knew the inevitable was only hours away.

Blodwyn was buried in Arnos Vale cemetery. Her funeral was frugal, just as she had asked. Only family flowers were allowed and there was no fancy service: just one hymn, her favourite, All Things Bright and Beautiful. The wake was held back at the house for anyone who wanted to come.

Patsy never attended her mother's funeral. She had already said goodbye just before Blodwyn died. She preferred to stay at the house and prepare the food that would adorn the table in her mother's honour. *She would be really proud of that,* she thought to herself, looking at the groaning table of neatly cut sandwiches, corned beef pie, sausages, quiche Lorraine, sausage rolls and scotch eggs; all made by her, fresh and tasty and accompanied by tea, beer, wine and her mother's beloved cream sherry.

"Don't be sad, grab and love your life; love and protect your children and your husband," were the last words her mother ever said to her. Patsy smiled, knowing she was around her. She could feel Blodwyn's presence, just as if she were looking over her shoulder. Blodwyn also told her to call out to her if she needed her and she would come.

"Okay, Mum!" she called out. "I hope you like the food. Please help look after me, Tom, Tinker and the new baby." She felt a tingle up her spine and smiled. Yes she was definitely there. She reached over to the sideboard, picked up her mother's beloved Clarice Cliff cup and poured herself a large sweet sherry.

Book Two

Shopping

It was a Saturday: shopping day. Patsy was down in the kitchen cooking crispy streaky bacon and eggs with toasted soda bread and tinned plum tomatoes. Heightened with ground black pepper and Worcester sauce, it was a real treat. She called to the children to come down. Toby, the beloved golden Labrador, who spent most of his time outside in the kennel, was sat in the kitchen, mouth drooling at the wonderful aroma of the bacon cooking. When the children came down into the kitchen his tail accelerated like it was a propeller and he was obviously delighted to be with the children whom he loved so much.

"Right," called Patsy, "everyone to the table." She placed platters of crispy bacon, fried eggs, toasted soda bread and a big bowl of steaming plum tomatoes on the table. All the children screamed with delight; this was a real feast.

"I want to see those plates cleared," she ordered. Toby was sat under the table now, hoping for some scraps to fall onto the floor and, of course he was never disappointed. Anything the children passed down to him was devoured within a second, without even a chew. Oh how he loved Saturday mornings!

After breakfast, Pasty called to the boys to take Toby for a walk, which they duly did. Megan
and her sister were to make all the beds, bedrooms were to be cleaned and vacuumed and the bathroom and toilet scrubbed with Vim until the enamel in the bath shone.

"Remember, do not put Vim and bleach in the toilet together," shouted Patsy, "or it will cause an explosion!"

That had happened on many occasions. The red tiles in the hall also had to be scrubbed and polished with a special red polish that was kept under the sink in the kitchen. The front room would also need polishing and vacuuming. When all this was underway, Patsy got on with the washing. It normally took about four hours to do all the bedding, towels and the mountain of clothes. Saturday really was the busiest day of the week.

By midday, all the chores were done. Lunch was homemade leek and potato soup with cheese sandwiches. The children ate with vigour.

"Tinker, Trixie and Shamus, you can all go out to play," said Patsy. "Megan - shopping."

"Okay, Mum," she replied, which caught Patsy off guard. She had forgotten the word 'mum'; it wasn't used very much in that house and gave her a little wobble.

Their house overlooked the school playing fields. To the left of the allotments, behind the house, were beautiful wild fields. It was a big hill with a sometimes muddy path running right up the middle which came out into the new housing estate and on to the shopping centre. It was quite a trek and in the winter when the weather was bad it would take even longer.

The shops were a new and modern block with a lovely outside sitting area right in the middle. There was a launderette, two greengrocers, two butchers, the Fine Fare supermarket, Brittain's toy shop, two newsagents, a bakery and a Barclays bank. Further down was a furniture shop, a large chemist, an off licence and a betting shop. Across the road was the very large and expanding doctors' surgery.

Megan's first trip up to the shops would be for the meat and veg. With a list and the money in her hand, she made her way down the lane by the allotment to the path up the steep hill and through the new housing estate which would bring her out at the launderette and her favourite: Brittain's toy shop. She would always stop and look at the mesmerising array of toys in the window. Mr. Brittain ran a Christmas club which Patsy usually joined; paying in five shillings a week, if it was spare. At the end of the year the payments would be totalled up and the toys would be purchased. Today it was half a crown: two shillings and sixpence was better than nothing!

"Hello, Megan," said Mr. Brittain, "haven't seen you for a while. Are you and the family well?"

"Yes thank you," she replied, handing over the half crown.

"Thank you," he said. "Tell Mum it will be a good Christmas for you all this year. It's already five pounds; here, I'll write it down for you." He handed over a handwritten note stating five pounds had been paid into the Christmas club. *That's brilliant*, thought Megan. *It was only two last year.*

She smiled to herself and wondered what Christmas morning would bring this year, as their stockings were virtually empty last time.

Next stop was the butcher. Vale's butchers slaughtered locally, which meant they could give the best possible prices. There was always a long queue outside the shop when Megan arrived.

"Hello, little angel," called out Darren, the head butcher. "Where have you been? We thought you had forgotten about us! We all missed you, didn't we lads?"

He called out to the other butchers who were busy cutting, chopping and serving the customers. It always amazed him: this little girl coming in with a list of meat. The other lads stopped what they were doing.

"Hey, little angel," they all called out, which made Megan blush terribly in front of the other customers, who were waiting and queuing for their meat.

"What will it be today?"

"Right," said Megan. "One pound of streaky bacon, six beef burgers, six belly pork slices, two pounds of pigs' liver, two pounds of pork sausages, six chicken legs and a nice piece of brisket for Sunday!"

"Tell, Mum, I've put a nice big breast of lamb in free of charge," said Darren.

"Oh," said Megan. "Half a pound of your cooked fore spur ham."

"I've also chucked in an ox heart as well," he winked as he passed over the change.

"Thank you," she said. "See you next week." She knew they all felt sorry for her: a little girl doing the weekly shop. *What in God's name did she know about the quality of meat?* they all thought. It was a good job they looked after her.

The meat was extremely heavy and the plastic carrier bags cut into her little hands. She looked at the list. She just could not carry everything at once, so another trip it would have to be, maybe three. *Oh well,* she thought and made her way to Paulette's veg shop.

"Hello, Megan, haven't seen you for a while, are the family well?"

"Yes thank you." She decided not to get all the veg on her list; she would come back for the rest. Paulette was a lovely lady and the shop was her pride and joy. Her husband had run off with one of her assistants some five years ago and she had decided to make the shop work in spite of him. He always went to the market in the morning and brought back the fresh veg but she used to get really annoyed at the quality sometimes.

"Wasn't there anything better? Could you not get a better price?" He would always be nasty to her and say,

"If you can do it better fucking well get on and do it." She had often thought, *I might just bloody well do that,* but she still let him take the reins and do the buying.

One morning, she decided that she would like to sell plants and flowers as well so made an appointment with a local agent. He would call early in the morning while her husband was at the market and, if she decided this was what she wanted to do, sod him, the stock would already be on sale when he got back and there would be nothing he could do about it. So, that morning, she got up earlier than normal. Brian would leave at 5am to go to the market and would normally return about ten. *Where the bloody hell was he?* she often wondered. He always seemed to have rubbish stuff, it almost seemed like leftovers. Well today she would be making the decisions and she would only choose the best. She arrived at the locked up shop at 7am. To her amazement, their van was parked outside. *What the fuck,* she thought, *what's up here?* She opened the back door to find the shop was quiet. She tip-toed through to the stock room; she could hear loud and rhythmic moaning. Throwing open the door, there was her Brian shagging the new assistant, Mandy.

"You bastard," she cried, throwing all sorts of vegetables at the pair of them. "You had better be gone by the time I get home tonight!" Of course he was, with the van, all the cash in the safe, the very expensive stereo system and, worst of all, their beloved dog, Stanley.

It was touch and go for a while but her mother helped and pulled her through. She had come from being a very ordinary fruit and veg shop, not really being noted for quality because he was always the bloody last in the market, to being the finest and busiest fruit, veg and plant shop in the whole area. Business was booming.

*

Megan was one of her regular Saturday customers. Paulette remembered her coming with her mother when she was small. Megan became the shopper, which often bothered her. Where was her mother, she always asked herself? Megan was smiling, as usual, and ordered apples, bananas and tomatoes. She spied a good value cauliflower that would be great for Sunday. She managed, with a push, to squeeze that into one of the bulging bags as well, paid for those items and told Paulette that she would be back for the rest later.

Every now and again Megan would stop at the newsagent's and buy herself a small ice cream scooped from the counter. It was always blackcurrants and cream; her very favourite. Patsy always counted the change to the last penny but sometimes the fruit and veg shop was so busy they could not give a receipt. She would have to be careful, though, and remember exactly how much the fruit and veg was before adding the cost of the ice cream on. It was her one and only secret pleasure. *Flippin' heck*, she often thought, *how could blackcurrants and cream taste so good?* She smiled to herself as she sat on the concrete public seat and licked away until it was all gone.

She started to make her way back through the housing estate to the top of the hill and, after about ten minutes, found herself walking through the alley that separated the houses to allow the path through. Soon she would be at the top of the hill and could make her way down the path towards her house. As she reached the top of the hill she could already feel her mother's eyes watching her every move; it quite unnerved her sometimes. She made it down the path and into the alley which led to the road, turned left then left again into the gate. She walked around the back of the house and went into the kitchen.

Her mother was sat on a stool, with a cup in her hand. The house and especially the kitchen were sparkling clean. Her brothers and sisters were out playing, so it was very quiet. She knew it would be wine or sherry in the cup and arguing with mother was not something you would want to do once the demon drink was in her.

"You took your time," Patsy snarled at her.

"It was really busy, I had to queue in the butcher's and the veg shop," she replied, dumping the heavy bags on the kitchen floor. They were instantly picked up by her mother and investigated.

"Good meat, where's the rest of the veg?" she snarled at Megan.

"I couldn't carry it all; I am going back now. Could we not have proper bags that won't break?" Megan asked.

"Can't afford them; remember, I am still trying to pay off the rent arrears," her mother tartly replied. "Here's the next list." Megan took the list, turned around and put a cardigan on before leaving, as the weather had turned chilly. *No,* Megan thought, *but you can afford a bloody litre of sherry every night.* Patsy growled and snarled at her, just as if she had heard her thoughts which, of course, she had. After a swift clip around the ear and with not even a drink of squash offered, or a five minute rest, she was unceremoniously thrown out the kitchen door. With a stinging face and a tear in her eye, she once again started to make the journey back down the lane and up the hill to the shopping centre. She knew her mother was sat in the kitchen, watching her every move, with a cup of something in her hand.

This time it was the chemist, the supermarket and finishing off the rest of the vegetables. She went to the chemist first for toothpaste and the very precious olive oil. It always made her giggle at the face of the assistant in the chemist who served her every week. Olive oil was sold in little bottles as a natural remedy for earache and, every week, she bought some. *God, thought the assistant when Megan bought another bottle this week, they must have some earaches in their house!* Next was the veg shop; Paulette served Megan very quickly as it was quietening down now in the late afternoon: potatoes, parsnips and onions. Then it was on to Fine Fare supermarket for tinned tomatoes, peas, carrots, cereals, flour, sugar and lard. It all filled eight carrier bags and she made it with two pennies to spare; not enough for another ice cream she frowned but, hey, she had already had one, which made her smile. She now had four carrier bags in each hand and was struggling to walk with them as they were so heavy. Every ten feet she had to stop for a rest and to ease the pain in her hands. After about the fifth stop the pain started to become unbearable and panic started to set in. It was getting dark and there was a little light misty rain coming in. She called out to her angels,

"Please help me, or I won't be able to make it." In an instant, the bags suddenly felt lighter, as if they were being held up for her.

"Thank you," she called up to the sky, and started to make her way home.

Rain was now falling, light, but wet. It was nearly 5.30 and it was getting dark; the rainclouds making it even more so.

"Right, get a move on!" she told herself and tried to up her tempo. The rain was now starting to fall more heavily but, with the heavy bags, she really was going as fast as she could. *Oh, God, I'll get another slap,* she thought. By the time she had got to the top of the hill, at the top of the meandering path, it had become very slippery and muddy. She stopped, looking down the hill, knowing and feeling her mother's stare. Just for one nervy, gut wrenching moment, she thought she heard a growl, like a dog. She looked around, but could see nothing.

"Oh feck!" she cried out. "Angels, I need you!" With that she started down the hill as quick as the terrain, and her little legs, would take her. She heard it again.

"Oh no!" she cried out, panic taking over.

"Here!" called Michael. "We are here."

"Oh thank God," Megan shouted out.

"Just keep going," they called back. She could see the lights on in her house but the growls were getting louder and nearer. She had to get home; then she heard a noise behind her. In her panic stricken moment she fell, bags of shopping spewing all around her. It all seemed to happen in slow motion: the lightning, the thunder, the booms, the screams and the horrifying sight of her mother like a charging elephant, her eyes glowing green with rage. She was running down the lane to the bottom of the hill, where Megan had finally stopped, and was heading straight for her. *Oh, God, I'm in trouble now*, she thought.

"Oh, God and angels please help me now!" she called out and with that her mother ran right past her into what sounded like a fight. All she could hear were loud screams and cries. She looked around, in the gloom, to see her mother was attacking something. She could see claws, tails, and teeth. They were jumping up and down like two fighting cocks with the angels looking on. Suddenly there was a flash of lightning; spears of light through the low clouds. Then there was nothing; quietness and no angels.

Her mother ran over to where she was sat in the mud heap and slapped her hard across the face.

"You dropped the shopping," she screamed.

"Sorry," Megan replied quietly, hiding her tears.

"Don't fucking do it again," her mum shouted back. Then, softening, she said, "Sorry, I shouldn't have shouted at you, come on." They both picked up all the scattered shopping and made their way up the lane.

Her brothers and sister were all gathered in the kitchen wondering why Mum wasn't there and the tea ready.

"It's okay," said Patsy to everyone gathered in the kitchen, "Megan just fell down the path with the shopping."

"What, in all that thunder and lightning?" asked Tinker. "You okay?" he asked, looking at Megan.

"Yes fine, silly thing to do."

"What's for tea?" her brothers and sister asked their mother in unison.

"Let me see, how about corned beef hash with creamy leek mash, spicy beans and onion gravy then apple and raspberry crumble for pudding? Did you get any tinned raspberries, Megan?"

"Yes," Megan replied.

"Great, that's it then; go and change," she told Megan.

Megan stripped her clothes off and had a good wash, even washing mud out of her hair. She had a funny thought: *Mum's not even wet or muddy...* She changed into clean clothes and suddenly felt exhausted. Her arms and hands hurt and there were red welt marks across the palms of her hands which seemed to be glowing. She was also ravenous and realised she had not eaten since breakfast, apart from the ice cream. No wonder she felt poorly.

"Tea!" shouted her mum.

"Coming," she called back and bundled her muddy clothes into a ball to put into the washing basket before making her way downstairs.

Their mother never ate with them at the table, preferring to sit in the kitchen with her cup of something. Megan often wondered if she ever ate at all. That night, however, they were all ravenous and the meal was delicious. When the meal was over, they were allowed to lie in front of the open fire, which was ragingly hot, and watch black and white television for a couple of hours before going up to bed. They all said goodnight to Mum and headed upstairs to bed. The second Megan laid her head on her pillow, the growling started again. Exhausted, she pulled the blankets up over her head and fell into a deep sleep, while quietly saying her prayers.

Sundays were the best days. She got up with the lark, had chores to do, then cooked Sunday lunch which was always the best and most loved meal of the week. Mr. Winters had popped some runner beans and leeks on the kitchen windowsill, along with a few beetroots and a couple of courgettes. School uniforms had to be pressed and hung up on the line ready for the morning and Sunday lunch would be served at about three in the afternoon.

"Don't forget to get the beef in the oven at 11.30," called out Patsy. It was all about timing and she was a master of it.

Mr. Winters, who lived next door, was a keen gardener and had left some vegetables on the kitchen windowsill that day but Megan's mum wanted carrots and cabbage from the growing patch which he helped keep up whilst Megan's dad was away working. Calling over the fence to him in the garden, Megan asked was there any cabbage that was good to cut and carrots to pull. He immediately came around into the back of the garden, smiled and selected some for use that day. He secretly fancied Patsy and was keen to help.

"Thank you, Mr. Winters," Patsy called out to him.

"Please call me Alan," he said.

"Thank you, Alan," Patsy called back. He shivered, right up his spine. She always made him feel that way.

"Thank you," said Megan and he returned to his own garden, peeking every so often over the garden fence, just to see if he could get a glimpse of that sassy Patsy Murphy.

Cabbages normally came with cabbage white caterpillars. It was Megan's job to pick them all off but she never killed them, putting them instead over the fence into the school playing field. She hoped that they would not die, just find something else to eat. The angels reassured her that they would. She chopped the cabbage and scrubbed the new carrots, not daring to take off the precious skin which held all the vitamins. *Oh what a feast,* she thought, looking over all the vegetables she had lovingly prepared. When she cooked the lady in blue always appeared and just stood in the corner of the kitchen by the back door, smiling, and pointing out any little thing she might have missed. Today she just watched and smiled, knowing that Megan knew exactly what she was doing. It was as though she was proud of her. *I hope she is,* Megan often thought.

The roast dinner was a triumph and on the table at exactly three that afternoon. There were Yorkshire puddings to die for and delicious thick gravy which was thickened with a mixture of flour and butter and all the juices from the baked onions and meat juices combined; the flavour was amazing. Hungry mouths mopped up all the gravy with the huge Yorkshire puddings and the meat melted in their mouths. Yes, everyone ate well that day and there would be plenty of leftovers for bubble and squeak for the following day. Megan was eyeing up the leftovers, as she was cooking the next day and was already planning their evening meal.

The next morning, Megan heard her mother leave for work at about 5am. She got up, cleaned her teeth, washed, dressed and made her way downstairs to the kitchen to put the oven on for the soda bread. As soon as she walked into the kitchen, the blue lady appeared.

"Good morning, child," she said. "Soda bread is it?"

"Yes," replied Megan, "and porridge and toast and berry jam."

"Lovely," she replied, "you will remember all of this when you are older."

Her mother had made them all packed lunches that day; they were in the fridge and Megan handed them out to everyone, keeping one for herself.

They all made their way to the door and out onto the garden path to walk to school. Megan hung back, turning round and checking everything was in its place before she pulled the front door closed behind her.

She didn't feel particularly well. That bloody thing had growled and scratched at the window all night and the footsteps seemed louder and longer than usual; it had sounded like a flippin' army going up and downstairs all night. She felt very edgy that morning, scolding her younger brother for spilling his tea and she felt bad about that walking down the road. She was approaching the school and her nerves started to jangle. *What are they going to do today?* she asked herself.

They were waiting for her and, within seconds, had surrounded her. The girls were chanting at her, giving her an odd slap here and there in front of their mothers who looked on.

Everyone looked away; no one did anything. This was now starting to spill over into lunchtimes and, each time it reduced Megan to a pile of shaking tears. Her mother constantly complained to the headmaster, Mr. Robert Davies, who really was not interested. He had once made a pass at Patsy and was flatly rebuked by her, which of course put a dent in his ego. He thought he was a good catch: good looking, single, high standing in the community, a car, a good salary and an even better pension. Yes, he thought he was a good catch but could never seem to keep a woman interested. He often flirted with the single, lady teachers but could never hold their interest. He just had nothing in common with any of them it seemed.

"I suppose you haven't met the right one yet," his mother would always tell him. What a bloody nerve Patsy Murphy had turning him down! He had only asked her out for a drink at the local pub. He was actually hoping for more than just a drink, and she knew it. He rather fancied her curvy figure, long legs and big green eyes. *Cheeky bitch!* He'd make her pay, make them all pay. So when Patsy called to see about the bully girls, he just dismissed her, labelling her as a troublemaker.

By the end of the week, Megan was a wreck, and always in tears, which of course the bully girls loved. They just seemed to get off on it. She was feeling sick all the time and would often sit in the nurse's room with a sick bowl when it was PE because that was the session that she would meet up with them all.

"How much more of this can I take?" she would ask her angels and they would always reply,

"You will be fine and triumph." The angels never left her side, even at school and that made her nervous because she often wondered if everyone else could see but no one ever seemed to acknowledge them. Megan carried on; each day getting worse and worse. She was losing weight and getting thinner and frailer; her food seemed like it was just passing through her. The demon child within her was getting weaker. Meanwhile, the bully girls just kept on going and going at her. She often questioned herself but never got an answer. Perhaps she already knew it but blocked it from her mind.

This intense campaign by the bullies to break Megan had now been going on for six solid weeks.

There were only another six weeks before she would finish at Briarwood school and start at her new comprehensive school but one particularly bad night, when Megan had been bullied all day, she felt she had finally had enough and could no longer carry on being at that school. She was desperately trying to talk to her mother who, of course, had her own problems to deal with. This kid wasn't her only priority. When Patsy's newfound half-sisters arrived that night, bearing bad news that Dizzy was pregnant by a man that did not want to know, all hell kicked off. The two sisters started fighting with each other. Megan was sat on top of the fridge in the kitchen. She normally sat there to watch her mother cook and it was levelling to be able to look straight into her mother's big green eyes as she spoke to her, but tonight her world was upside down. Thin and frail from the bullying and mentally fragile, all she really needed was Sally to hug her and tell her she was loved. But Sally had not been in touch since they had come home and Megan was missing her. Her siblings were not interested in her. All they cared about was playing and their toys. Little Megan felt so alone.

She screamed out loud,

"Does anyone really care about me?" and threw herself off the fridge.

She landed head first, on the hard kitchen floor which had a concrete base. The two sisters stopped fighting immediately and ran to the unconscious little girl. Blood was pouring out of her head so they ran next door, screaming for help. Patsy begged Mr. Winters to call an ambulance which, of course, he did. She ran back to the kitchen, suddenly bursting into tears and screaming,

"Please, Lord, don't let my little Megan die."

She didn't die, but had a fractured skull with lacerations to the scalp. She remained unconscious for two days.

The Summons

"Tom, Tom! It's the telephone for you; someone called Dizzy is asking to speak to you," shouted Mrs. Brown to Tom who was in the garden planting beans and potatoes in the vegetable patch. Tom put his shovel down and walked towards the house. Taking off his shoes at the kitchen door and thanking Mrs. Brown for the use of the telephone, he answered the phone.

"Hello?" said Tom quietly, worried who could be on the other end of the line.

"Tom, it's Dizzy, Patsy's sister; you have to come home. Megan is in hospital, she's got a head injury. Tried to kill herself she did," a very concerned little voice spoke into his ear.

"Oh God is she bad?" he asked as he started to quiver inside, his stomach juddering from the bad news.

"Yes, still unconscious," Dizzy replied.

"How's Patsy?" he asked, not really wanting to hear any more bad news if possible.

"Just about managing but there are some rent problems." He shut his eyes and said a quick prayer asking for some divine intervention with this problem.

"Okay," he said, "I will be back as soon as I can arrange something here. Thanks for the call."

"Bad news?" asked Mrs. Brown, realising this was more than a little problem at home.

"Yes, my daughter has had an accident," he said, not wanting to tell the full story or arouse anyone's interest in his family.

"Is there anything I can do, Tom?" she asked with a willing heart.

"No, but thank you all the same. I will go and have a word with the foreman tomorrow. I might need to go home for a while," he said.

"Well don't worry about your room here," she said, making a cup of tea and passing it to him. "It's yours even if you are away for a year. I don't care; it doesn't worry me, Tom. It's yours until you say so."

"Thank you," he meekly replied, starting to make his way back out to the garden.

"Oh, by the way, a letter came for you this morning. It's on the dresser in the kitchen," she called out to him as she set the table for the workmen's evening meal. Tom carried on in the garden, finishing the planting. Megan and Patsy were heavy on his mind.

He sat on his bed and fingered the envelope, almost as though he was scared to open it. He had noticed the Irish stamp on the front and was praying that it was from Father Thomas Jones. *Thank goodness,* he thought, heaving a sigh of relief that it was. Finally he could get some help for Patsy and, most of all, get rid of this bloody secret he had been carrying around with him for years, before anyone else found out.

The letter read:

Dear Tom,

Thank you for your letter which I received two days ago. This is the first time I have had a chance to reply to you as the church diocese here is very busy and I have many parishioners to attend to who all seem to want me at the same time.

I am so pleased that you have contacted me with regards to Patsy. As I said before, anything I can do to help, I will; that's what I am here for. I will take the early morning train to Rosslare and the first available ferry. I should be with you some time on Thursday.

Keep strong, I am praying for you all.

Thomas Jones

Tom read the letter again and again, suddenly realising that it was Wednesday and he would be there tomorrow.

"Oh thank you, Lord!" he said out loud.

Bright and early next morning there was a knock at the door. A shiny blue car stood outside the house in the street. Tom opened the door and both men hugged.

"A lovely welcome for a weary traveller," said Father Thomas, warmly smiling at the sight of Tom.

"Come in, come in, Father," said Tom.

"Call me Thomas," he said, smiling and following him into the house.

"Can I get you some tea, Thomas?"

"Lovely, thank you, just what I need." The kettle was already boiled and the tea made. Tom was now making breakfast for them both. It was seven in the morning and Mrs. Brown would normally stay in bed until about 11am. All the other men had gone to work so they had time and privacy to talk about everything. Three hours later, and two more pots of tea, they were still going. Mrs. Brown smiled at them as she entered the kitchen to make a cup of tea and grab a slice of toast. She liked Tom, had all the time in the world for him in fact. He was a good man; not many about like him, she often thought. She knew he had trouble in the family and, God only knows, she understood that. She had most certainly had her fair share of it in her life and wished only the best for him. Mind you, if she was younger she would most definitely make a play for him but he was married and had lovely children. He always spoke about them and she was now an elderly lady... but she could still dream.

Father Thomas had borrowed a car from the Bristol diocese and so was able to drive Tom home to Patsy and the family, leaving Mrs. Brown feeling a little lonely now as a good friend and brilliant gardener had just left her home.

Tom arrived home in the early evening, saying goodbye to Father Thomas outside the house, so as to not rattle Patsy. Both agreed to keep in touch and meet up again as soon as Thomas had sought out the help he was looking for. He was going to meet up with his old lecturer from Oxford University, William Rutstone, who was a specialist in the occult. They had already spoken on the telephone and William was keen to help. Father Thomas drove away from Tom to try and find some answers to this terrible problem.

The family gathered around their father in the kitchen, excitedly hugging and kissing him in turn. Patsy was in tears, so glad to have him home: her man mountain, her love. For the first time in months they were all reunited as a family but the funny thing was no one mentioned Megan, his baby girl, ill, in hospital with a head injury. It was too late to go to the hospital now so he decided he would go first thing in the morning, which sent Patsy into a rage. The mention of Megan was ruining the harmonious family reunion. But go he would. He would see his little daughter whether Patsy liked it or not!

Her father's face was the very first thing that she saw when she eventually woke up.

"Dad!"

"Shh now, Megan, you need your strength. How are you feeling, love?"

"Groggy," she replied. There was a drip in her arm which was linked up to a big machine that beeped and made lots of different noises. She was sporting two black eyes and a bandage that went all around her head and, Tom said, made her look like a panda, which made her giggle. The nurses were bustling in and out of her room, which was nice. She had a side room all to herself with a little radio and television.

"On the mend at last," said Sister Williams. "We have been waiting for you to come around, Megan. How are you feeling, my darling?"

"Okay," she replied.

"And tell me, who is this handsome man standing at your bedside?" she asked, looking at Tom and wishing she had a man that looked that good.

"He's my dad," she replied proudly.

"Well lucky you," Sister Williams smiled, wondering if she looked okay and thinking she should have put some more lipstick on that morning. "Well the doctor will be here soon," she said, still looking at Megan's father and starting to blush at the thoughts running through her mind.

"Hello, young lady, you gave us all a fright," said the doctor. "You have a fractured skull, so you will be here with us for at least another two weeks. We can feed you up and get some weight back on you; then make sure that you are fully recovered. Okay?"

"Yes thank you," replied Megan.

"Mr. Murphy, can I have a word outside?" he asked, pointing to the door which was just out of earshot for Megan.

"Mr. Murphy," Dr Stapleford said, "I really don't know how your daughter survived trying to take her own life but she is a very lucky girl. I am now pretty sure that with the right nursing and treatment that she will make a full recovery. She's also emaciated, very underweight. I believe she has had a lot of trouble at school being bullied and she has been asking for her mother. You are the only visitor she has had. I am arranging for a nutritionist and a child psychologist to come and see her; meanwhile while she is here with us she can have anything she wants to eat and drink. I will have a word with the school board to investigate what's going on and get her some physio to help with her neck movements. Oh, and Mr. Murphy, your daughter has a very rare blood group; I want all the family to be tested to see if they are a match just in case in the future, she ever needs blood."

"Thank you, Doctor," Tom replied and went back into the room to give his little girl the great big cuddle she obviously needed!

Megan had a wonderful time over the next three weeks. She spent them in the children's ward of the hospital and made an amazing recovery. She had put on some weight and, by the third week, was having full time lessons with a relief school teacher who called in every day. The teacher was amazed at how polite and intelligent she was.

Not once in the five weeks that Megan was in hospital did her mother visit. It was just as well her dad was home; he came in every single day on his way home from work, sometimes not getting home until nine at night, to the wrath of Patsy.

She was finally allowed home after five weeks in hospital. So that Tom could afford for them both to catch the bus home, he walked the ten miles to the hospital to collect her. His wages had dropped since he left the power station and he was still sending money home to Ireland, so money was now tighter than ever. Patsy had got them into rent arrears; what did she do with the money he sent home every week, he asked her constantly?

They got off the bus and started walking down the hill towards a large set of steps which led to the pathway up to their road. Megan had slept well in hospital and had no paranormal experiences at all except for her angels who would pop in and out to check on her. It had been bliss but, as they were walking up the hill towards the house, her stomach started churning and anxiety set in. She looked up to her dad who smiled at her, trying to give her some support. Somewhere in the distance she once again heard that call: the growl. Oh yes, they knew she was back. Her dad squeezed her little hand.

"Don't worry, I'm here now." They slowly made their way up the hill to the house. When inside, her brothers and sister made straight for her; cuddling her and thanking God that their little sister was home and safe. The smell of food cooking was all through the house and very tantalising. The hospital did look after her, and the food was fine, but never ever a patch on her mother's home cooked fare.

They all sat down to roast capon with homemade sage and onion stuffing, Yorkshire pudding, new potatoes, roasted potatoes, cauliflower cheese and freshly podded peas with a lovely orange and thyme gravy. It was all washed down with Patsy's apple and cinnamon crumble with thick clotted cream.

It was a real feast and so lovely to be at home again with her family. Megan's dad made her heart sing and she was excused any chores that day. Mr. & Mrs. Winters from next door knocked and brought in the biggest bar of Cadbury's chocolate she had ever seen to welcome her home. Her mother, though, never acknowledged her at all; not a word. Still, she went to bed happy. Later that night, however, the growls and scratching started outside her window, the baby started crying again and the footsteps began, up and down the stairs. *Perhaps,* she thought to herself, *this is it; this is my life; how it's meant to be.* Just then Trixie clambered into her bed and they cuddled down under the blankets together to muffle the noises. Both fell asleep almost instantly.

The next morning, Megan's dad was downstairs in the kitchen making everyone breakfast as Patsy had already gone to work. Megan giggled at the sight of her dad in his vest and underpants making porridge and cooking bacon. He was amazed as Megan very quickly made a loaf of soda bread and had it in the oven in about five minutes. She laid the table, then went and tidied the front room, putting all the cushions in exactly the places that Patsy liked. Next, she went to wake her brothers and sister. Washed and toileted, they all descended down to the warm kitchen to have breakfast and dress for school. This made things click in Tom's brain, just how much his little daughter did, at 9 years old. She really was a second mum to her siblings. Guilt, frustration and rage erupted in him at the same time so he shouted hard at her brothers and sister to get on and eat their breakfasts and not to play Megan up. He told them all he would be coming to school today, so everyone was to be ready in ten minutes.

Megan was delighted that her dad was coming to school. He was a massive, and very handsome, 6 feet 8 inches tall and man mountain himself. The bullies, teachers and that flippin' Mr. Davies, the headmaster, had never met him before. She giggled to herself. Hopefully now, with her dad at her side, she would be taken seriously and they would all leave her alone.

They walked in line: the two boys in front and Megan and her sister behind them with their dad walking at the rear. It was quite a sight to see the very clean and smartly dressed Murphy clan turn left into the school gates, up the steps and into the playground. Everyone stopped and looked in disbelief. Megan was now holding her dad's hand and the bully girls' mothers just drooled at this gorgeous hunk of a man walking across the playground holding little Megan's hand.

"What the fuck!" cried out Sylvia to Maureen. "What's he doing holding that brat's hand?"

"Don't know," said Maureen, "but he can bloody well hold mine any time, and anything else he wants to!" Tom winked at Megan.

Right then, where's this Mr. Davies?" he asked her.

"This way," she said. He was so tall he had to duck in through the doorway into the gym. They crossed the gym and all the dinner ladies stood in shock, mouthing to each other,

"Who is that with Megan?"

At the school office they were greeted by Maxine Giles. She had been the headmaster's secretary ever since he was awarded the position some twelve years ago. She had been secretary to two previous headmasters and ran the school under the strict orders of the headmaster. She ruled with an iron fist, tolerating absolutely nothing unless Mr. Davies had first said it was okay.

"Mr. Davies, please," Tom boomed.

Mr. Davies nearly wet himself on seeing the man mountain stood before him in his office with little Megan. He spluttered,

"Yes, I am Mr. Davies." Maxine burst in behind them, nearly knocking Megan over.

"Sorry, sorry, Robert he just ignored me when I said you were busy."

"It's fine, Maxine, I'll deal with this. How can I help you... Sir?"

"I am Megan's dad, and I have come to talk to you about the bullying my daughter is experiencing. Apparently you are doing nothing about it; in fact, no one is doing anything about it."

"Now, now, Mr. Murphy," said the headmaster, "it's nothing, absolutely nothing. It's just children being children and Megan is so sensitive she overreacts to everything." Tom walked over to a very shaky Mr. Davies and picked him up by his shirt collar so he was at least two feet off the ground. He held him up to his face and looked him in the eye.

"Mr. Davies, you and your staff are full of shit! How could you let my little girl be so bullied that she tried to kill herself rather than come to your school?" he boomed right into his face. The headmaster went limp, nearly fainting. He was choking, as Tom had his shirt collar wrapped around his huge hands. "I am telling you," continued Tom, "I am making you responsible for the safety of my little girl and if I hear one more bad thing about this fucking nasty nest of vipers' school, just one more report of anything..." he boomed into Robert's face, "I will be back. By God I will be back for you and fucking God help you if I do."

"I'll call the police, I'll call the police," Mr. Davies shakily replied.

"Yes, please do. Then we'll have all you bastards sorted out: one by one. I know enough coppers to sort your lot out, let's call them now!"

Maxine Giles was listening to all of this going on and she was shaking.

"God he really means it," she said to herself.

"Mr. Murphy, please put me down.

You need fear for nothing more. I will take this matter in hand and you will have no further need to contact me with these concerns, I assure you."

"Well," roared Tom, "this had better be the last and only time I have to come to this godforsaken school and have this conversation with you because if I have to come back again, you will all know it and I will take matters into my own hands; do you understand?"

"Yes, please don't shout, you will upset all the other children and we don't want any more fuss." It was too late, as all the other teachers had gathered about the office and were witnessing this scene; drinking it all in and seeing this giant of a man lift Robert Davies off the floor by his shirt collar.

"Go on, give it to the bastard," shouted one of the teachers, much to Maxine's disgust.

"Who was that?" she called, "I'll have you disciplined!"

Then, as suddenly as he had arrived, Tom turned around, kissed little Megan and made his way across the gym. By now the dinner ladies were clapping him. As he crossed the playground, where all the bullies and their mothers were gathering, two teachers dashed out after him in case of any trouble. But Tom didn't intend any trouble; he was just firing a warning shot across the bows, hoping they would take note of who he was. Megan was still with him as he reached the gate. He turned to say goodbye and said to her,

"Show me who they are, point to them."

"No, Dad," she replied.

"It's okay; they now know who you are."

He bent down and picked her up in his massive arms, kissed her and said,

"Have a lovely day, see you tonight." With that, he put her down and was gone, making his way to the bus stop to go to work. Megan smiled and looked over to where the bullies and their mothers were standing. She nodded to them and thought proudly, *yes that's my dad.* The bell went and everyone dispersed to the classrooms to be signed in the attendance register.

Megan not only had a great day, she had a fabulous one. Still there was the odd poke and slap but she could put up with that. They left her alone for the whole week and Megan suddenly came alive again. She looked forward to the weekend and her chores, especially the cooking. There was only one more week of school to go and she would be free, yes free!

The Final Week

The weekend came and went really quickly. All the chores and shopping were done on Saturday, and Sunday seemed to pass in a blur. The family all got up early and attended the 6am mass then came back, did chores, cooked lunch and, once again, attended the 6pm mass some five miles away. They walked to church but had the luxury of catching the bus home; getting them back in the house for 8.30pm where Patsy was waiting with plates of toasted cheese and onion sandwiches. Then it was early to bed to be ready for the week ahead.

Monday morning was back to normal. Both parents had gone to work, so Megan got up early, made the soda bread and tidied the front room. It was now so automatic that she didn't even think about it; it just happened. She got her brothers and sister up for their breakfast, then washed and dressed. While they were eating she made the beds: situation normal.

Everything was done by 8.30am on the dot and they left for school together. Megan was smiling to herself, really looking forward to another nice day at school. But as she turned into the school gates, heading up the steps to the playground, she was immediately jumped on by the gang, pulling her hair and kicking her in the shins.

"No big daddy with you today, Smelly Murphy," one of the girls shouted. They,

once again, surrounded her, chanting and slapping.

"No, please!" she cried out. The bell rang and a teacher who was watching called over to the bully girls to move on, which they did, still calling Megan names as they ran to their classrooms.

Little bitches, thought Brendan Swallow, one of the teachers who was on playground duty that day.

"You okay, Megan?" he called out.

"Yes fine," she replied, with tears trickling down her little cheek as she tried to wipe mud off her socks and the bottom of her skirt. Once again, nobody did anything and it happened again at lunchtime. At the end of the day, she ran out of the back of the school, taking the long two mile trek home, rather than having to face that lot again.

Tuesday was exactly the same, so was Wednesday and Thursday. They kept at it with no respite.

"What is it with these teachers?" she would ask the angels. "Surely they can see what is going on, why can't they help?"

"Don't worry, child," they would reply. "Have faith please, all will be well."

She couldn't help but worry, though, and felt very alone.

When she eventually got home, after running as fast as she could all the way, she found no parents, her siblings upset and the electricity off.

"Oh good God, that's all we need now," she screamed to herself. "Okay, okay, I'll sort it myself. I'm here, just let me get changed and I will sort it all out." She rushed upstairs in double quick time to change then ran down into the kitchen and reached up on to the top of the dresser for the little, blue egg cup that was filled with the filed halfpennies for the meter. *Good,* she thought, there were four. She put two into the meter and the electricity returned, much to the delight of her brothers and sister.

"What's for tea?" they all called at once.

"I don't know yet," she replied sharply and nearly knocked into the blue lady who had just walked into the kitchen. "All of you go and watch the television or do your homework and I will sort out something." She opened the fridge and groaned; it was Thursday so there wasn't much left. She would have to be creative.

She made toast and topped it with butter and homemade bramble jam. Together with some tea, she took it all into the front room where they had gathered around the open fire.

"This will have to do until I can cook us tea." They all smiled and thanked her, greedily devouring the sweet, jammy toast and drinking the hot, sweet tea.

"Right then," she said to herself, "that will give me time to make something nice to eat!"

She quickly made some shortcrust pastry. She loved making pastry; she had good cold hands and handled it with ease. When it was done she popped it in the fridge to rest until needed.

Next she buttered and floured her mother's favourite big, square pie tin, opened two tins of corned beef and sweated off two large onions, to which she added a tin of mixed vegetables, salt and black pepper. Then she crumbled in two stock cubes and a trickle of water to get it all going down and nicely sloppy before lining the tin with pastry and adding the cooled mixture, which she had placed outside on the dog kennel to cool it quicker. Next, she cooked up some leek mash and made onion gravy, topped the pie with more pastry, brushed it with milk and popped it in the oven to cook for forty minutes. While it was in she pulled some carrots and a cabbage from the garden and cooked them, timing it all perfectly so that everything came together and she could put a meal on the table for them all. She thickened the onion gravy with a little butter and flour and it was done. Pudding was a chocolate Angel Delight, which was easy and all she could find.

"Tea!" she called. Just before the rabble appeared in the doorway, the blue lady said to her,

"Megan, put two more meals out, your parents will be home soon." There was plenty of everything so she put the two meals in the oven with a plate on top.

Just as she had finished washing up, the key went in the door. Tom and Patsy fell through, laughing and crying at the same time. They had been to a funeral at the

Concord pub and both had been drinking. It was unusual and heart-warming to see them being nice to one another. The children were ready for bed and Megan rushed them all upstairs so their parents could have some time together on their own.

Just as everyone was settled in bed, the bedroom door opened; it was their dad. Trixie and Megan both got out of bed and jumped into his arms.

"Megan, did you really cook that meal for everyone tonight?" he asked her.

"Yes, of course, the blue lady always helps me cook when there's no one here with us. She said you would be back and to put some dinners up for you," she replied. He kissed and cuddled them both again, then tucked them both in.

"Please don't go away again, Daddy, we need you," Megan said, looking at him as he left their bedroom.

The house went quiet, in fact eerily so. Megan lay in bed and realised there was no noise, nothing. Where was the baby's cry; why wasn't anyone walking up and down the stairs and rattling the door handle like normal?

"What's the matter, what is it?" Megan called to the angels. Gabriel appeared.

"Yes, Megan, what is it?" he asked. Michael suddenly joined them.

"Tomorrow, Megan you will be fine; all will be well."

"Trust us and yourself," they said in unison. "You will be fine."

"What are you saying? Help me... please!"

"Don't worry about tomorrow, we love you and will be with you, Megan." With that they lifted up and swept up through the ceiling.

"Oh, God, help me please," Megan called out in her fear and confusion. She pulled the blankets over her head and said her prayers, asking the Lord and the angels to protect her parents and her brothers and sister. Most of all she asked them to protect her when she attended her last day of school tomorrow. God knows she would need it!

Revenge

It was the final day at school and everyone was really happy, saying goodbyes to their teachers and talking about the new secondary schools they would be attending in September. There were seven weeks of holiday now then a step into the big, wide world awaited them all.

It was a funny day for Megan. She had got up as usual and done all her chores before waking and feeding her brothers and sister. Unfortunately, there was no money in this household for gifts for the teachers. It was as much as Patsy could do to feed the family at times, so expensive gifts for teachers were out of the question. Anyway, they were paid; it was their job, she always said, so a simple thank you would do: end of discussion!

She walked down to the school gates, where the usual crowd awaited. Her stomach churned in anticipation of what this lot would do to her today but she managed to slip past them unnoticed, or so she thought. They had seen her but were engrossed with their mothers, who were talking with the teachers about the new school and showing off the new uniforms they had bought. The bell rang and they all went to assembly. The last day at this school had started. She made a point to go and speak to every one of her teachers and thank them for all the hard work they had done for her, even though one or two of them dismissed her, uninterested. Some of them were like that but most thanked Megan for being a good student and told her it was a pleasure to work with her and good luck for the future. That was it, her part was done. It was a quiet day that seemed to drag on: clearing out their lockers, taking all their work off the wall to take home, collecting all their workbooks. This was precious stuff to Megan as she had tried hard and was proud of her work, especially her paintings and poetry which adorned the classroom wall. Yep, all of it was coming home; she would keep it for her children and proudly show them in years to come.

After lunch, she returned to the classroom for the last time to wait for the final bell to ring which would signal the end of this hell for her. It had been three years of being bullied every, single day with no support from either her mother or the teachers, especially the headmaster. It had nearly pushed her over the brink but, thankfully, she had survived and only had a couple of hours left to endure. All the bully girls were going on to another school, Brislington, while she was going to Hengrove. Goodbye to Sharon and all the bully girls. Yeh! Happy thoughts, but was she getting ahead of herself? An angel appeared in the classroom and her stomach started to churn. *Trouble,* she thought. Then another angel appeared. *Oh, God help me; what's up?* Next came a growl but still she couldn't see anything. Parents were already gathering in the playground and Megan was looking out of the window. Sharon's mother, along with all the other posh snobs, was there: smoking, chatting and taking the world apart as usual. Cars lined the street ready to take their children home and away from Megan forever.

The bell rang.

"Wait," said one of the angels, "be last to leave!" So she stayed at her desk and watched. She heard the growling again and nerves made her shake. *What was going on?* She waited twenty minutes and the angels had gone, so she left. She walked down the steps of the Nissan hut- style classroom and started to make her way past the throngs of schoolteachers, parents and children saying goodbye.

"Where do you think you're going, Smelly?" Sharon shouted. Screams of laughter filled the air and, within seconds, watched by their parents and teachers alike, they once again encircled Megan, joining hands so she could not get out. They started chanting, "Smelly Murphy, Smelly Murphy," just as if performing for all to see. This was their usual thing, but today it was more aggressive and nastier. The mothers were screaming with delight and thought it was really good. This was the last time they could do this to her, so let them have their fun. Megan felt different today: stronger and fed up of all this crap that she had endured for so long. So, instead of trying to bash her way out of the circle, she stood still, looked up and silently asked, *if there's anyone here today to help me, please this is the time. I need your help now.*

At that precise moment, Sharon, who was getting really bored because Megan had not reacted, decided to smack her across the face. Her mother was looking on and she knew it would make her proud but this turned out to be her kiss of death. Something just snapped inside Megan; it was as if that had just released a volcano. Her neck swelled, she welled up and became taller, her fangs started to drop and her talons protruded. She grabbed Sharon by the hair and, in one move, swung her round to hit all the other girls in the circle. They all went down like a row of skittles. Then she picked up Sharon again by the hair, and did it once more, dropping them like stones. They tried to fight back but she was stronger, bigger and as fast as lightning. Sharon was screaming to her mother now,

"Get her off me!" All the other girls were shrieking and running in all directions but Megan would not let go of this nasty, cruel, vicious and vindictive bitch. She had to have her, so she swung her by her precious hair and big clumps of it came out in her hands. She pushed her to the ground and put her arm behind her back, just like Sharon usually did to her.

"How do you like your own medicine, you evil bitch?" Megan screamed into her ear before biting it. "I haven't finished with you yet!" She did not really know where the strength or words were coming from, but it was a massive release and made her feel even stronger. At that moment, five teachers came running, not believing what they were seeing. Little Megan Murphy, who had suffered at the hands of Sharon and her gang, whilst they had watched for amusement over the last three years, was literally kicking their asses and there was nothing anyone could do to stop her.

They managed to stop Megan from swinging Sharon around by her hair and released her to her screaming mother who ran forward and slapped Megan across the face.

"Look what this girl has done to my Sharon!" she screamed, holding up a massive lock of hair with some scalp attached. "I'm gonna fucking kill her and her family. I will have them all!" she screamed. The other girls were all crying with shock at what had just happened to them and started screaming at their mothers to get her, that bitch that had just hurt them all! It was mayhem.

"Call the police, call the police!" Sharon's mother screamed. Just then the headmaster appeared. He seemed shaken but authoritative.

"Take everyone into the gym," he ordered the teachers, "whilst we sort this mess out." With that he slapped Megan around the head.

"And you!" he said. "Thank God I never have to see your snivelling little face again!" He frogmarched her into the gym. The throngs of other parents were aghast to what they just had witnessed, and some of them were cheering,

"Well done, Megan; stood up for yourself at last. Well done!"

"Silence everyone!" screamed Mr. Davies. Before he could say any more a rather large man, dressed in black from head to foot, appeared at the doorway as if from nowhere.

"Hello, Robert," he said. Robert Davies seemed to shake from head to foot with surprise at the appearance of this man. "I have been waiting and watching you for a very long time," he said.

"Get the police and arrest that bitch!" Sharon's mother once again screamed.

"Quiet!" boomed the man in black. "Yes, we will get the police, as there is rather a lot to sort out here. Someone ring the police now!" he shouted to one of the on looking teachers. Then he looked in turn at Sharon, her mum and all the other mums and girls who were crying and screaming. He shouted,

"You lot just shut up or I will have you all arrested!" They went quiet.

"Hello, Phillip," said Robert Davies rather shakily. "Look, it's just a misunderstanding. I am sorting this problem out right now, it happens all the time with this riffraff family the Murphys."

"Robert," Phillip said. "I have been watching you run this school for some time, you nasty, evil bastard. Over the last three years you have been guilty of consistent child abuse. You have allowed this little girl to suffer, mentally and physically. She has nearly lost her life, trying to kill herself because of the pressure from this evil bunch of girls and their disgusting mothers. How much were you paid to look the other way? Especially that one," he pointed to Sharon. "She has been expelled from five different schools for exactly the same thing. All the other schools in the area refused to take her and her gang. How much were you paid?" he asked, his face right up to Robert's.

"Now then," blurted Robert, "that's none of your business. Who says any money passed hands?"

"Well, we will let the police decide that shall we?" He turned to Sharon, her mother and the others.

"And as for you lot," he said, "the social services will be visiting you all and I will hand this matter to the police for investigation to see if any charges will be brought." At that moment the police arrived. Robert Davies was taken into his office and read his rights as he sobbed his innocence. The door was quietly closed so no one could hear the ongoing conversation. The mothers and girls were all led outside to an awaiting police van, into which they were bundled and driven away. All eyes were on the gym door. What on earth was going to happen next?

The school nurse approached Megan with a wet cloth to wipe the blood from her face and her knees.

"Let me help you, pet," she said.

"Get off her, you bitch of a woman," shouted Phillip. "You are as bad as the rest. Over one hundred times in the last two years, Megan has called in to you for help and you chose to ignore it. Call yourself a nurse?" Brenda Wilkes broke down into a heap and sobbed.

"I'm sorry, I'm sorry... the headmaster, he said Megan was trouble and I was to ignore her. I am so sorry, I didn't realise."

"Well," said Phillip, "it's too late now. You will be lucky to keep your job after I have dealt with you."

Phillip looked into Megan's bewildered eyes.

"Are you all right?" he asked her tenderly.

"Yes I think so," she replied.

"You did it! Well done, Megan, at last, you stood up for yourself. Your life will change now for the better. Look out anyone who messes with little Megan Murphy. I am so very proud of you, but sorry you had to go through so much pain. Really, I'm very sorry that there has been no one here for you, especially at this school which has let you down so badly. I wonder also how many others have been let down? Well, if I have my way, no one will be let down again, I will make it my pledge." He put his hand on her shoulder and said,

"Go home now." He called to the two angels that had been waiting in the corner of the gym. "Michael, Gabriel, take her home now, right to the door! The angels nodded. "Megan," said Phillip, "I just wanted to tell you that you really are very loved. You were loved from the day you were born. You know you are different, but it is in a good way. Never let anyone tell you any differently. As always, the angels will be there for you. This is a bright new start for you now, take it by the hand and run, run with it, Megan. Keep strong and you will be okay, promise me."

"I promise," said Megan. He kissed the top of her head and waved to the angels to take Megan home.

"Go now, child, I have work to do here, sorting this mess out." The angels took her by the arm and off she went.

They walked through the door of the gym to a crowd of people who had been waiting and watching to see what was happening. As Megan emerged they clapped and shouted.

"Well done, love; about time those bullies got their comeuppance!" She had crossed the playground, gone down the six steps to the road and turned right to walk to her house when she heard a growl, almost a call.

If you could see through my eyes, you would see a little girl walking arm in arm with a big, beautiful angel on each side. You would see a little gold tail twitching behind her, little stubby wings, fluttering with anticipation, and three gold bumps going down the back of her neck. Of course, anyone else looking would see little Megan Murphy walking up the hill on her own. She was feeling wonderful, free, freeeeeeeeeeeeeeeeeeeee!

She smiled to her angels, who smiled back and hugged her closer. Then, again she heard the growl, louder this time, just like a lion's roar. She stopped, slowly turned and looked into the biggest pair of green, demon eyes she had ever seen. They were staring at her, calling her and, with a flash and a faint smile, her big, green demon eyes flashed right back.

To be continued...

Lightning Source UK Ltd.
Milton Keynes UK
UKOW04f2059020216

267641UK00001B/105/P